*HOIRS

NORTH WALES
MALE VOICE
CHOIRS

Meurig Owen

Foreword by
Alwyn Humphreys MBE

Also by Meurig Owen:
Ways with Hazel and Horn (with Bob Gruff Jones)
A Grand Tour of North Wales
Gordon Wilyman – Memoirs of a Welsh Halfbred
(with Gordon Wilyman)
Brenhines y Bryniau
Hedges, Sticks and Baskets
Cofio'r Cefn – Cefn Remembered (ed)
William Parry Jones: Nant Meifod, Cresco, Tyn Rhyl

First published in 2009

© Text:: Meurig Owen

ISBN: 978-1-84524-154-4

Cover design: Sian Parri
Cover photo: Côr Meibion Dwyfor

Published by
Llygad Gwalch, Ysgubor Plas, Llwyndyrys,
Pwllheli, Gwynedd LL53 6NG
✆ 01758 750432
🖷 01758 750438
✆ lona@carreg-gwalch.com
Web site: www.carreg-gwalch.co.uk

Contents

Acknowledgements and Thanks

My warmest thanks are due to the many people who agreed to share their thoughts and memories about Male Voice Choirs in North Wales. I was privileged to hear of their joy in the camaraderie of choir membership, of their loyalty as well as the sheer dedication of choir conductors. Without their enthusiastic co-operation responding to my incessant enquiries, this book would simply never have come about. They spoke frankly of their dreams and achievements as well as some of their problems and fears. Some choirs on the crest of a wave, others facing a decline in membership – particularly of the younger age group. But unfailingly there was a great sense of optimism. In writing this book I endeavoured to reflect the feelings of people within this great Welsh Choral tradition. I found it very buoyant with loads of fun and bonds of friendship.

It will be evident in the North Wales Male Voice Choir story that the choristers and conductors I interviewed are named in the text and I thank them profusely. Invariably they looked through the transcripts for accuracy and were kind enough to put me right when there was any misunderstanding. There may be the odd omission because most were speaking from personal recollections – memories are fallible after all!

I must thank Rhys Jones for his invaluable help on the background and development of the choral tradition in the 19th and 20th centuries, J. Elwyn Hughes who pointed me in the right direction concerning the choir tradition in the slate quarrying district of Caernarfonshire and Dr Alwyn Humphreys who graciously agreed to write the foreword. Finally my wife Menna has been a constant help casting a critical but constructive eye at every stage in the book's production.

My hope now is that you'll sit back and enjoy – all in all I think you'll find it a happy and enjoyable read.

Meurig Owen

Foreword by Dr Alwyn Humphreys MBE, Conductor Emeritus – Morriston Orpheus Choir

(Described by the Secretary of State for Wales as 'A legend – not only a credit to the world of music, but to the Welsh nation', Alwyn Humphreys was Musical Director of the internationally-acclaimed Morriston Orpheus Choir for 25 years. Born in Bodffordd, Anglesey in north Wales, where his father sang tenor in the local male choir and which his uncle conducted, Alwyn was Principal Violist of the National Youth Orchestra of Wales before graduating with honours in music at the University of Hull and Trinity College London. His musical arrangements for male choir, now numbering over 200, are much in demand from choirs worldwide, with publications in Britain and America.)

The sound of a Welsh male choir is unmistakable, easily identified from amongst any other similar ensemble in the world. And yet, any attempt to define it in mere words is a virtually impossible task. The most frequently asked question by radio and TV presenters the world over to a Welsh male choir conductor on tour is: 'How do you achieve that incredible sound?' My response has always been: 'If I knew the answer to that I would be a millionaire, going around every country under the sun selling the magic formula'.

Naturally there are theories, citing Wales's richly emotional religious history where a need to express deep feelings overcame any shortcomings in musical ability. A Welshman will often say: 'I sing because I have to, not because I want to'. Added to this is a complete lack of embarrassment in feeling moved by the singing experience. Many a time I have known a tough burly chorister admit that the hairs on the back of his neck were tingling during a performance and his legs reduced to jelly. The effect on an audience can be even more electrifying, and I know many people whose lives have been dramatically changed by it.

I'm not sure if it's true, but certainly I have heard it said, that Wales – at one time at least – had the greatest proportion of male choirs and choristers per head of population in the world. The inevitable result of such a situation is that the phenomenon is taken for granted and its value under-rated. Let's not mince words: the Welsh male choir tradition is a national treasure and has been one of the most positive and respected characteristics of our country for many years. It has concentrated the minds and talents of innumerable men over the years, has helped people to face unimagineable hardship, and lifted them to a higher and better place.

One of the inevitabilities of such a common feature of Welsh life as the male choir is the lack of reading material about it. Meurig Owen has performed an invaluable service in creating this volume and its appearance could not be more timely. Not content with mere statistics and lists he has produced in this fascinating book a portrayal of real people who have been – and still are, many of them – instrumental in furthering the cause of male choirs in Wales. A choir may well be a musical ensemble first and foremost, striving to achieve perfection in those rich harmonic sounds, but it is far more than that: it is a family of people bound together, sharing joys and sorrows. One thing is certain: if you're in a male choir, when it's time for your exit from this world, you'll get the best send-off possible this side of heaven.

After all – and I'm choosing my words carefully here – the sound of a Welsh male choir is the most powerful musical expression anywhere in the universe. There I've said it! And I wouldn't make such a rash claim if I didn't believe it. The Welsh male choir sound reaches the parts of the human condition that other music cannot. The range of notes produced may be limited (far more limited than a mixed choir, a brass band, or an orchestra) but the range of colour and emotion is far greater.

Sadly, there is one ommission in this book – and it is not the author's fault. Côr Meibion Bodffordd, the Bodffordd Male Voice Choir, is not mentioned as it came to an end in 1967. My father was an ardent 1st Tenor member, who often got up at the crack of dawn, spread his sol-fa music copies over the kitchen table and lost himself in them. His brother, my Uncle Willie, was the conductor. They were typical of the ordinary dedicated people who made music as if their lives depended on it. In many ways they did. I owe them so much, and I feel that this book is a tribute to them amongst the many, many others who took the same journey.

The Male Voice Choirs of North Wales

Wales – Land of Song

It is a knowledge easily taught and quietly learned, where there is a good Master and apt scholars.
Singing is delightful to Nature and good to preserve the health of man.
It strengthens all parts of the breast and opens the pipes.
It is a singular remedy for stuttering and a stammering in the speech.
It is the best means to procure a perfect pronunciation.
There is not any music of instruments whatsoever comparable to that which is made of the Voices of Men, where the voices are good, well sorted and ordered.
The better the Voice is the meeter it is to honour and serve God therewith; and the Voice of man is chiefly to be employed to that end.

William Byrd 1588

Did the pilgrims on their way to Bardsey, Island of the Saints, burst forth in song? The Welsh, a Celtic nation, are wont to express their emotions musically, whether in the Arms Park spurring the national team to glory with *Calon Lân*, or equally, singing that same hymn at the Cymanfa Ganu (Hymn Singing Festival) to crown a glorious week at their National Eisteddfod. It would be nice to know if perhaps they jollied along merrily towards Bardsey to crwth accompaniment! But what evidence is there for such a fanciful notion?

Peter Crossley-Holland in *Music in Wales*, a book he edited in 1948 said: 'From as early as the sixth century the poets-musicians of Wales were an indispensable part of life in the halls of noblemen. The bard comforted, entertained and incited to valour, enhancing the effect of his poems with harp and voice. He was minstrel, historian and ambassador, and was rewarded generously by his lord.

'Music and poetry reached a high degree of development and organisation in early Wales as compared with arts in stone and wood, which was not surprising in a race constantly on the move during a period of wars.'

Gerallt of Wales (Giraldus Cambrensis) in the 12th century, tells us in his *Description of Wales* that 'in their musical concerts they do not sing in unison like the inhabitants of other countries, but in many different parts; so that in a company of singers, which one frequently meets with in Wales, you will hear as many different parts and voices as there are performers'. What price for a visit to the mansion of a native Welsh Prince to satisfy our curiosity, to hear once more those musical strains! Unless perchance a scientific device is created to recall that music at some future date, it will all remain a matter of pure conjecture.

There is one further clue from a yet later date which still challenges the scrutinisers and that is the Robert ap Huw Manuscript from about 1613, which is in the possession of the British Library. Robert ap Huw, a descendant of the Tudors of Penmynydd in Anglesey, a distinguished roving minstrel, was harpist to King Charles 1st. And was the author or copyist of a manuscript which is virtually the only guide to Welsh harp music in medieval times. But all attempts to transcribe the music into modern notation have so far been thwarted. One day when this document, which has references to an earlier period, is fully deciphered a clearer indication will emerge about the quality of early Welsh music.

Peter Crossley Holland maintains 'that the accession of the Tudors in 1485, although of Welsh descent and at first hailed enthusiastically in Wales after two hundred years of English oppression, had the dolorous result of slowly destroying a great part of Welsh culture'. The most influential of the gentry made 'English their language and the majority of the harpists who remained in Wales virtually had the choice of employment with English speaking families, or of gaining what pittance they could in the Welsh speaking peasants kitchen. In this way the old Welsh musical science received a mortal blow'. According to this submission Welsh music became fragmented so that concerned parties: bards, clergy and a few Welsh gentry met 'to review and restore the canons of poetry and song' at what is known as the Caerwys Eisteddfod of 1523 and 1568. Legislation to protect the qualified bards from the competition of inferior minstrels was introduced.

It is evident that the decline in musical standards continued, the havoc caused by the Tudors unabated. To quote Crossley Holland again ' . . . in the eighteenth century Welsh musical culture was to suffer a further blow. This time it was struck by the more fanatical element in the Methodist Revival. Dancing and instrumental music were actively suppressed and folk song, with its not always polite words, was hardly encouraged. The best harpists continued to go to London; the harpists and fiddlers who remained in Wales were on occasion even driven out of the inns'.

The story of music in Wales at best can be described as sparse. To quote another authority W.R. Allen the influential Gregynog Choirmaster: 'Printed publications were rare. The records of the seventeenth and early eighteenth centuries are sparse; the eisteddfod of the time was evidently unmusical and the singing attempted in places of worship deplorable.'

But with the rapid rise of non-conformity in the nineteenth century Allen says that 'the (choral) tradition began to develop around the hymn-tune and the influence of the church is evident'. In South Wales Rosser Beynon known as the 'Apostle of Congregational Singing' is active while in North Wales David Roberts (Alawydd) with his Welsh language grammar of music makes a sinifigant impact. Soon names familiar now as the great composers and leaders of music come within our radar: John Roberts (Ieuan Gwyllt born 1822) who compiled a hymn book containing the best tunes from other countries and realised the value of the tonic sol-fa method; Ambrose Lloyd (1815-1874); Tanymarian (1822-85) and Emlyn Evans (1843-1913).

A profound statement from Crossley-Holland probably sums up the development of Welsh music best of all:

'Despite the privations suffered under the military conquests of the early centuries, despite the losses experienced under the Tudors and the great changes brought about by the Reformation, and the Revival, and despite the existing economic hardship . . . Wales truly remains a land of song.'

John Curwen's Modulator Set New Standards

'Thank the Lord, we're a musical nation!' is the sentiment immortalised by the Reverend Eli Jenkins when he perchance heard Polly Garter sing the praises of her paramours in Dylan Thomas's *Under Milk Wood*. Did he express the truth about the Welsh love of music, or was it a declaration that as a nation we also have a bizarre sense of humour? At least the widely travelled George Borrow touring Wales in 1854 was impressed, observing uniquely that 'the Welsh sing in harmony'.

Rhys Jones, the well known Welsh musician, believes that Welsh singing came of age when musician John Curwen (1816-80), the apostle of the Tonic Sol-fa system, began his advocacy of the practice in 1841. A conference in Kingston upon Hull had noted the declining standards in congregational music and there was a resolve that something should be done about it. Curwen, who later became an Independent minister at Plaistow, had heard of a new way of teaching children the rudiments of music employed by a Norwich lady, Sarah Glover. He had investigated and discovered that the children sang in perfect harmony, taught using, not the Old Notation but a 'new' style, the Tonic Sol-fa method.

Rhys Jones says that this wasn't strictly a 'new' idea, it was basically the revival of a method used in Italy in the 11th century by a priest, Guido Arrezzi, who had composed a psalm of praise to John the Baptist. Arrezzi could see that by using his way, the forerunner of what we now know as the Tonic Sol-fa but using different symbols, the scales could be easily adjusted upwards or down: he realised that the scale could be set anywhere. It was a system that could be easily learnt and understood by the ordinary singer, and is indeed still used in Italy to this day.

John Curwen's *Grammar of Vocal Music* appeared in 1843; his promotion of the Tonic Sol-fa had begun; and in 1864 he gave up his role as a pastor, devoting himself wholly to the cause. Whereas before, music belonged to the privileged rich who could afford the tutelage – Curwen now brought it within reach of everyone, here now was a method that could be taken up by the world at large – even by people of very limited literary attainments. The revolution had begun: John Curwen's Tonic Sol-fa Modulator changed the face of choral music. It now came within reach of the masses, and how they embraced it! By 1880 40,000 copies of the modulator had been sold for the 'Messiah' alone. 'It was a musical language my father mastered completely,' says Rhys Jones.

It opened up the joys of choral singing, choirs sprang up all over Wales, freed now from the restriction of old notation which few of them neither followed or understood. Welsh chapels eagerly took up the cudgels, the Modulator was a feature of every vestry and schoolroom: it was invaluable as a routine preparation for the Cymanfaoedd Canu, the Singing Festivals. Indeed choirs, both male voice and mixed, became an important part of religious life. The modulator and the piano became a prominent feature of the 'cegin orau', the Welsh drawing room; competitions in the eisteddfodau challenged the ability of competitors to range up and down the modulator. The religious revivals of the late mid 19th and early 20th centuries capitalised on the Tonic Sol-fa system where the four voices: tenor, bass, soprano and alto became an essential part of congregational singing.

In industrial parts of Wales, during the hey-day of mining for coal and slate, where large numbers of men worked together, male voice choirs sprang up in epidemic proportions. Likewise in the countryside, dependant on manual labour to farm the land, every village could boast a choir. The Tonic Sol-fa was so easily understood and embraced, ambitiously their repertoire was extended so that even Handel's Messiah and the Gilbert and Sullivan light operas came within their orbit. Moreover the choir was a communal thing, which drew people together. Rhys Jones argues that 'a choir is the ideal community, it is a close one where everyone works in obedience to a conductor that they trust'. He continues, 'It all came from a basically illiterate society – unable to read even, especially in a musical sense. John Curwen was the great influence which brought about the change'.

All this chimed in with the Welsh eisteddfod tradition, something which did not exist in England. True the English have their festivals such as the one in Blackpool for example. 'But they don't have local competitive festivals as we do,' says Rhys Jones. 'There used to be an eisteddfod in every village and the chapels held their competitive events. The standards might not have matched the larger eisteddfodau, but it was a nursery where people could perform, and were given confidence to face an audience.' This is what stimulated choral singing; in the eisteddfod they were given a platform, and through the adjudication, a baseline for comparison with others in their class. Winning at the larger eisteddfodau was a passport to sing at concerts 'and the grand concert used to be part of the way we lived'.

Much of Rhys Jones's observations about choral singing reveals, that despite the fact that in North Wales alone there are at least 40 male voice choirs plus countless ladies, mixed and church choirs who meet weekly to rehearse, we have already seen the zenith days. For example he has in his possession the 'Day Programme', Rhaglen y Dydd, of the 1938 National

Eisteddfod of Wales which was held in Cardiff. Its contents are very revealing, in the open class for mixed choirs of 150-200 members, there were 8 choirs competing. Four of the leading choirs in that competition appeared together on the Wednesday night of Eisteddfod week to sing Brahms German Requiem Mass with Sir Adrian Bolt conducting. 'How things have declined since then,' he reflects.

Many things have changed since those times, gone are the days of heavy industry, the mines and the quarries who were very large employers, and the comradeship of the workers and their families in close knit communities. All this and more may have contributed to the decline from the halcyon days of the big choirs, but Rhys has another regret. 'In the mid 20th century,' he says, 'musicians who should have known better argued that choirs should stay with "old notation" because tonic sol-fa, they said, limited their repertoire.' He is adamant: 'The result is that by today comparatively few people can read music. It must be the most boring business of all having to sing by rote, as if practising your maths tables. What happens now is that choir conductors select people who understand Tonic Sol-fa or old notation to stand next to those who don't, in order to achieve their objectives. The abuse historically of the custom of sol-fa teaching means that many cannot now follow sol-fa or old notation. Now belatedly there are musicians who have recognised the problem, and in such places as the William Matthias Music Academy in Caernarfon sol-fa is again being re-instated.'

Male Voice Choirs: 19th Century Influences and Developments

Robert Williams of Cae Aseth, Llanbedr in the Conwy Valley, born in 1791 can be regarded as a very important influence on choral singing in the quarrying area around Bethesda in Gwynedd. As a young man he had come as a farm worker in 1819 to Talysarn Farm, but after a short time there had obtained work at the Penrhyn Slate Quarry.

It is evident that he was a highly intelligent person with an enthusiastic musical flair and drive, essential qualities in a man of pioneering spirit. He had readily absorbed *Gamut*, William Owen's musical treatise, even copied its contents word for word. Soon he was running classes, attracting youngsters from Llandygai and Llanllechid on Saturday afternoons and on Saturday evenings rehearsing the hymn tunes for the following day's chapel services. The congregational singing at Carneddi became a by-word throughout Wales and crowds of people came there simply to hear it. John Elias 1774-1841, the most famous Welsh preacher of his day said: 'I don't expect to hear better singing anywhere this side of heaven than what I hear at Carneddi Chapel in Caernarfonshire'.

Robert Williams was killed in an accident at the Quarry on October 30, 1828 at the age of 37, but for nine years in a short life he had taught and inspired musical conductors which were set to raise the standards of congregational hymn singing in Welsh Chapels. A musical trust set up in his memory was to build on his legacy: an assurance that voice training continued at Carneddi.

People who came under his influence directly or indirectly included Griffith Rowlands (Asaph) and David Roberts (Alawydd) both of whom were to go on to lead the singing at Carneddi. Others were William Roberts, Tyn y Maes who composed the hymn tune *Andalusia* and William Owen Prysgol, *Bryn Calfaria*. Another was Owen Davies (Eos Llechid) who was born at Caerffynnon, Llanllechid in 1828.

At the beginning of the nineteenth century it was a standard custom for choirmasters to visit churches to oversee the choral singing, and one of the more influential of these was John Hughes, Dolgellau, who is credited with raising standards at Llanllechid. Owen Davies's interest in music was first nurtured at the Sunday School there, where he also, in the main, learnt to read. At thirteen years of age he began studying John Mills (Ieuan Glan Alarch) Llanidloes's hand book on the rudiments of music, *Gramadeg Cerddoriaeth*. At twenty years old he was appointed Choirmaster at Llanllechid Church, and as a thirty-four year old left his employ at the Quarry to devote all his time to conducting and training Choirs in the Church Choral Union in both North and South Wales. In 1859 he conducted the Bethesda Choral Society in a performance at Penrhyn Castle in the presence of Queen Victoria. So impressed was Her Royal Highness that she sent him a silver cup valued at over one hundred and fifty pounds as a mark of her appreciation.

* * *

The role of chapels and churches through their enthusiasm for improving the standard of singing in their congregations also helped promote the Welsh Choral tradition. Often in the slate quarrying areas of Caernarfon just as in the Wrexham Coal-fields, these twin influences were in evidence, the inherent dangers in both industries creating a need for spiritual uplift and comfort.

Powerful preachers too such as the 'Remarkable Dr Arthur Jones', (Yr Hynod Ddoctor Arthur Jones) who was for thirty years the minister at Ebeneser Chapel in Bangor and also ran the Dr Williams School, in their various ways promoted the choir culture. He had married a daughter of Twm o'r Nant, often referred to as the Welsh Shakespeare.

It was his staunch opposition to the 'demon drink' and his dramatic preaching style which led to the forming of a branch of what was called 'Y Clwb Du' (The Black Club), which was a kind of banking system for converts, to open a savings account. This led, following one of the Doctor's crusading meetings, to the forming of 'Y Côr Dirwestol' (The Temperance Choir) with William Morris, a former member of Alawydd's Ysgol Gân (Voice training school) as conductor. The singing by Côr Braichmelyn, as the choir was called, during their temperance campaigns brought in further converts – marching through the Ogwen Valley with a large upturned beer glass held aloft displayed the strength of their resolve! Although it has to be said there were a few waverers and some of the songs they sang were often at variance with their cause!

All this clearly chimed in with the spirit of the period and the choir sang in many parts of Wales as well as in Liverpool and Manchester. They were invited to sing at the Great London Exhibition of 1851 and having led the temperance parade with their action songs through the streets of London, they performed in the capital's Exeter Hall.

The temperance movement spawned many choirs of which Côr Braichmelyn led by William Morris was the best known: others were to follow. As for the Braichmelyn choir: in 1853 more than fifty of the choristers emigrated with their twenty-eight year old conductor. Braving the Atlantic following a grand farewell by kindred choirs, they set forth in July of that year on board *HMS Universe* from Liverpool for America, settling at Peach Bottom (now known as Bangor) in the quarrying district of Pennsylvania.

* * *

And so we see through the efforts of ordinary quarry workers how the choral tradition developed, capitalising by the middle of the nineteenth century on John Curwen's Modulator and the Sol-fa System. Here we see the green shoots of highly disciplined singing by male voice choirs emerging. Choirs which still flourish today grew out of the harsh conditions, both physically and economically, in the mines, quarries and rural communities of Wales.

Of all choral developments the one about the Penrhyn and Dinorwic Choir which was formed to compete at the Eisteddfod held at the World Fair in Chicago 1893 deserves particular mention. It was conducted by Dr Edward Broome (1868-1932), born in Manchester the family had moved to Bangor, North Wales, when Broome was very young. He became a member of Bangor Cathedral Choir before he was seven years old, and later having served a seven year apprenticeship under the Cathedral organist Dr Rowland Rogers, was appointed organist at St Mary's Church Bangor. He forged a brilliant reputation as a musician and was invited as a twenty-three year old to conduct the Choir destined for the World Fair in America.

There had been other occasions when quarry workers had gone to America to seek a better life, one such example already referred to – but none simply to go there for a month! In our day it's a fairly common occurrence to go there by air in a matter of hours. At that time it was a far more hazardous journey taking at least nine days. Nor was arrival at the destination guaranteed. Still remembered was how the *Empress of Glasgow* had sunk on the high seas with the loss of Penrhyn quarrymen seeking a better life in 1854. For many the risk factor equalled in our day to a space voyage to the moon. Such was the anxiety felt by wives left at home. One of the quarrymen, Jacob Williams, Graig Lwyd, had assured his wife that the ship would only sail during daylight hours within sight of the shoreline, seeking secure harbour for the men to sleep safely on dry land at night-time! It was all so much beyond their comprehension, many had hitherto scarcely ever travelled beyond Llandudno or Rhyl. And what of the cost? Fund raising concert performances were held throughout Wales during 1892 and finally a Grand Concert at Hope Hall, Liverpool with

Ffrancon Davies a famed singer in his day, a native of the quarrying district – making the journey from London to support his kinsmen, waving his fee and donating twenty guineas towards their costs. Lord Penrhyn contributed three hundred pounds towards the journey, which was said to cost well over a thousand pounds.

The World Fair was a show, 'the largest in the civilised world', to exhibit the very latest in industrial and scientific developments which America had to offer. The three thousand Welsh people who lived in Chicago at that time organised a great Eisteddfod, in a seven thousand seat amphitheatre, as part of the celebration. The two set pieces for male voice choirs (of not more than sixty choristers) was *Cambria's Song of Freedom* and *Cytgan y Pererinion* (The Pilgrims Chorus) by Dr Joseph Parry with a first prize of $1000, equal then to two hundred pounds. Seven choirs competed, two from Wales – 'Penrhyn and Dinorwic' conducted by Edward Broome, and 'Cwm Rhondda' conducted by Tom Stevens. The Cwm Rhondda choir from South Wales won, with Penrhyn and Dinorwic placed second – a decision that rankles still!

The Choir gave two further concerts in Chicago before going on to Canada and a performance in Montreal, returning home on the *Oregon*. And what memories! How in old age they still recalled the wonders they'd seen at the World Fair: one could boast that he'd seen a phonograph, another had been to a circus and seen the real Buffalo Bill with his cowboys!

* * *

The strike at the Penrhyn Quarry from 1900-1903 showed the choirs in yet a further dimension. Briefly, the dispute was between Lord Penrhyn and the workers and how he had reneged on an understanding agreed with the men in 1874 by his father concerning a system of work allocation known as *Y Fargen*. Furthermore their rights as craftsmen and members of a union was being outlawed. The dispute escalated into an exceedingly bitter situation causing great financial hardship for the 3000 men and their families. This was where the choirs, with fund raising concerts throughout the country were able to alleviate the distressed. Between January and the end of March 1901 a hundred concerts were held in all parts of Wales: little did they realise that ten more such concert tours would be done by August 1903, travelling to all parts of the United Kingdom – the final concert being held at Crewe.

It was a dispute which was to cause havoc to the slate industry and community upheaval in the quarrying district of Caernarfonshire.

Part Two

Male Voice Choirs Reveal Their Stories

Côr Meibion Aberystwyth
Aberystwyth Male Voice Choir

'The choir was first formed as a social amenity for GPO workers in Aberystwyth,' says Glyn Jones, a former telephone technician there. The Aberystwyth GPO back in 1962 included the telephone as well as the mail service and employed 30 men. 'A committee was called to discuss the formation of a male voice choir one Thursday,' Glyn recalls, 'the upshot of which was that all who were interested were asked to meet in the GPO Welfare Room on the following Thursday evening'. Twenty-five turned up and GPO electrician James Morse, a talented musician who had once sung with the Charles Groves Madrigals, became their first conductor, while Gwyneth Adams wife of the chief mechanic in charge of mail vans became their accompanist. 'We were all very raw amateurs,' says Glyn as he recalls their opening choir session, when Morse called for all with bass voices to put their hands up, three hands went up; when he called for baritones, there was only one! 'All the rest were tenors,' so there was a dreadful imbalance which meant that the net had to be drawn wider to include men from outside the service. That was how the choir got off the ground in August 1962. 'At first we practised fairly simple works like *Deep Harmony, Crossing the Plain* and *Comrades in Arms.*' But James Morse was now looking for greater challenges, the choir was getting larger and the big Pant y Fedwen Eisteddfod beckoned. 'In those days Pant y Fedwen had a special competition for male voice choirs within the county,' says Glyn, 'and James Morse wanted to go for it.' That was the beginning of successful outings under his baton: they won that competition three years running, which meant that the Pant y Fedwen Cup was theirs outright. The choir was now growing, its place very well established in the town and winning accolades. In 1980 Aberystwyth linked up with St Brioche, their twin town in Brittany, for a celebration in which the choir naturally took part. This proved to be the last time for Mr Morse to lead the choir, because two days after coming home he suffered a heart attack from which he died. Brittany proved to be his swan-song: he had led his men to glory and a bundle of laurels, the choir would go on with pride and confidence.

He was succeeded by David Griffiths, a choir member, while Howard

Williams took over as accompanist from Gwyneth Adams, who had retired. David highly regarded as a musical perfectionist, and Howard recognised as a fine pianist and organist in the town, carried on the good work. David Griffiths continued until he left the area in 1987, but rejoined the choir two years later. By then Margaret Maddock had picked up the baton and under her lead, the competitive spirit was restored: in the 1991 National Eisteddfod at Ruthin they picked up the second prize, and in 1992 at the National Eisteddfod in Aberystwyth they scooped the top accolade. In subsequent years they often came close to winning again and at Bala in 1997 they succeeded in doing so. Margaret's term, which ended in 2003, had shown the choir's competitive vigour.

She was succeeded by Carol Davies, a native of Pont Rhyd y Graith in Ceredigion. After Tregaron, Carol had gone to the University of Wales Cardiff and a degree in Welsh, thence to Aberystwyth to do her teacher's training. Following which she had appointments in various Ceredigion Junior Schools before becoming Head Mistress at Capel Cynnon Ffôs Trasol for twenty-four years. With her husband Ainsley Davies, who was Headmaster at the Dyffryn Teifi School in Llandysul, she had for many years been heavily involved in the Aelwyd yr Urdd Branch preparing youngsters for the Urdd Eisteddfodau, in both choral singing which was Carol's main interest, and reciting, her late husband's speciality. She is a mezzo-soprano who, when under twenty-five in 1966, won the coveted Blue Ribband at the National Eisteddfod at Aberafan. Now well settled at the Aberystwyth rostrum, she never ceases to be amazed at the choristers enthusiasm. 'There are regularly thirty-five to forty choir members at the rehearsals every Thursday night,' she says, 'some are in their eighties, but they still come for the sheer joy of singing.'

The Aberystwyth Choir is widely travelled: on a 15 day Canadian visit to Ontario in 1982 they did five regional concerts, while in 1987 David Griffiths led them on a visit to the United States to sing in the choir centre of the World, Salt Lake City. Other itineraries have included Brittany (Pontivy), Holland, and Germany where they sang in Cologne Cathedral. They also do their share of, charity and test concert appearances within Wales.

Their chairman is Thomas Henry Jones of a Llannon seafaring family, who for much of his life was a sea captain; then in 1984 headed a shipping agency, firstly in the Middle East for four years, and then South America for fifteen, before retiring in 1998. Their secretary, Mervyn Hughes is, appropriately, the son of a GPO postmaster who had roving commissions at Machynlleth, Rhyl (where Mervyn was born) and Porthmadog. Mervyn who retired in 2003, worked in the Civil Service in London in the

1960s before his transfer to Aberystwyth to join the staff of Ancient Monuments. Retired postal technician Glyn Jones, a founder member of the Choir, is the deputy musical director and conductor.

So what is the kick that they get from choir membership? All three are agreed: it's a close, friendly crowd and they get a great thrill from singing to their uttermost ability, giving it their all. And there's great comradeship ; the men now come from assorted backgrounds and professions, a few live and work in the town, some at the college, there are solicitors and teachers, there's even a pathologist! Many are retired: the membership is drawn from within a twelve mile semi-circle of the town.

And what goes into the art of conducting? Glyn Jones reckons that there are two essentials. 'First you must have endless patience – often the choir can practice week after week trying to perfect their performance, but still make the same mistakes! Secondly you must have the ability to get the best out of your choir, and that's a very special gift.'

The Choir

Tapes and CDs: Tape Cassette released in 1983 (Solar Sound). CD released in 2002 Celebrating 40th Anniversary.
Catchment: The Choir members now numbering 42 are drawn from a 12 mile distance of Aberystwyth, including Penrhyn Coch and Tal-y-bont.
President: Gareth Rowlands
Chairman: Thomas Henry Jones
Secretary: Mervyn Hughes, 47 Ger y Llan, Penrhyncoch, Aberystwyth, Ceredigion SY23 3HQ. Tel. 01970 828001
Treasurer: Geraint Jones
Musical Director and Conductor: Carol Davies BA
Deputy Musical Director and Conductor: Glyn Jones
Accompanist: David Evans

Rehearsals are held at the RAFA Club Aberystwyth
every Thursday evening 7.00-9.00.

Côr Meibion Ardudwy

'I aim for a repertoire that is popular with audiences, and is easy and relatively quickly learnt,' says Aled Morgan Jones the forty-two year old conductor of Côr Meibion Ardudwy in North West Wales. 'I'm drawing on my own experience when I was a young chorister. I found then how difficult it was to keep up the interest in choir practice when the pieces that we rehearsed were not ones we liked. So the tunes selected are ones the lads enjoy and in that way they sing all the better; and the better they sing, the more audiences will warm to their performance.' There's a lot of psychology there too because a good performance by the choir gives Aled that extra bit of confidence. He's been a member of the choir for most of his adult life but it was only in 2006 that he was appointed conductor. Of a farming family, he now farms the family farm in Cwm Nantcol near Llanbedr, his musical talent is genetically inherited and his experience as a very competent solo performer strengthens his resolve with the choir. 'When I sing on my own and I sense a good audience reaction, my singing performance also goes up a gear,' he says. 'It's exactly that way with the choir,' and the audience is happy, 'on the way home from a concert the choir will be aware of that and their confidence is boosted.' This is Aled's homespun philosophy and his intention is to attract more choir members, especially younger ones to join in what is evidently an exhilarating experience.

'We must be doing something right,' he says, 'because the choir has been going since 1953!' Evie Morgan Jones, Aled's father, was there almost at the start and remembers how he was persuaded to join, in 1954, by a neighbouring farmer in Cwm Nantcol, Robert Ieuan Richards. Mr Richards was the enthusiast in 1953 who had entered his mixed choir for the Good Friday Eisteddfod at the local Gwynfryn Chapel, but had then decided to split it to form a ladies choir and a male voice choir. That was how the choir came into existence. In the early years it was called Côr Meibion Glannau Artro, Banks of the Artro Male Voice Choir, named after the river which flows through Llanbedr. Later, as the choir grew with a membership reaching all parts of Ardudwy, from the Mawddach to the Glaslyn rivers, ranging from Barmouth across to Penrhyndeudraeth and Minffordd, near Porthmadog, a change of name to Ardudwy became inevitable. Robert Ieuan Richards, their first conductor, was of a musical family; his father Ifan Bennett Richards before him – in the days when every village had at least one choir, was also a conductor. But poor health two years later meant Robert Richards had to give up. He had set the choir on a firm footing. Many recollections come to mind of eisteddfodic experiences in the locality as they sang pieces like *Cymru'n Un* and *Cytgan y Pererinion* (Dr Joseph Parry) at Llanegryn and Llanfachreth. And further modest successes at Llanrwst in 1955 when they were better placed than the Penrhyn Male Voice Choir! Evie Morgan Jones recalls all this with a great deal of relish because he was there, part of the fledgling choir which was quickly establishing itself in a wider arena.

Losing the services of Mr Richards meant a key person was off the scene, but within three weeks we find Mr R.O. Jones the schoolmaster at Llanbedr stepping into the breach. His tenure too proved short lived and by 1958 farmer Edward Edwards (Cilcychwyn) was holding the fort. The difficulty of finding a suitable permanent conductor by 1960 sees the choir having to suspend their activities although they had a full compliment of leading officials still in place, John Parry as secretary and E. Emyr Davies as treasurer. That abeyance was to last two years. And the answer to their problem came at the Barmouth Hymn Singing Festival, Cymanfa Ganu, in 1962, which was conducted by Rhyddid Williams, the music master at Ysgol Ardudwy in Harlech. So impressed was Mr Williams at the quality of the singing that he declared from the rostrum: 'There are the makings here of a first class choir'. This led to a fresh beginning for the Ardudwy Choir, Rhyddid Williams becoming the conductor, took on the challenge which was to lead to a resurgence of ambitious eisteddfodic activity and concerts. At Llan Ffestiniog 'Jubilee Eisteddfod' beating off Côr y Brythoniaid to win with their rendering of *Morte Christe*, led them to reach out for greater challenges. The Welsh National Eisteddfod held at Newtown in 1965 and the Pantyfedwen in the same year gave them worthy adjudication. A memorable concert at the Harlech Memorial Hall in 1963 with soloists Maldwyn Parry (twice a Blue Ribband Winner), renowned cerdd dant winner Llywela Davies and the Ardudwy School Children's Choir, led to the release of their first cassette tape.

When Rhyddid Williams took up a new teaching appointment in South Wales in 1968 there was an impasse. For a while the Ardudwy Choir took on a youngster, Dafydd Lloyd Jones, a pupil of Rhyddid's, as conductor before appointing Gwilym Jones, originally as a stop-gap. But evidently taking on Gwilym, a native of Ruthin and a founder member of the choir with a great fund of latent talent, was a very wise move for he held the role for ten years! In 1976 Elfed ap Gomer, a twenty-two year old student teacher at Ysgol Ardudwy, a member of the group Pererin who had also successfully conducted Ardudwy school girls choir, became conductor of the Ardudwy Male Voice Choir. It proved a successful episode with concerts at Shell Island and bank holiday events at the

Llanfair Quarry underground caverns near Harlech, with their magnificent acoustics. Successful Eisteddfod forays too, and in Killarney at the Pan Celtic Festival, a win in 1979. He was followed by Dafydd Bryn Roberts who worked at Trawsfynydd Power Station, and was deputy conductor of Côr Meibion y Moelwyn but had previously conducted Trawsfynydd Mixed Choir for fifteen years. This proved to be a period when foreign travel became a popular feature of their agenda: Ireland – three times to Galway, Germany (Huchfeld near Stuttgart) and to Denmark. When Dafydd Bryn left, Gwilym Jones took up once again and was followed by Sylvia Campbell who had been the choir's accompanist.

Aled Morgan Jones, who had served as Sylvia's deputy took up the baton in 2006.

The Choir

CDs and Tapes: *Hedd yr Hwyr* (Sain);
Pan Ddaw'r Nos yn Hir (Sain)
Catchment: All parts of Ardudwy, from the Mawddach to the Glaslyn rivers, ranging from Barmouth across to Penrhyndeudraeth and Minffordd, near Porthmadog.
Choir Officials
President: Eddie Lloyd, Galway
Chairman: Bili Jones
Vice-Chairman: Ifan Lloyd Jones
Secretary: Goronwy Davies, Llys Artro, Llanbedr, Gwynedd. Tel. 01341 241714
Treasurer: Bryn Lewis
Conductor and Musical Director: Aled Morgan Jones
Deputy Conductor: Gwilym Rhys Jones
Accompanist: Idris Lewis
Compere and PRO: Phil Mostert

Rehearsals are held on Sunday evenings
in Neuadd Llanbedr 7.30-9.30.

Côr Meibion Dinas Bangor
City of Bangor Male Voice Choir

The City of Bangor Male Voice Choir's visit to Chicago in September 2006 at the invitation of their Welsh communities is a measure of how much they have grown in stature since their formation in January 1988. From a nucleus of twelve who braved that stormy night in response to an advert in the local paper has developed a fifty strong choir, one of the most widely travelled in Wales. Fact is, they thrive on travel! 'I have no interest in competitions at Eisteddfodau and so on,' says their conductor and founder James Griffiths, 'travel is what I prefer.' That firmly stated policy has paid off for them and their fame is spreading. They were chosen to go to the Annual International Toronto Caravan Festival in 1995, a major event in which a myriad of nations show examples of their native cultures. There they were given the 'Best Traditional Entertainment' award in that year out of the 48 countries represented. And honoured to be at the Lorient festival of 2003 in Brittany which hugely celebrates Celtic culture. Interspersed with all that, there have been visits to the Tyrol in Austria twice, Malta where they sang in the Cathedral in Valetta, Cyprus performing in the Kurium open air amphitheatre to over 2000 people, Northern Ireland (Londonderry) and Soest in Westphalia (Germany), a town with which Bangor is twinned.

Given James Griffiths' lifestyle, perhaps it's not surprising that travel is so high on the choir's agenda. As an examiner for Trinity Guildhall he spends a great deal of his time abroad; his commissions take him to places as varied as Hong Kong, China and New Zealand. And always he's on the lookout for places to take the choir! His role as an examiner involves him in assessing students through grades one to eight and for diplomas.

Following his early retirement from teaching in Benllech on the Isle of Anglesey, he had become deputy organist at Bangor Cathedral, a position he held for forty-three years. His mentor was the renowned long-time organist at the Cathedral, Dr Leslie Paul. For James Griffiths music has been his life, for seventeen years prior to founding Bangor Male Voice Choir he had been the accompanist for Côr Meibion Y Penrhyn. It's his musical links with the world at large which now make him an ideal ambassador for the Bangor Choir and for Welsh culture.

Often it's meeting Welsh ex-pats abroad that leads to a concert tour in that country, thus their Chicago visit had taken in the town's great Celtic Festival as well as a performance in their multi-storey Temple Church. Going on to Madison, capital of Wisconsin, there had been further Welsh links as descendants of the early settlers rekindled ancestral roots. Likewise at Fort Wayne in Indiana. Although worldly travelled there is an evident sense of wonderment about all he discovers during the concert tours. At some of the chapels, built by early Welsh settlers in Ohio – at Gomer and Venedocia – there is still that feeling that you could so easily be back home in Wales. Commemorative coloured windows are a reminder of the founding fathers, graves bear Welsh names, Welsh Sunday School books and bibles, chapel minute books are there as part of the heritage. 'You could so easily be back home in Wales,' he says. But there is no Welsh spoken, only the enthusiasm for all things Welsh and a particular love of singing. All of their forays abroad create links with other choirs, for example the Tyrolean visits have formed a close bond which has led to the Austrian choir Kufteiner Singkreis coming over to sing with them at Bangor Cathedral. Similarly Pro Musica the German choir from Westphalia.

It's Mr Griffiths' good fortune to have Lowrie Robert Williams who was deputy head of Bethel School, near Caernarfon, as a long standing choir accompanist. 'She is an exceptionally good musician and teacher, and has also conducted hymn singing festivals, cymanfaoedd canu, several times,' he says. While his deputy is the well qualified Gwilym Lewis, who is also the conductor of Holyhead Male Voice Choir. Choir. Members come from a wide spread around Bangor including Llanberis, Caernarfon, Llanfairfechan and Anglesey and have good solo performers among their numbers, Bob Thomas, Huw Hughes a Blue Ribband winner, Norman Evans, David Hughes and Gwilym Jones. The compere being David Price, former Choir secretary.

The Choir

CD: *CASGLID* released in 2000 and again in 2006.
Catchment area of choir members: Bangor, Llanberis, Caernarfon, Llanfairfechan and many from Anglesey including Newborough and Holyhead.
Choir Officials
President: Mr Cledwyn Jones
Chairman: Gwyn Hefin Jones
Secretary: O. Myfyr Parry Williams, Rhiwena, Nant y Glyn, Llanrug LL55 4AH. Tel. 01286 676512
Treasurer: H.H. Williams

Accompanist: Lowrie Robert Williams ATCL
Compere: David Price
Conductor and Musical Director: James Griffiths, FLCM, Hon. TCL, LLCM
Deputy Conductor: Gwilym Lewis, M.Mus, LRAM, ARCM
Compere: David Price

Rehearsals are held at Ysgol y Faenol, Penrhosgarnedd, near Bangor from 7.30-9.30 every Wednesday evening.

Betws-yn-Rhos Male Voice Choir
Côr Meibion Betws-yn-Rhos

The Choir began as a party of men who came together on 13th of November 1974 to practice for the choir competition in the Dydd Calan Eisteddfod at Betws-yn-Rhos, the New Year's Day Annual Eisteddfod. Nerys Jones, who is the present choir mistress, says that there had been a tradition of friendly local rivalry between parties of ladies and men, usually singing light hearted pieces. But now the men were going for the 'big time' with Nerys as their accompanist. Their first inspirational conductor was Emyr Jones who was the headmaster at the village school. He was born at Waen Fawr, Caernarfonshire, and had left school at an early age to work in the Dinorwic Slate Quarry, but later studied at Cartrefle Training College before taking up an Abergele teaching post. He then came to Betws-yn-Rhos to be headmaster. He was a distinguished writer: his two books on the history of the quarries had won him acclaim, as had his two published novels. The one about John Evans of Waen Fawr's search for the 'Welsh Indians', *Grym y Lli*, had won him the 'Prose Medal' at the National Eisteddfod of Wales in 1969. But he was also an enthusiastic musician, and apart from the choir, the schoolchildren also benefited from his conducting skills. Nerys Jones remembers how he brought the discipline and spirited gusto of the Quarry Bands of his youth into the choir at Betws. 'He was a great sol-fa man too,' she says, 'he set great play on that.'

The success and enjoyment of that first eisteddfod experience ensured that the choir continued and grew, with regular Thursday evening practices in Hyfrydle Chapel Vestry. By 1975 they had started turning out to help various chapels and voluntary organisations by singing at their concerts, and in the following year began to do likewise during the Summer Season at St Johns Church Llandudno, a custom which still continues.

Emyr Jones retired in 1978 leaving the area for his native Caernarfonshire, whereupon the baton was passed on to Trebor Lloyd Evans, a choir member. Trebor, who worked at the Midland Bank at Abergele, was a native of Llangwm and possessed a very fine voice. He continued raising the choir's singing standards and expanding its repertoire. Under his stewardship he saw a steady growth in membership. In 1978, upon his receiving a posting to the bank at Denbigh and leaving the area, Nerys Jones who had been the choir's accompanist from the beginning succeeded him as conductor, while Vera Evans became the choir's pianist.

The two ladies brought their own brand of enthusiasm and dedication; during the following year membership grew to forty and the choir joined the North Wales Association of Male Voice Choirs. They began learning the programme for the 1988, 1000 voices concert at the Royal Albert Hall in London.

In 1988 the choir embarked on its first trip to Europe having been invited to sing at Westerstede in Northern Germany. Since then they have toured extensively, performing in France, Germany, Holland, Scotland, Cornwall and South Wales.

Nerys Jones claims no academic musical qualification beyond a sol-fa certificate, the result of a training course with Evan Jones, Tan y Marian as a child, and brought up in a musical family at Betws. Both her parents were gifted musicians and her grandfather was the tenor known as David Owen Cynant. Although Nerys never received a music lesson, she's an accomplished pianist able to play any score by ear, and to transcribe old notation sheet music into sol-fa for the choir's benefit. Her day job is as cook at the village school of 70 children, which she took on qualifying at a domestic science course at Llandrillo Technical College. Even that is still only part of her interesting life because married to Wyn, who formerly worked at Coed Coch, home of the late Miss Brodrick and her World famous Welsh Cob ponies, they also have their own 'Nerwyn' Welsh Ponies which still carry the Coed Coch genetics. And Wyn is an authority on the breed, judging not only in the Royal Welsh Show, which he did in 2004, but also in Australia and New Zealand.

So what are the qualities needed to be a successful conductor? 'Plenty of patience and I try to be very clear, even though I don't use a baton, that the choir knows exactly what I expect of them. With me there's no fancy jig-me-rolls!' she says. Hefin Evans, the choirs 53 year old secretary who works as an undertaker in Colwyn Bay says, 'Nerys always chooses the right choral pieces bearing in mind the size of the choir and their capabilities.' Hefin took on the secretarial role in 2002 following John Eric Hughes, a retired Abergele Headmaster. He regards music, playing the organ (often helping out at local chapels and churches) and walking as his main leisure interests. At Penmachno, where he was brought up, he played the cornet in the brass band, and later at Old Colwyn played the trumpet in the Silver Band.

Vera Evans retired from the position of accompanist in 1994, and was succeeded by Gaynor Morris and Gwenno Mererid. But now they too have retired and the present accompanist (2007) is Meirwen Hughes from Abergele, wife of John Eric Hughes the former choir secretary.

On the 13th of November 2004 the Choir celebrated its 30th birthday with a concert in the Betws-yn-Rhos village hall, where they were joined by the Llanrhug Silver Band. Their enjoyment undiminished! This is something that Nerys Jones is very pleased about – 'whatever worries members may have is soon blown away in the fervour of choir practice,' she says.

Betws-yn-Rhos is on the B5381 road about 3 miles south of the North Wales coastal town of Abergele.

The Choir

CDs/Tapes:
Côr Meibion Betws-yn-Rhos (cassette 1989)
Côr Meibion Betws-yn-Rhos (cassette 1992)
Mae Yna Wlad (cassette 1996)
Bryniau Aur Fy Ngwlad (CD 2003)
Catchment: The members are drawn from Abergele, Betws-yn-Rhos and the adjoining villages including Eglwys Bach and Llangernyw.
Officers
President: Ena Wynn
Chairman: Gwynfor Davies
Secretary: Hefin Evans. Tel. 01745 823 948
Treasurer: Gwyndaf Roberts
Musical Director and Conductor: Mrs Nerys Jones
Deputy Conductor: Wynford Davies
Accompanist: Meirwen Hughes
Compere: Gareth Davies

Rehearsals are held in Hyfrydle Chapel Vestry, Betws-yn-Rhos
Every Sunday and Thursday 7.30 to 9.30.

Nerys Jones left the choir in March 2008,
and was succeeded by Ian Woolford.

Ian Woolford, a native of Rhosllanerchrugog, is a professional baritone singer trained at the Royal Manchester College of Music by Freddie Cox and Rowland Jones. His career as a singer followed a period in the North Wales Police. Since the job switch Ian has had an exceedingly busy time. After his period with English National Opera he decided to concentrate on solo performances, which took him to all parts of the world including Australia, Italy, Germany, Israel, Malta.

Although he claims his speciality is the classics, he says 'I've done the lot – the whole range.' This includes shows with Vera Lyn, Charles Asnavour, Harry Secombe, Stuart Burrows and Bruce Forsyth. On top of all that he's done other things too. In 1986 Ian started up Côr Meibion Llanrwst, and then, when he moved away to Colwyn Bay, conducted Côr Meibion Colwyn from 1994 till 1997. And then conducted Côr Meibion Cyndeyrn at St Asaph until that came to a natural close in 2007. With his friend Colin Jones, he was in on the ground floor in 1991 helping him set up the North Wales Choir – Cantorion Colin Jones. Now he's fully focussed with Côr Meibion Betws-yn-Rhos. Hey, how old is he to have packed in so much? 'I'm 54 and I haven't finished yet,' he says hardly pausing for breath. He has ambitions for Côr Meibion Betws, they now practice twice a week; 'It's essential, so that I can firmly establish the male voice sound I want from them.' He's able to demonstrate by example. 'They were able to sing well on the lower register but when it came to increasing the volume the sound became raucous – they're now producing a good male voice sound,' he says. 'The Choir think the world stops at the Betws parish boundary, I want to show them that that isn't true.' The National Eisteddfod beckons. 'I want to build up their confidence, that was what they've lacked . . . '

Côr Meibion Hogia Bodwrog

How do you get younger people to join a choir? Break down the image that choirs are for oldies, full stop. Mission impossible? Well over at Llynfaes in the parish of Bodwrog in central Anglesey, Arwel Jones is proving, with Hogia Bodwrog, that it can be done. Miracles do happen: they number twenty-six (and increasing) with an age range from twelve years old to over seventy.

Five minutes in his company is enough to tell you how and why it's happening. He's thirty-nine years old, but looks much younger, and has a musical zest which is highly infectious.

He was born in Carreglefn near Amlwch where his parents ran the post-office. It was evidently a musical environment, strongly influenced by grandparents; granny being the chapel organist while his 'Taid' was a keen soloist who sang at all the local eisteddfodau. Arwel was inevitably taken along as a slightly bored young child, until that is, he began competing too and started winning pocket money! That changed matters until at Llanddeusant Eisteddfod, while singing solo as a twelve year old, his voice broke. And oh, the embarrassment. That was when he turned to competing as a piano player.

It was a natural progression that he went on to study music at Bangor University under Professor John Harper, Marian Bryfdir and John Hywel for his Bachelor of Music (Hons) degree. Greatly influenced too by the charismatic Dr William Matthias. He was encouraged to give organ and pianoforte recitals at the University where he also gained experience accompanying soloists and conducting choirs. His future destiny was firmly mapped out and his rather adventurous musical taste truly fixed.

Going from there to study further at the University of Wales Aberystwyth for a Post Graduate Certificate in Education specialising in Music and Special Education Needs. He then began to teach at Anglesey Comprehensives partly fulfilling his vision of the future, before taking up his present position as a roving envoy in the county's junior schools. This is where he's energising tomorrow's choirs, giving them a taste of being part of highly theatrical performances. Scaling such achievements as a performance of *Bugsy Malone* with four hundred school children, many of whom had done nothing like it before. And bringing back John Curwen's Modulator on to the schools' musical syllabuses.

Music is Arwel's life, he thinks and dreams of nothing else, he's been with choirs for as long as he can remember. For several years he shadowed Gareth Glyn as conductor of 'Lleisiau'r Frogwy' and was their regular accompanist. He gives piano lessons to about twenty youngsters.

His taste in music is distinctly cosmopolitan with a penchant for the classical; Bach being a favourite for his uncluttered melody. 'An intricate score jars on the ear. Many modern composers produce work that's too flowery,' he says, 'and it distracts from the ultimate enjoyment.' But given a choice between melody and the sound of words, he comes down strongly in favour of word clarity. 'The way that you sing the words is more important than the musical sound,' he says. Within all these confines he still leaves room for an element of exploration, adventure and excitement. His repertoire with Hogia Bodwrog is continually expanding and now number over eighty pieces. Arwel resolutely believes in the choir learning new songs, many of which are his own arrangement. 'I like doing new jazzed versions of traditional hymns, the tunes are easily recognised but the accompaniment is different.'

'We have a guitarist as well as a trumpeter, with myself at the piano conducting – which gives it all a great deal of oomph.' Soon he expects to also have a harp! Doing the conducting and playing the piano at the same time relies on a great deal of body language, which the choir have now come to understand. 'But the trick is the instruction and training I give them before hand,' he says. Since taking over as choir master twelve years ago the mutual bond of respect between Arwel and the choir has grown; he regards this as vital to the choir's success, adequately demonstrated by how the choir has gone from a concert party of twelve lads to its present twenty-six members of all ages. Often former school pupils remember him and want to rekindle the choir experience. Twelve year old Iwan, one of Arwel's star piano pupils, is rapidly becoming part of the act and usually plays with him in a duet. This has gone down well, especially at their concerts, because Iwan is a small child (they even had difficulty kitting him up with a 'Hogia Bodwrog' jersey that was small enough) while Arwel sitting by his side is positively giant size!

Glyn Owen a veteran choir treasurer and former secretary at seventy years old, remembers how the 'choir' started in the 1960s at the local Youth Club with the Rev. Dewi Jones, minister at the Independent Chapel in charge. 'We competed at local eisteddfodau including the Urdd Eisteddfod,' he says. 'But it was mainly a "noson lawen" party at that time.' Then a lull, when much later it became an elocution group which competed at the National Eisteddfod.

When the National Eisteddfod came to Anglesey (Llanbedrgoch) in 1999 a decision was made to revive the choir once more, which is when Arwel Jones came on the scene – and there's been no looking back. 'We went from strength to strength, often performing in three or four concerts a week all over Anglesey and the mainland,' he says. 'It was really hectic so we then decided to restrict to two concerts a month.' Arwel admits that at first it was fairly undisciplined, and that his main task was 'to impose his own stamp on the choir, and to get them note-perfect'.

So what of the future? 'We are not a competing choir,' he says, 'but singing to a high standard will always be our first resolve, equally we want to preserve the Welsh language and culture in this area and beyond.'

The Choir

Catchment: Llangefni, Llanfair PG, Gaerwen, Aberffraw, Rhos-y-bol, Carreg Lefn.
CD: *Tyrd yn Ôl*
Officers
Chairman: Dafydd Parry
Vice Chairman: Dafydd Roberts
Secretary: Elfed Hughes, 4 Maes Twrog, Llynfaes, Llangefni, Anglesey
Treasurer: Glyn Owen
Assistant Treasurer: William Jones
Compere: Elfed Hughes
Musical Director and Accompanist: Arwel Jones, B.Mus (Hons), ARCM, AMusLCM, PGCE (Wales)

Rehearsals are held every Wednesday night in
Neuadd Goffa, Llynfaes, Anglesey at 8p.m.

Brymbo Male Choir
Côr Meibion Brymbo

Brymbo once known for its steel works and proximity to the Wrexham coalfields, Hafod and Bersham collieries in particular, would years ago have had a choir. The old folk would talk of such, but no records were kept.

So the Brymbo choir of today, established in 1959, was re-formed from the embers of the past by Tommy Andrews, the organist and choir master at St Mary's Church, while Dilwyn Roberts, of the Welsh Church in the village, became accompanist. All of those who helped reform the choir were choristers at St Mary's Church and included Harold Davies, Ken Davies, Emrys Harrison, Arthur Johnson, Robert Arthur Lloyd, Jack Morris, Ron Matthias, Norman Roberts, Ted (Bantam) Roberts, Harold Schofield, Gwilym Williams, Johnny Williams, and the Rev. D. Saunders Davies, who was then Vicar of Brymbo.

When Tommy's health deteriorated (he died in 1961), Dilwyn took over as conductor with Alan Wynne as accompanist. But it was 1966 before a committee was formed, with Alec Owens as secretary and treasurer, Jack Morris chairman, and Emrys Davies, Managing Director of the steelworks as president, a position he held until 1973 when his son Neville took over; the choristers now numbered thirty five and performed 'in a few local things'. Some two years later, 'due to pressure of work and his imminent departure from the area, Dilwyn Roberts left'.

So Glyn Hughes, the highly respected organist at St Paul's Church Pentre Broughton, was appointed conductor in 1966, a role he continues to this day. A native of Cerney, near Brymbo, he worked first of all at the National Coal Board for eighteen years, before later joining the accounts department at Brymbo Steel until the works ceased. His love of music goes back to his school days: he remembers how the teacher, sensing his interest, asked if he would like to have violin lessons. 'I immediately jumped at the chance,' he says. But six months on, having sent his widowed mother – his father died when Glyn was five years old – and grandparents to distraction with the screeching instrument as he played *Ba, Ba, Black-sheep* and *Fight the Good Fight*, he realised the violin was not for him! But Glyn's grand parents had a piano and an organ in their house and with the help of his grandfather he had piano lessons from Sybil MacCarthy and successfully got his 'Associate Diploma'. By the age of fifteen he was playing the organ at the 'Independent Chapel' and six months later likewise at the Cerney Mission, and as time went on trained the Sunday School Choir for anniversary events. Meantime he studied with Raymond Williams (from Rhos) and went for singing lessons from Ernest Davies, Wrexham, the London Royal Academy of Music trained singer. He then joined Broughton and District Choral Society, 'famous in its day, they won at the National': just turned sixteen he was their youngest member. After a few years he became deputy conductor and deputy accompanist. 'Things happen and Brymbo asked me to be their conductor in 1966,' he reflects. 'That's when I gave up the Broughton Choir.' He clearly remembers the first practice with Brymbo when 'twenty-one turned up, but before long numbers increased dramatically peaking at over a hundred.'

Appointed organist at St Paul's Pentre Broughton in 1968, he trained at St Asaph Cathedral with organist Dr Myddleton. And he also has a festival choir which every two years performs the *Messiah* or *The Creation*. In 2007 he received a special award from the Archbishop of Wales, the Right Reverend Barry Morgan, for his dedication to church music.

In 1971 Kelvin Leslie took over as accompanist until his departure for University, when a young man Ian Belton became the Choir's accompanist, with Rhiannon Hughes a music student at Keale as deputy. Later Ian left the area for a while but 'he's back with us now'.

Within six years the choir had grown to a peak of 110 members, the 1970s marked the beginning of their glory years. Gwilym Hughes, formerly a laboratory technician at the Steel Works, who joined the choir at this time, and for twenty years was their Publicity Officer, in 2008 becoming chairman for the fourth time, has vivid memories of those times. About how they appeared on Hughie Green's TV show 'Opportunity Knocks', winning the contest on the night and two years later invited back for a Gala Performance. It was at this time that they made their first cassette. Gwilym recalls how composer Mansel Thomas and the head of Decca Records were looking around for a choir to sing songs (which Mansel had arranged) for the American market. It was a collaboration which delighted Mansel leading to a friendship and his becoming a vice president of the Brymbo Male Choir.

'From then on things took off,' says Gwilym, 'everything seemed to come together. We were doing adverts for radio and we went to our first Albert Hall Concert with the London Welsh Society, in all we've been eight times.' In the year when the Wrexham Football Team were up for the 'cup', it was the Brymbo Choir's earth moving song 'I'r Goal' (which topped the Welsh charts) that boosted the morale of the team's supporters.

Brymbo is predominantly a concert choir. 'We were never a big competition choir,' says Gwilym Hughes, 'we won the Bolito Memorial Trophy once at the Morecambe Festival, the Nicholson Cup in the Chester

Music Festival and came in second at the National Eisteddfod at Wrexham. But it's on the concert platform that we really excel.'

They're a favourite for the big occasion and sang in Neil Kinnock's famous Labour Conference at Blackpool. Memorable too, their St David's Day concerts for the Welsh Exiles in Oxford – 'Treorchy Choir sang there only once,' says Gwilym, 'but they've invited us back **three** times!'

Their first foreign tour was in 1971 to Kreisiselohn, Wrexham's twin town in Germany, a place they've visited three times in all. They were also invited to the 17th Berlin Music Festival – the only UK choir represented, in an international event where 70,000 singers from many nations sang together in West Berlin's main street! In 1979 America, the first of four visits which have included performances at Vancouver (America), Canada, Seattle, Washington (in the Capital's State Building) and at the new centre in Oregon called Hope Site. 'Its a special theatre, really marvellous, we placed a brick in the wall saying: "Brymbo Choir was here".' Other American tours have included visits to Florida at Disney World, Miami and Fort Lauderdale. One way and another the word gets around.

Europe, particularly France and Germany, have been favoured stamping grounds. The Black Forest in Germany, while in France, they've sung in Rheums Cathedral and the Notre Dame in Paris. Many of the concerts have come through contacts and friendships made at Llangollen International Eisteddfod where Gwilym's wife Alwenna arranges accommodation for the thousands of overseas competitors who perform there each year.

'Although today down to 42 choristers, we're still a very good concert choir,' says Gwilym, 'and the lads really enjoy singing.' Many changes have occurred in Brymbo since the choir was first formed. For a start the Steel Works closed in the early 1990s, and although Gwilym says that it was not a choir of steel men, there's no denying the goodwill shown by the GKN company towards them. They often rehearsed in the works canteen, sometimes slightly bent company rules by having an unofficial short committee discussion in the factory lab during work time! 'You just couldn't take singing out of the business,' says Gwilym. The bosses dealt with it all with the utmost diplomacy. Indeed the choir was a positive asset to the company, making for a friendly workplace, and the choir in turn, wonderful ambassadors; in their way promoting Brymbo and the company to the world at large. In fact the Steel Works helped to finance the choir's overseas tours. And it was customary for the Managing Director to be the choir president. Even now, although the works are closed, the friendly contact with the directors continues. 'We did a concert recently for Director Terry Wiggin at his church in Stoke on Tem, they were very proud of the choir. Former Managing Director Neville Davis and Director John Marsh are still serving the choir as Vice Presidents.' So there's no gainsaying that closure of the steel works and the coal pits had an adverse effect on the village, but regardless, the choir remains in robust health. Plans are afoot for a great 2009, the Choir's 50th Anniversary Year, when a French Band and Scottish Pipers will be joining them in a special celebration at the Brymbo Social Club. Also a joint exchange visit concert with the Castleford Male Voice Choir from Yorkshire is on the year's agenda. As well as an European tour to include 'a German Festival near Strasbourg'. It's going to be a great year for this big hearted choir.

Two rehearsals are held each week: in Tan y Fron Community Centre on a Thursday, and on Sunday night in Broughton Church. 'That way we have the experience of singing to both piano accompaniment at Tan y Fron and at the Church to organ music.' Glyn Hughes is a stickler for practices: the first half hour at Tan y Fron from 7 to 7.30 will be devoted to a workout with the tenors section one week, bass the next, and for the remainder of the evening until nine o'clock he will take the choir as a whole. On the Sunday night at the church it will be a general rehearsal for the whole choir.

The Choir

CDs/Tapes: *Eich Hoff Ganeuon; Songs you have loved*, Decca 1972; *Côr Meibion Brymbo Male Choir; En-Core – ENCORE; 'F'anwylaf un – Dearest of all; I mewn i'r goal – We're gonna score; 40 glorious years* – CD and Tape
Catchment: Wrexham area including Leeswood and Mold
Officials
President: Peter Furber
Chairman: Gwilym Hughes
Secretary: Alan Beynon. Tel. 01244 571497
Treasurer: David Evans
Conductor and Musical Director: Glyn Hughes MBE, AWACM, ALCM, LLCM
Compere: Gwilym Hughes
Accompanist: Ann Owen BA (Hons)

Rehearsals are held twice a week, every Thursday night in
Tan y Fron Community Centre, and on Sunday night
at Broughton Church from 7 until 9 o'clock.

Côr Meibion Y Brythoniaid

Meirion Jones has always had a tremendous interest in the sound of Male Voice Choirs. That came about back home in Blaenau through listening to Côr Meibion Dyffryn Nantlle and the Noson Lawen Programme on the wireless. That fascination led to the Eisteddfod scene.

He remembers going to Gŵyl Fawr Aberteifi and realising that seven choirs who had entered for the main choral competition were all due to perform during the evening session. Listening to them, for Meirion, was an earth moving experience. He was by then already a solo baritone performer (trained by W. Matthews Williams and Madam Ann Hughes Jones, Glan Conwy) and conducted the local girls choir. But the Aberteifi experience was big time and Meirion was smitten.

At Hyfrydfa Chapel in Blaenau they used to have their competitive evenings with singing groups, men versus the women. This was Meirion's chance to try out his expertise! That was it, he'd found his metre, the music bug had entered his soul. And enjoying the process of moulding the voices. He well remembers that party of ten young men of Blaenau, 'half of them could sing and half of them hadn't a clue'. It was the challenge that was needed, and he just loved the experience.

The next step in his progress upwards was an event at the Forum Cinema in Blaenau where there was a call for a party of fifteen voices to perform three set pieces. There's a shimmer of excitement in his voice as he recalls the occasion: 'We really pulled the house down,' he says. He had passed the litmus test and the lads wanted more. 'Lets have a proper male voice choir now,' they implored. That was in 1964 the year Côr y Brythoniaid was born, the result of Meirion's infectious enthusiasm. Personal magnetism played its part, soon the choir was forty and the new members had very fine voices. As the choir grew, so did the quality improve. It was a sound that pleased the maestro.

1966 was the next milestone and their challenge: to enter the choral competition at the great Butlins Eisteddfod held at the camp in Pwllheli. In its day this was ranked as the best eisteddfod in the North – could they cut it in the big time? They were now a choir of 49, challenging leaders like Froncysyllte and Newmarket (now Trelawnyd), choirs of over 100 voices with formidable reputations to match. Y Brythoniaid were the last on stage: the final ovation was a mighty eruption of applause from the audience of 2500. And the adjudicator agreed too. 'This is what a male voice choir should really sound like,' he said. This marked the beginning of their golden years as they went on to four more repeat successes at Butlins.

In the three years that followed, they competed 26 times in all parts of the country, and on only three occasions did they fail to get the first prize. The only hurdle left was the National Eisteddfod. 'This was my abiding aim, I wanted to see a Blaenau choir win at the National. That was the driving force,' he says. At Bala in 1966, placed 3rd: but then in 1969 with Schubert's arrangement of the 23rd psalm they came first and an observation by adjudicator Terry James, 'If Schubert himself was here he would be absolutely delighted with that performance.' Meirion Jones was to take the choir to further National Eisteddfod successes in 1971, 1977 and again in 1985. There's a saying that 'success breeds success': that was certainly true with Côr Meibion y Brythoniaid. They were now over 100 voices and at their peak numbered 116. This was a choir that was going places.

In the 1970's at the Pontrhydfendigaid Eisteddfod they won the challenge cup four times. It was a period charged with excitement. One analyst has likened it to 'the euphoria at Man U today!' Meirion lists the big stars who have sung with the choir: Willard White from America who sang with them at Neuadd y Brangwyn in Swansea; and on television; Harry Secombe (Highway) and (Pebble Mill); Shirley Bassey (the Shirley Bassey Show) and Bryn Terfel. Singing Brahms Alto Rhapsody at St David's Hall with the BBC Welsh Orchestra conducted by Owain Arwel Hughes. And on one momentous occasion, at the William Aston Hall Wrexham, Meirion Jones conducted the Brythoniaid Choir and the Brighouse and Rastrick Band together. That was in the year that the B and R Band became the World Champions. The piece was *The Soldiers Chorus*, and their conductor said to Meirion: 'You go and do it lad!'

Meirion at the rostrum could weave his magic and inspire his singers. At Harlech Castle entertaining Her Majesty the Queen during her Jubilee Tour in 1977.

Foreign travel beckoned: California in 1980 and America again in 1990, to Pennsylvania. California came about at the instigation of John Elfed Jones, the then head of Anglesey Aluminum. On a visit to Anglesey, one of the Vice Presidents of the parent company, Kaiser and Oakland (California), was brought to hear the choir at rehearsal. Instantly besotted he said, 'I'd like you guys to come over to sing in the States.' It was to open doors to new experiences, wowing America with the Brython sound and in the course of visits, meeting and staying with the ex-pat Welsh. Memories, memories – Meirion has loads of them, singing in Disney Land in an empty auditorium and before finishing the first rendering finding the place filled to capacity, drawn by the deep harmony which is part of the magic of the Brythoniaid sound.

In Hungary too, a momentous tour when they sang at the Academy of Sciences in Budapest, followed by a three day respite at Lake Balaton.

In 2001 after 37 glorious years at the rostrum, Meirion Jones retired. In 1994, in recognition of his 'considerable contribution to choral music' he was made an honorary member of the National Eisteddfod Bardic Circle and in 1997 conferred a MBE.

His place was taken by John Eifion Jones, a musician of distinction who had won the Open Tenor Solo Award at the National Eisteddfod five times, and at the National Eisteddfod held in Anglesey, the David Ellis Memorial Prize – the Blue Riband for vocal soloists. Under his guidance the choir went on to win the Chief Choral Competition at the National Eisteddfod at St David's in 2002, and again at Faenol Park (2005) as well as at Pontrhydfendigaid Eisteddfod. Hugh Trefor Jones, the Choir secretary since 1999, speaks highly of him 'as a good communicator who has an excellent rapport with the choir. He's very enthusiastic, and is able to demonstrate by example'.

John Eifion Jones joined the Brythoniaid following seven years leading Côr Meibion Dwyfor and one and a half years conducting Côr Meibion y Penrhyn. 'I was recruited to conduct the Dwyfor Choir when I was only twenty-two and totally inexperienced: I had no idea how to do it and what to do with my hands,' he recalls, 'the very idea of conducting a choir had never ever previously entered my head.' He had been approached by the choir's secretary, Gwilym Meirion Jones, Tremadog (father of the singer Rhys Meirion) in 1987. It was perhaps not a totally unlikely development given that Melfyn Jones, John Eifion's father, was a founder member of the choir, and Garndolbenmaen, their base, was also John's growing up village. So ever one up for a challenge he'd said: 'OK I'll give it a try.'

'I wanted to be sure that I would enjoy doing it and that the singers would be happy too with me as conductor. It's a two way relationship,' he affirms. 'I also said that I would like to increase the choir from its then sixteen singers to around thirty.' For John conducting was a totally new experience but one he says that 'was always very, very enjoyable.' Then as now music is a hobby which gives him immense pleasure. 'I'd had piano lessons, and while at junior school, played about with the fiddle and flute, and that was about it.' At Dyffryn Nantlle Grammar School he'd dropped music as a subject for serious study in favour of science. Even so for him as a child – one of four – with his parents Melfyn and Ann, home life was a melee of music. They formed a concert party which entertained at village events throughout North Wales and as far as Liverpool and Manchester. In fact here was a family where the genes from all sides spelt music, music, music. One of his mates from those early days is Bryn Terfel who went on to international operatic fame.

Conducting a choir is a skill which he's picked up as he went along, listening and watching how others do it and always ready to learn more. He's not afraid to seek advice and he has his role models. 'I have a lot of respect for Meirion Jones (the former Brythoniaid conductor), he gave me the opportunity to go with Côr Meibion y Brythoniaid as a soloist on a foreign concert tour,' he says. 'And when I sang with Côr Meibion Caernarfon, I learnt a great deal watching Menai Williams conducting. And I'm very impressed with younger conductors like Islwyn Evans from South Wales: in the way they control the response from their singers and how they interpret the score.' It seems like an act of faith for John Eifion: 'I'm learning something new all the time, asking and watching and welcoming another point of view. Everyone has a different opinion. I believe it's a healthy attitude to take.'

Following Meirion Jones as conductor of Côr Y Brythoniaid was very daunting but 'we're moving forward' the impetus is being maintained. Numbers are going up and new members have included a younger element. 'We're working hard on the distinctive Brythoniaid sound, and that's a great deal more than just opening our mouths.' He's very conscious that the choristers come voluntarily from their different occupations in their leisure time to the practices, so it's important that they enjoy the experience. 'There's never a practice without its lighter moments as we rehearse, and if the lads are getting some enjoyment, then there's a very good chance that the singing will be better too.'

John Eifion asserts that y Brythoniaid will remain firmly in the competitive arena. 'That's all important, it's the way to raise standards – there's no doubt about that and I'll argue with anyone who says otherwise!' he says. 'It gives us a target to reach out for: if we don't win we'll know how to improve, while on the other hand, winning challenges us to maintain the standard.'

Practices are held at Ysgol y Moelwyn, Blaenau Ffestiniog each Thursday evening from 7.30 to 9.30 at which visitors are encouraged to come and listen. Concerts, tours and the competitive spirit will always be a feature of the choir's retinue. Their eight LP/CDs output has yielded a Golden Disk Award. And the high standards set by Meirion Jones are more than maintained under John Eifion's command.

The Choir

Tapes/CDs: See Website
Catchment: Cricieth, Harlech, Tywyn, Blaenau Ffestiniog, Pentrefoelas, Porthmadog, Trawsfynydd.
Officials
President: Elfyn Pugh
Chairman: Billy Lloyd
Secretary: Hugh Trefor Jones, 25 Y Ddôl, Porthmadog, Gwynedd, LL49 9HY. Tel. 01766 512863
Treasurer: Wyn Simmonds
Conductor and Musical Director: John Eifion Jones
Accompanist: Elizabeth Ellis FRCM, ARCM
Compere: John Eifion Jones

Rehearsals are held every Thursday night in Ysgol Y Moelwyn, Blaenau Ffestiniog from 7.30 to 9.30.

Côr Meibion Caergybi
Holyhead Male Voice Choir

Holyhead born Gwilym Lewis is the conductor of Côr Meibion Caergybi. He looks the part too, Gwilym is the identikit maestro, his flowing side-whiskers are the ultimate persona. Educated at Caergybi, he went on to the University of Wales Cardiff for his B.Mus. degree, and was awarded a University of Wales Studentship for a Master's Degree in Music. He was then appointed Senior Lecturer in Music at Kirkby Fields College of Education Liverpool. His next move, in 1973, was as Director of Music at the British School in the Hague where he remained for fourteen years.

Then came an unlikely career switch, leaving the cap and gown of academia, Gwilym became a concert pianist and entertainer, on the Royal and the Regency Cruise Liners. Here he gave two classical concerts per cruise and there would be sessions with the resident band ranging from boogie to the classics.

Five years later in 2000 he returned to Holyhead to be with his sister Olwen Lewis, now best remembered as TV singing star of the sixties and the 'Blodau'r Ffair' harmony group. Olwen, formerly a music teacher at Ysgol Botwnnog, had taken over as conductor in 1990 from Dewi Francis, headmaster at the local Llanfawr Junior School, who had founded the choir in 1955.

The choir originated at Capel Bach Millbank, an off-shoot of Hyfrydle the Welsh Presbyterian Church in Holyhead. It quickly became established as a choir of over forty voices, drawing further members from nearby Trearddur Bay and Bodedern, with Nansi Parminter as one of the first accompanists. Nansi had received piano lessons from Eluned Williams Pwllheli back in Botwnnog, and on her marriage to a Holyhead chemist, had been ideally located for her role with the choir. She was to continue those duties until her death of cancer in 2007.

It was never a competing choir as such, rather an entertaining one, ever happiest when on the concert platform, so when the Albert Hall Thousand Voices concerts began Dewi Francis took them there. Côr Meibion Caergybi scores the remarkable achievement of having sung in every Thousand Voices Concert held in the Albert Hall and in April 2009 Gwilym guest conducted the massed choir singing the well known hymn tune *Gwahoddiad* by John Tudor Davies. So it's a tradition that continues as part of their regular weekly rehearsals, taken up practising the chosen set pieces for the next London event. The choir now has about twenty members so Gwilym always welcomes the chance to join in with other choirs for the more robust choruses. Preparation for London offers just such an opportunity. The participating choirs from the north will come together for periodic rehearsals with Alwyn Humphreys, a personal friend from school days when Gwilym played the viola with him in the Anglesey County Orchestra. Dewi Francis asked Gwilym in 1963 to make a musical arrangement of the well known hymn tune *Weimar* for the choir. That arrangement has since been published and accepted in the portfolio for male voice choirs. Another proud moment for Gwilym was to sit at the pianoforte in the Albert Hall in 2004 to accompany the massed choirs singing his arrangement of the hymn tune *Coedmor* to celebrate the occasion when both North and South Wales Choirs first joined together. 'For a few seconds I glanced across at them as the conductor raised his baton. That was the most thrilling moment of my entire life,' he says.

As a deputy conductor of Côr Meibion y Traeth he took centre stage in Lorient Brittany in 2005 conducting that choir together with a five hundred strong massed Pipe Band rendering *Amazing Grace* in their huge stadium before an audience of twelve thousand people, an event which was relayed on national television. Recalling the event now he says he was surprised the next day to find how so many people in the street recognized him, even though he was far away from them on stage. 'Hello Maestro' was their friendly greeting from all quarters. Then it was pointed out that his face was shown on a big screen for the benefit of the Pipers and all the Celtic Festival audience!

So here is a man of many talents: conductor, pianist, viola player and guitarist (those two latter instruments now idle up in the attic) composer and showman. All talents put to exemplary good use when the Holyhead Choir give their concerts locally for various charities or for the holiday makers at the 'Vic' in Llanberis. His experience entertaining on cruise ships and teaching have equipped him well as a good communicator with the ability to raise the 'hwyl', the *bon viveur* which is the essential of a good evening's choral entertainment.

The Choir

The Catchment area: Holyhead and North West Anglesey
Choir officials
Conductor and Musical Director: Gwilym Lewis M.Mus.,LRAM, ARCM, 154 Ffordd Llundain, Caergybi, LL65 2RB. Tel: 01407 762467
Treasurer: Richard Parry

Rehearsals are held at Ysgol Llanfawr (Primary School) Holyhead on Tuesday evenings at 7.30.

Côr Meibion Caernarfon

The Caernarfon Male Voice Choir started life at Ferodo, the brake and clutch linings factory mid-way between Caernarfon and Port Dinorwic on a site overlooking the Menai Straits. In 1967, the year of its formation, 600 people worked there. Emlyn Jones a former employee explains the broad bones of its beginning: 'Elfed Davies and myself, working in the tool-room at Ferodo Ltd posted up notices at the works in early October 1967 seeking interest in forming a works male voice choir. Much interest was shown and after a meeting chaired by Elfed, with myself as secretary, it was decided to give it a go'.

John Hughes, also a Ferodo employee, was invited to be the conductor, and on November 5th 1967, the choir held its first rehearsal at the Young Farmers Hall in Pepper Lane.

The choir had no accompanist to start with, but after moving rehearsals to Llanrug in 1968, Miss Mair Foulkes became the accompanist. In the early years it was known as the Ferodo Male Voice Choir but as time went on membership was opened out to men from outside the factory. This increased membership of the choir and also gave it a better voice balance. Later for a while, practices were held at the Liberal Club, and then moved to Caernarfon Conservative Club, which proved convenient and had a nice social ambience, an essential element in the choir culture. John Hughes' work giving the choir a sound basis had by the early 70s ended, and the new conductor Haydn Davies, Director of Musical Studies for Caernarfonshire, was in the saddle. Although his expertise and background was in the brass band tradition, and was an accomplished cello player, Haydn was to take the choir to yet higher standards. Choir membership peaked at 80, and in 1975 they went on their first overseas concert tour, to Toronto, returning in early August for their second National Eisteddfod success, at Bro Dwyfor. Their first success being in the National Eisteddfod at Haverfordwest in 1972. Haydn Davies left the area in the early 80s on being appointed HM Inspector of Schools. Subsequent conductors have included Bill Evans, a particularly good pianist and violinist who was a teacher in Caernarfon; Dalwyn Henshall who was studying for a doctorate of music at Bangor, John Hywel from Bangor University's Music Faculty and Gareth Hughes Jones.

1993 saw Menai Williams, formerly Côr Meibion y Penrhyn Deputy Conductor, of the Music Department at Ysgol Syr Huw Owen Caernarfon, taking the baton. She brought with her a wealth of experience having already conducted Hogia'r Ddwylan (1966-1988) and Côr Meibion Y Penrhyn (1970-1974). Born at Bylchau near Denbigh when her father Rev. T.J. Hughes was minister at Tan y Fron (1937-1942), there had been several family moves as her father responded to pastoral calls. From the Vale of Clwyd they went to Waenfawr, before moving briefly to Rhyl and then to Penrhyndeudraeth, 'my growing up years', from there to Rhos and thence finally to Bethesda. Her first teaching post on leaving the University of Wales Bangor was as head of music at Ysgol Dyffryn Ogwen, later ending her career at Ysgol Syr Huw Owen Caernarfon, joining Mona Meirion Richards who was head of music there. This was ultimately to bring her to Côr Meibion Caernarfon. It began a period when the choir scaled new heights of success: from 1994 to 2003 taking the National Eisteddfod laurels no less than five times. She also introduced Cerdd Dant singing into the choir's repertoire, an unusual departure from main stream pieces, which turned out to be very popular with members. In this she had the good fortune of having Mona Meirion Richards an accomplished harpist as accompanist. Mona was the National Eisteddfod and Urdd Eisteddfod harpist for 30 years, while Menai too is an acknowledged expert. Mona has been with the choir for a period exceeding 25 years and Menai for 15.

The rehearsals are now held in the centre of musical excellence, 'Y Galeri', which was opened at the beginning of the 21st century as part of a dockside development in Caernarfon. Côr Meibion Caernarfon was the first choir to sing there, putting the building's very fine acoustics to the ultimate test.

They're a well travelled choir: in 1982 they wowed America accompanied by Bryn Terfel, the now World famous baritone, their patron, whose home is on the edge of Caernarfon, as soloist.

When Bryn Terfel launched 'Gŵyl y Faenol', the Faenol Festival, at the end of the 20th century, drawing the cream of the World's musical talent to an open air event in the Faenol Park, they were there too. Indeed their travel itineraries read like pages from a Thomas Cook brochure: apart from Canada where they've toured twice; they've been to the USA twice, once as guests of the annual Baltimore Gymanfa Ganu, Welsh Singing Festival, with Bryn Terfel and soprano Mary Lloyd Davies as soloists (1982); to Germany in 1979 and 1992; Holland 1990 as part of a massed choir of a 1000 voices from Wales who joined up with a 1000 voice Dutch Choir in a choral extravaganza, and in 1994 in the company of Archbishop of Wales, Alwyn Rice Jones, singing in a cathedral in Holland to celebrate 50 years since the country's release from Nazi oppression by the 51st Welsh Division; the Sligo Festival in Ireland too has been a popular venue where they have twice scooped the top prize. In 1998, a visit to Malta to

Côr Meibion Maelgwn, conducted by Trystan Lewis, winning the first prize in the choirs over 45 in number at the National Eisteddfod at Bala, 2009.

Trelawnyd Male Voice Choir with Neville Owen their conductor from 1955 to 1969 and accompanist Rhona Davies

Côr Meibion Dinas Bangor with accompanist Lowrie Roberts Williams, conductor James Griffiths and deputy conductor Gwilym Lewis, 2006

Cymau Male Voice Choir with their accompanist Alwen Lloyd Enston and conductor Christine Williams. (2007)

Llanddulas Male Voice Choir with their conductor/ accompanist/harpist Eirlys Dwyryd, 2005

Côr Meibion Orffiws y Rhos published a celebrity brochure on their fiftieth birthday in 2007

Eirlys Haf Jones (formerly Turvey) has been Flint Male Voice Choir's accompanist since the choir's formation in 1975

Meibion Llywarch at the Gwyl Cerdd Dant

52

*North Wales Association . Officials of the organisation committee for the
Festival of Massed Male Voices 1997: Back row L to R. – J. Cheshire
(Ticket Secretary); E. Roberts B.E.M. (Stage Manager); P. Harrison
(Programme Secretary); E. Williams (Chief Steward); Front row L to R.
– J.R.Davies (Association Treasurer); I.M.Jones (Association President);
E.Roberts (Festival Committee Chairman); G.Hughes (Association
Chairman); G.W.Roberts (Association Secretary)*

*Denbigh Male Voice Choir with conductor Arwyn Roberts, accompanist
Joyce Davies and deputy accompanist Ann Edwards, 2007. Choir (left to
right back row): D. Carter, H. Jones, R.M.Jones, T.L.Jones, P.Harrison,
G.D.Edward, T.Brookes, G.Roberts, E.Evans. Second row L to R.:
R.Jones, D.Wynne, A.Roberts, L.Jones, A.B.Jones, D.K.Jones, J. Raine,
R.Davies, I.Davies, G.Edwards, A.Davies. Front row L to R:
H.T.Williams, A.Davies, A.Jones, D.Hards, R.Jones, R.W.Lloyd,
T.Prytherch, D.L.Jones, E.Birch, G.Davies, A.S.Jones,D.B.Jones*

An early picture of Hogia'r Ddwylan with their conductor (from 1967 to 1988) Menai Williams at the harp

Hogia'r Ddwylan and friends celebrate their fortieth anniversary in style cruising on Menai Strait, 2006

Massed Choir rehearsal in Corwen July 2000, preparing for the Royal Albert Hall Concert in London

Côr Meibion Bro Glyndŵr circa 1990 with accompanist Alice Evans and conductor Paul Johns

*Côr Meibion y Traeth with their conductor Gwyn L. Williams at the
National Eisteddfod, Llangefni 1983*

*Cledwyn Rowlands, founder
member of Côr Meibion y Traeth
who received a long service
citation from the choir on
completing over 45 years
membership*

*John Eifion conductor of Côr
Meibion y Brythoniaid since 2002
and the accompanist Elizabeth
Ellis*

Côr Meibion y Brythoniaid with their conductor John Eifion and accompanists Elizabeth Ellis and Caryl Roberts. (2002)

Côr Meibion Dinas Bangor lead the parade at the Lorient Celtic Festival in Brittany, August 2003

Flint Male Voice Choir with their concert accompanist and deputy conductor Aled Wyn Edwards and conductor Huw Dunley , centre. February 2006

Four ladies who've in turn conducted Hogia'r Ddwylan : Ilid Anne Jones, their present conductor; Mari Pritchard, Sioned Webb and Menai Williams

Hogia'r Ddwylan August 2006, Ilid Anne Jones conducting

Côr Meibion y Moelwyn 2006. L to R (Back Row): Glyn Jones, Owen Evans, Gwyn Jarman, Gareth Jones, Tom Wrench, David L. Jones, Tecwyn Williams, Meirion Ellis, Dwyfor Williams, Evie Roberts, Eifion Morris, Anthony Mc Nally. Front Row: Meredydd Ellis, Melfyn Hughes, David Williams, Vernon Jones, Sylvia Ann Jones (conductor), Gwyn Vaughan Jones (accompanist), Cyril Lewis, Idris Roberts

Oakeley Male Voice Choir circa 1960. Back row: A.W.Evans, R.Jones, A.Parry, E.Thomas, R.Evans, H.Barlow, E.Jones, D.Owen, W.Jones, T.Davies, W.O.Williams . Second row: G.Jones, J.Thomas, H.G.Jones, G.Woolford, D.Lewis, V.Jones, A.Lewis, I.Jones, D.Roberts, G.Crump, J.R.Jones. Front row: J.G.Jones, W.J.Morris, J.M.Richards, T.Williams, T.Owen Thomas (conductor), Mrs George Guest (accompanist), M.Jones, G.Ellis, H.Williams. Inset: R.J.Williams, R.D.Roberts, G.Parry, C.Hughes, R.Pugh

Côr Meibion Pen y Bont Fawr with their conductor Tegwyn Jones and accompanist Lynda Thomas. (1995)

Cantorion Colin Jones

61

Phylis Dryhurst Dod conductor of Denbigh and District Male Voice Choir from 1988 to 2001 and massed choir accompanist John Tudor Davies of Rhos

John Glyn Williams, conductor of Rhos Orpheus Male Voice Choir, at rehearsal for the Millenium Thousand Voices Albert Hall Concert

Trystan Lewis, conductor of Côr Meibion Maelgwn

Côr Meibion Dyffryn Peris with accompanist Hefina Jones and conductor Dafydd Roberts. (2007)

Côr Godre'r Aran, 1954. Back row L to R. John Morris, John T.Jones, Dennis O Derbyshire, Morris Roberts, Idris Edwards, David Pierce Jones. Second row. W.Gittins Owen, Ifor Roberts, Martin R.Jones, Trefor Edwards, Emrys Williams, Einion Edwards, Arthur D.Jones, Arthur Edwards. Front row. Greta Williams, harpist (Telynores Uwchlyn); Tecwyn Jones, D. Lloyd Jones, Harold Morris, Tom Jones, conductor; Evan Roberts, Richard O.Edwards, John Roberts. Most were among the first Godre'r Aran choir members

Betws yn Rhos Male Voice Choir emblem

Cor Meibion Betws-yn-Rhos

Côr Meibion Bro Dysynni with accompanist Mair Jones and conductor Eirian Lloyd-Evans. The Choir L to R : Geraint Evans, Bryan Davies, Ian Evans, Arthur Williams, Reg Davies, Ifor Lewis, Kevin Arnold, Cynlais Pughe, Glyn Rees, Gareth Evans, John Plumb, David Evans, Ronnie Roberts, John Meirion Richards, Graeme Cox, Gerry Jones, Sulwyn Jones, 2006

Cor Meibion Bro Dysynni, 1970. Back row L to R: W.Humphreys, Ron Davies, G. Kirkham, P.Parker, Glyn Rees, G.Roberts, W.Murfin, D.Jones, J.Jones, Sulwyn Jones, E.Williams, B.Jones, J.M.Evans, M.Jones, T.Williams, W.Davies. Front row L to R: D.Jones, I.Jones, Phil Jones, G.Roberts, R.Roberts, I.Thomas, Gwynorydd Davies (conductor); Gwenda Hunter Graham (accompanist); S.Roberts, R.E.Williams, Emlyn Williams, Ron Roberts, J.Humphreys, Basil Jones.

Côr Meibion Caernarfon and their conductor from 1993 to 2008 Menai Williams, and accompanist Mona Meirion Richards

Newtown and District Male Voice Choir with their Deputy Conductor/ Accompanist Gill Owen, Musical Director Christine Roberts and Peg Morris Accompanist , centre left to right. (2007)

Côr Meibion Llanfair Caereinion with their conductor Lynda Gittins on the left and accompanist Jane Lewis, right. (2005)

*Phylis Dryhurst Dodd at an open air rehearsal with Llanfair Caereinion
Male Voice Choir on their way to the Powys Eisteddfod at Glyn Ceiriog in
1957 where they took second prize*

Meibion Dwyfor at Plas Tan y Bwlch

*Côr Meibion Llanfair Caereinion : conductor D. Emlyn Evans,
accompanist Doris Roberts. (1975)*

*Corwen Male Voice Choir, circa 1920 – conductor Arthur Roberts,
accompanist Gwyneth Roberts*

Gobowen Orthopaedic Male Voice Choir, 2003

Côr Meibion Pen y Bont Fawr with their conductor Emyr Lloyd Jones and accompanist Lynda Thomas. (1993)

Côr Meibion Dyffryn Ceiriog, 2005, with conductor Peter Simpson Davies

Llangollen Male Voice Choir with their conductor Rhonwen Jones, centre left, and accompanist Alwen Enston. (2007)

Meibion Llywarch with Dan Puw their conductor, left, and second from right, accompanist Eirian Jones

Côr Mebion Bro Dyfi with their conductor Gwilym Bryniog Davies and accompanist Catrin Jones, 2008

sing in the Palace of the Governor, was a wonderful experience. A weekend visit to Norrkoping in Sweden for a concert came about, in 2006, as the result of TV people from that country hearing them rehearsing in the 'Galeri'. Of such incidents are links from across the globe formed.

On relatively home ground there have been many happy moments, as when the choir sang at the Millennium Stadium in Cardiff on the occasion of the International Rugby Match between Wales and Scotland, shortly after the stadium opened. The choir sang well there, but even so the home team lost in the rugby game which followed!

Singing, at the opening of the Hydro Electric Works at Llanberis by HRH Prince Charles in 1984, was another great occasion, their voices rebounding magically within the huge cavern. Another happy recollection for the choir was performing in the opera *Fidelio* with the Bangor University Choir conducted by John Hywel. Playing as the Prisoners Chorus, they appeared bare footed dressed in rags (rustled out of torn up ancient pyjamas, dyed black), each one sporting home grown whiskers as they came out of captivity singing *Oh Happy Morn*! For weeks leading up to the performances, choir members were instantly recognised about the town by their whiskery beards.

The Choir

Tapes and CDs: *Tydi a Roddaist* – Cambrian Recordings Ltd
– Côr Meibion Caernarfon a Seindorf Ffestiniog Cymreig,
Sain 78;
Ar Lan y Fenai – Tape – Sain;
Côr Meibion Caernarfon – CD Sain 1979;
Yn Ninas Diniweidrwydd – CD Sain 2004.
Catchment: Caernarfon and surrounding villages; Llangefni, Llanfair PG and Tŷ Croes in Anglesey; Dinas and Morfa Nefyn in Lleyn.
Officials
Patron: Bryn Terfel CBE
President: Dr Huw Roberts
Chairman: Owain Wyn
Secretary: Dafydd J. Jones, Maes yr Haf, 3 Bethel Road, Caernarfon,
Gwynedd LL55 1HB. Tel. 01286 672633
e-mail: jdacid300@aol.com
Treasurer: Alwynne T. Jones
Conductor: Menai Williams B.A.

Accompanist: Mona Meirion Richards BA, LRAM
Compere: Wynford Lloyd Davies

*Choir rehearsals are held in Y Galeri, Caernarfon
every Tuesday evening 7.30-9.30.*

National Eisteddfod of Wales winners nine times since 1972.

Menai Williams left the choir in July 2008 and was succeeded as conductor by Delyth Williams in September 2008.

Delyth Williams, the twenty-nine year old head of music at Ysgol Eifionydd Porthmadog, was appointed to succeed Menai Williams at the beginning of September 2008. She is a native of Groeslon near Caernarfon where she still lives, and studied music at the University of North Wales Bangor taking the Conductor's Module; and tutored by Wyn Thomas, she left with a B.Mus. degree. Delyth is well experienced in conducting and training her school choir for Welsh League of Youth (Urdd Gobaith Cymru) events, and preparing youngsters for yr Ŵyl Gerdd Dant as well as for musical shows at Ysgol Eifionydd. She also plays the piano and the saxophone. Conducting Côr Meibion Caernarfon is her first experience with an adult choir, but she's been well received by the choristers and readily acknowledges the valuable help and advice she's receiving from the choir's accompanist, Mona Meirion Richards.

Côr Meibion Caerwys
Caerwys Male Voice Choir

The Rev. T.R. Jones came to Caerwys, his first and only pastorate, in 1909 and served that community for over fifty years. Such was his standing in the Vale of Clwyd Chapel Convention that he became known as 'Archesgob Henaduriaeth Dyffryn Clwyd' (Archbishop of the Vale of Clwyd). He was a genial kindly person and his preaching voice had a musical lilt. Indeed he's still remembered by the older people of Caerwys for his love of children and how he'd round them all up to be taught the tonic sol-fa. Generations of Caerwys children grew up knowing their scales.

For much of his life T.R. was a bachelor and lodged with Tommy Williams, Bell House the local butcher. Tommy was the conductor of the Caerwys Mixed Choir, so as the children grew up, they could read music and were ready to join in the choir, Côr Caerwys. 'Caerwys was noted for its singing,' says John Rees a native of the town who benefited from T.R's sol-fa exercises. 'He taught my father and grandfather too,' he says, 'we could all sing.' The choir sang in the Rhos National Eisteddfod and in 1951, at the Festival of Britain. 'At the same time Howel Matthews started a youth choir which flourished for about three years.'

But by the middle 1950s, influenced by the Coronation, 'people bought television sets and all those things stopped, they didn't want to sing – and they didn't want go to listen either'. For almost fifty years: nothing!

* * *

Just imagine a dark Monday night in mid-winter: location St Michael's Church Caerwys which easily dates to 1537. It's eight o'clock, and within this double aisled church with its massive military tower at the west end, there's the sound of music. Walk the gravelled drive, the coloured lights shining from stained glass windows beckon you on. Curiosity leads you to the ancient doorway. Inside familiar tunes fan your interest, draw you towards a choir practice in the church vestry – a kind of large annex. There a cheery crowd of men seated in a semi-circle are responding earnestly to the conductor's bidding. There's a good feeling of bon-homie. The conductor Elizabeth Hughes from Ruthin, retired from her teaching career at Maes Garmon after fifteen years in 1991, had produced musical shows at the school but this was her first time with a male voice choir. It's a role she's taken on since September 2007 and establishing an excellent rapport. Although many now do not read music 'they pick things up so quickly,' she comments.

* * *

The Caerwys choir, founded in 1999, is one of the youngest in Wales. As the new millennium approached, the people of Caerwys wanted to make it a memorable occasion. A small male voice choir was formed to sing on a makeshift stage and to perform at the striking of the hour of the new millennium. That event was filmed by an international news team and by means of a satelite link, while the choristers sang traditional Welsh songs – the performance was broadcast live throughout the world. The choir members called a meeting in February 2000 and decided to continue the choir. There were only eight members originally, with Robert Goodby as the conductor and lead tenor. However, with enthusiasm and good singing the word got around the area and members of other choirs joined the Caerwys choir.

Bob Goodby, who laid the foundation, was succeeded by Islwyn Jones from Mold, a much respected and experienced member and conductor of choirs for over forty-five years. It was he who improved the choir to its present standard. When Islwyn retired in 2007 to become a member of the First Bass section and elected president of the choir, Elizabeth Hughes a musician and composer in her own right took over as Musical Director. 'She has taken the choir to new standards of performance,' says Roger Jenkins, the choir secretary. The accompanist is Margaret Williams. From an initial group of eight the choir has grown to forty members and is a member of the National Association of Choirs. At the Treyddyn Chair Eisteddfod in February 2006 they won the Choir competition. The choir appeared on the National Eisteddfod stage at Mold in August 2007 as both guests and competitors, and in October 2007 performed at the Kilkenny Celtic Festival in Ireland.

Once more Caerwys is alive with the sound of music.

The Choir

Catchment: Mold, Caerwys, Tremeirchion, Cefn Meiriadog and other villages within an approximate ten mile radius.
Officers
President: Islwyn M. Jones
Chairman: Tim Erasmus
Secretary: Roger Jenkins, 2, Park Grove, Caerwys, Flintshire, CH7 5BX. Tel. 01352 720637
Treasurer: Huw Voyle
Musical Director and Conductor: Elizabeth Hughes BA, ATCL
Accompanist: Margaret Williams
Compere: John Arfon Davies
Website: corcaerwys.org.uk

Rehearsals are held at St Michael's Church, Caerwys every Monday night 7.30 to 9.30.

Cantorion Colin Jones
The North Wales Male Chorus

'My boss in the Royal Manchester College of Music, Freddie Cox, used to say to me: 'Jones, you can help a voice, you can't make one – otherwise Bartelli, Gigli's teacher in Italy, could have made a thousand Giglis, yet we only have one!' Colin Jones still remembers that piece of advice from the time when he was a lecturer training opera singers, a role he played from 1967 until 1975.

Colin Jones might easily have become a professional singer himself, in those days he had a very fine voice and sang, as he recalls, in *Othello* with Elizabeth Vaughan and Sir John Barbirolli. 'But teaching people in the technique of voice production had the greater appeal,' he says.

He was born in Rhosllanerchrugog where he still lives, the one time mining village within the Wrexham coalfield. It's a place that has changed much during his lifetime. He remembers the days when ninety percent of the men there worked in the mines, walking the short distance to the Hafod Colliery, and the twenty-six chapels flourished. It was the environment which influenced his destiny: the Sunday schools had their music classes and home life was centred around the piano. Colin was already playing the piano when he was six years old, and as a youngster of fourteen won at the Llangollen International Eisteddfod in a competition open to the World's best pianists. Later he went for Saturday morning piano lessons at the Mathay School of Music in Liverpool for extra qualifications. Then came a further crucial decision: it was the time of conscription for national service and for Colin a choice to either join the army and 'be posted to Egypt or wherever', or to go down the coal mine 'as a Bevin Boy'. He reckoned that if he joined the army he would lose two years of valuable piano tuition, so inevitably he took the other option and 'went down the road to the Hafod colliery' where he worked for nine years. By then, a twenty-six year old, he decided to do a three year degree course at the Royal Manchester College of Music, at the end of which he was offered a post there as Senior Lecturer in Vocal Studies. It was an exiting time for the young Colin honing his expertise and training student singers in voice production. And every week-end training singers who entertained at Mediaeval Banquets at Ruthin, Manchester, Tadcaster, Lumley Castle, Caldicot Castle and Coventry.

In 1976 Colin Jones was appointed Principal Lecturer and Head of Music at the North East Wales Institute of Higher Education (NEWI) at Wrexham, a position he held until 1993. By then NEWI was concentrating more on the sciences and when Colin was offered early retirement with a 'golden handshake', he took it.

His choir involvement had begun in 1952 when for five years he was the accompanist for the Rhosllanerchrugog Male Voice Choir, then at twenty-one, appointed Musical Director. His work with the choir enhanced its quality for over thirty years, winning major prizes at the Welsh National Eisteddfod and proclaimed BBC Choir of the Year on more than one occasion. For many years he was principal accompanist at the Llangollen International Eisteddfod, and many eminent soloists including Sir Geraint Evans, Stuart Burrows, Elizabeth Vaughan and Bryn Terfel have requested his services. His role as a guest conductor has taken him to the London Palladium; the Opera House, Chicago; St David's Hall Cardiff, and the Liederhalle, Stuttgart.

He left the Rhosllanerchrugog Male Voice Choir in 1987. In 1991 he was the guest conductor at the Thousand Voices Concert in the Royal Albert Hall. Preparation for this wonderful event had meant rehearsals in all parts of North Wales, but already singers wanted to know what Colin's plans were in the long term. On his rehearsal circuit he had heard a cross section of the elite voices of the north, and it was this, together with the call for one great North Wales Male Voice Choir that spurred him on to form 'Cantorion Colin Jones'. Essentially they were hand picked, the very best of what he had heard in North Wales. As a Choir this was to be the tops, selecting would be a highly exacting process. Using all of his now considerable experience, it would be a choir to set new standards. Some of the singers were already known to him as soloists he had coached for events such as the National Eisteddfod and the International at Llangollen. His expectations were high, they would be moulded as only he knew how.

During 1991 there was much hard work to be done as the singers from all parts of North Wales, from Anglesey in the north to Machynlleth in the southern parts; from Harlech on the west coast, to Wrexham and the border country, responded to the call from Maestro Colin Jones. Rehearsals held centrally at Betws-y-coed would be disciplined and intense.

From the outset Colin stipulated that the choir would number a maximum fifty-five singers and their aim to be a high standard concert and touring choir. It would not enter the eisteddfodic competitive arena, on this he had very definite views. His time with the Rhos Male Voice Choir had shown him that the adjudication at the National Eisteddfod was flawed, 'often the Rhos Choir won a competition without deserving the honour – at other times they lost when they should have won!' He seriously despairs of the system, because 'given its inconsistency in the value and quality of the adjudication, it fails to raise standards'. He argues fiercely that 'a choir's worth should be judged by a musically enlightened audience: that is the way to raise standards' and with his new choir he would prove the validity of his contention.

Their first concert was in 1992 at the William Aston Hall Wrexham and in the following year a performance at the Malta Musical Festival. Over the succeeding years they have made many overseas tours; their itineraries read like pages from a Thomas Cook World Travel brochure: Singapore and Australia in 1996 with concerts at Sydney, Melbourne and Adelaide. 1999 saw them on the West Coast of America and a concert tour which began in Minneapolis and Minnesota before flying on to Seattle in Washington State. Thence to Victoria on Vancouver Island before going on to Vancouver in Canada. 2000 took them to Finland in December! 'All the lads talked about how they would have to deal with the expected three hours of daylight and the knee-deep snow and how they would have to pack double thickness thermals in their cases,' says Colin, 'but in the event this was the first time in fifty years that Finland had no snow, and the choristers walked about happily in their shirt sleeves.' In 2004 and 2005 America beckoned once more, in the first instance, two weeks in California and three concerts around San Francisco, then down to Los Angeles to do three more. In 2005 they were invited to sing at the Gymanfa Ganu to be held in Disney World in Florida. Then on to Orlando for a concert and another Gymanfa. 2007 and 2008 France and a programme of three concerts on each occasion. Understandably the invitations come thick and fast 'but like many other choirs the choristers and their Musical Director are getting older, so future tours are likely to be shorter ones to European countries,' says Colin.

So here is the story of a World class choir and their musical director whose name is synonymous with choral music par excellence. What's the secret? 'It's building up the confidence that's important,' he says. 'Each one must listen to the next one to him, there are some very powerful voices here and it's essential that they don't stand out individually but blend in.' It's part of Colin's philosophy never to use copies at the concerts. 'I never have a copy at the rostrum,' he says, 'nor will the choristers, it all comes with experience.' He continues: 'I'm lucky to have a choir who can read music and they learn quickly.'

'I must have a well disciplined choir who respond to my command – that's terribly important. And I must draw the music out of them, a look at them is often enough – I'm not one to move about much at the rostrum, just raising a finger or an eye, that's enough.'

The Choir

CDs: See Website: cantorioncolinjones.com
Catchment: The Choristers come from all parts of North Wales.
The Choir Officials
President: Dai Jones, Llanilar
Chairman: Terry Brockley
Vice Chairman: John Puw
Secretary: Steve Gardner
Treasurer: Gordon Price
Stage Manager: John Roberts
Committee: Roger George, Arwyn Roberts,
Tudor Rowlands, David Price and Gareth Oliver
Accompanist: Olwen Jones LWCMD
Compere: John Rogers Jones
Conductor and Musical Director: Colin Jones GRSM, ARMCM,
LRAM, ARCM
Website: cantorioncolinjones.com

*Rehearsals are held once a fortnight on Sunday afternoon
at St Mary's Church Betws-y-coed at 2 o'clock.*

Colin Jones retired on November 8th, 2008 after 52 years as conductor, 17 of these with Cantorion Colin Jones.

John Daniel GRSM, ARCM, who graduated from the Royal Manchester College of Music in 1971, where he studied piano and voice, succeeded Colin Jones as conductor in November, 2008.

In January 1971, at the age of 22, he was appointed Musical Director of the Froncysyllte Male Voice Choir where he stayed for about twenty years. He took the Fron choir to a notable double in 1977 winning at both the Llangollen International Eisteddfod and the National Eisteddfod at Wrexham.

Up to his retirement in 2006 he was Head of the Faculty of Expressive Arts at Ysgol Morgan Llwyd, Wrexham where, with the school choir, he won many prestigious awards. In 1998 he was appointed Musical Director of the newly formed Rhos Ladies Choir and yet further accolades, notably a National Eisteddfod first prize.

Following this in 2005 he was appointed conductor of Rhos Male Voice Choir which he led to a first prize at the inaugural 'Golden Nightingale' competition in Bournemouth.

He leads a very full musical life, tutoring singers and pianists as well as giving master classes to other choirs and choral societies on voice production, choral techniques and musical interpretation. Probably his proudest achievement is seeing both his sons, which he taught, as graduates of Royal Colleges of Music, the one in London and the other at Manchester.

Côr Meibion Colwyn

Gwyn Roberts joined the Colwyn Male Voice Choir when it was reformed in 1972, on its fifth re-incarnation since male voice choirs were first talked about in Colwyn in 1899.

That original choir performed for Queen Victoria, a Royal Command so to speak, at the magnificent Crystal Palace in London. It was a choir with a lot of kudos conducted by one, Theophilus Jones, and were eisteddfod victors at Abergele, Llandudno and at Caernarfon, the premier award winners of twenty-five pounds and a silver cup! Much later, in 1926, taking the first prize of forty pounds at Pentrefoelas.

Fast forward to July 1997 and another exciting command, this time to appear with Clarissa Dickson Wright and Jennifer Paterson, TV stars of the 'Two Fat Ladies' cookery series. They were doing a programme at Llandudno and Patricia Llewelyn, the show's Welsh producer, wanted a Welsh Choir. The format was to be a picnic prepared by the 'Ladies' on the Great Orme. And the choir to sing *Nant y Mynydd* (Mountain Stream). As they went up the spectacular Llandudno hillside, Jennifer began to sing in her memorably deep and low baritone voice 'clang clang clang went the trolley, ding ding ding went the bell' with the entire choir joining in. Then a spontaneous burst of *O Gymru* (From Wales), the choir's signature tune.

All of which illustrates the versatility of their appeal. And over those years despite all the fits and starts, when for various reasons they disbanded and reconvened, this is a choir in fine spirit.

Gwyn Roberts took over as a 'stop gap' conductor in 2001 and he's 'still at it'. Of a musical family, his mother Janet well in her eighties still regularly plays the organ for Sunday worship at the Baptist chapel in Llanelian while his sister, Margaret Jones, sings with Côr Glan Alun and Denbigh Choral Society. Gwyn's musical experience amounts to having done the eisteddfod rounds with his brother John – now a lead tenor in the choir – as boy sopranos, during their growing up years at Llansannan and later in Capel Garmon near Llanrwst. 'I haven't sung solo since my voice broke,' says Gwyn. But he's done a lot of choir singing, is a member of the elite Colin Jones Choir and proving to be a very competent conductor. 'I was a bit nervous at first,' he says, 'still am to a degree – but having nerves is not a bad thing.'

At the rostrum in the Old Colwyn Community Centre where they have their weekly practices every Sunday and Wednesday night, he shows great flair and authority. He admits that he's learnt a lot by watching Colin Jones, noting the understated hand movements of the maestro. Choir members are happy in his company. He smiles encouragement when they've pleased him. The hand gestures are minimal, the movement of a finger or even a thumb, even approval or otherwise in his facial expression shows his command. He accepts that conducting is an art form which is giving him great satisfaction.

He obviously has a fine musical ear and a good grasp of the four voice range as well as the harmony. He knows the words and how and where the volume should vary. Each exercise at practice improves the overall sound. Even the mere sound of words, intoned and correctly pronounced, receive his detailed attention.

So is the conducting business a gift? It certainly appears so for Gwyn. 'I know many very good pianists and musicians, who can't do it,' he says. But rather surprisingly adds that a good accompanist could be more important than a conductor! In saying that, he acknowledges his debt to the present accompanists, Richard Hibbs and Gwyneth Macdonald – and also salutes Joyce Davies who left the area in 2008 after two years service with the choir and prior to that Mary Darling for a job well done. 'Truly invaluable.'

Gwyn upholds a fine tradition. The first conductor of the re-formed choir back in 1972 was Gwilym Davies, who was by profession an accountant; of a musical family, he was also a very good singer. The choir was formed as a youth choir to compete in the Urdd (Welsh League of Youth) Eisteddfod. So basically at that time it was known as Côr Aelwyd yr Urdd Hen Golwyn. Gwyn remembers Gwilym as a naturally easy going sort of person who possessed the ability for good choir control. Occasionally he would scold, but was never harsh with them. The Choir flourished during his three year stewardship which ended when he died suddenly in 1975.

The rostrum was then taken by Neville Owen, a music teacher at Prestatyn, who was formerly choir master of Côr Meibion Trelawnyd. He was to take the choir up a gear and numbers increased. His enthusiasm for the eisteddfod scene took them to success at the National Eisteddfod in 1976, and again at Caernarfon in 1979, winning the 'chief choral', against strong contenders Trelawnyd, Llanelli and Côr Meibion Y Brythoniaid. In the same year taking the laurels at the Cork Music Festival in Ireland, by which time the choristers had increased to 'over a hundred'.

Choir accompanist at this time was Mercia Howard, daughter of the local Baptist Chapel Minister, who was formerly the particularly gifted music teacher at Penrhos College in Colwyn Bay. She was renowned for her ability, having once had sight of the music score, to accompany the choir without a copy. This enabled her to concentrate more easily on the conductor's instructions. She was to serve the choir well for a good number of years with subsequent conductors.

When Neville Owen left in 1981, Jefferson Thomas a Rhyl music teacher took over, remaining until 1986. He was followed by Geraint James who was head of the Design and Creative Arts Faculty at Eirias High School in Colwyn Bay (now Director of Education for Conwy) and was joined as deputy by Roby E. Davies in 1988, a successful composer and Organist at Llanrhos Parish Church.

Geraint was to take the choir to a first prize at the National Eisteddfod in Porthmadog (for choirs of 41-60 voices) in 1987. And in 1988 led them in a special recording for Gordon Lorenz under the Kingsway Label, to mark the 250th anniversary of John Wesley's conversion. Singing a selection of Wesley hymns at the Huddersfield Town Hall, they were joined by TV personality Moira Anderson and the Alan Simmons Singers.

In June 1989 the choir represented Wales at the Toronto International Festival, and in August of the same year took part in the premier of a specially commissioned new Welsh opera at the Llanrwst National Eisteddfod – *Dagrau Pengwern* by Geoffrey Thomas, which was introduced by Sir Geraint Evans.

Geraint James continued until 1992, to be followed for short periods, by the Welsh diva Myfanwy Roberts, and Gareth Hughes. During Gareth's tenure the choir competed at the 5th Malta International Choral Festival in 1993, returning with a Bronze Award. It was at this event that the choir formed a close friendship with the Gold Medal Winners, the Moscow Engineering and Physics Institute Male Voice Choir, which resulted in the Russian Choir visiting Wales in 1995. But a joint concert of the two choirs held at the Rhyl Pavilion Theatre was not without its moment of pure drama. That occurred because of the almighty thunder storm, the worst in years, that struck the area. And when Côr Mebion Colwyn were singing the line ' . . . and when darkness fell on the earth . . . ' from Willy Richler's *The Creation*, a lightening strike blew the fuses, leaving the theatre in total darkness. The timing couldn't be better, and the choir sang on!

The next musical director was Ian Woolford, formerly conductor of Côr Meibion Llanrwst, and the possessor of a fine baritone voice. He drew on his experience in voice training at the Manchester School of Music to take the choir on to yet higher standards.

When Ian left, the baton was taken for a short time by the Wrexham soprano, Beverly Jones. Gwyn Roberts took over as a 'stop gap conductor' in 2001.

Their story continues, foreign travel such as visits to the 2000 seat

Palau de Musica in Barcelona singing on stage with representative choirs from five other nations. 'We'd like to do that again. It's a mini Albert Hall,' says Gwyn, 'and the acoustics are superb.' And further visits to Ireland, their favourite of all, for the unique festival of Celtic Nations – Gŵyl Pan Geltaidd. They've done Ireland seven times already, on three occasions as guests of the Mc Cormic Singers in Limerick.

The Choir

Tapes/CDs:
Côr Meibion Colwyn 25th Anniversary Concert 1997
O Gymru (From Wales) June 2003
The Choir
Catchment Area: From Rhyl to Llanfairfechan
Officials
President: Sir Philip Mayers OBE
Chairman: Alun Hughes
Secretary: Charles Cooksley, 21 Allanson Road, Llandrillo-yn-Rhos, Colwyn Bay, LL28 4AN. Tel. 01492 548670
Treasurer: Alwyn Williams
Conductor and Musical Director: Gwyn Roberts
Accompanists: Richard Hibbs and Gwyneth Macdonald
Compere: Alun Hughes/Brian Jones/Gwyn Roberts

Rehearsals are held every Sunday and Wednesday night
7.30-9.30 in the Community Centre, Old Colwyn.

Côr Meibion Cymau

Côr Meibion Cymau started life as an ENSA choir, the Cymau Glee Party of twenty voices in 1938, which entertained the troops during the war in Army Camps throughout North Wales. They developed into a mixed voice choir conducted by John Henry Lloyd, an employee of Aerospace at Broughton, who took them to success in the 1947 National Eisteddfod held at Colwyn Bay. The choir was disbanded for a while, eventually to be revived in 1972 as a male voice choir, with some members from the original group incorporated. The person who breathed new life into the choir was Miss Marian Jones, a music teacher from Cymau, who taught at Ysgol Daniel Owen in Mold. She was an influential person in the village, and played the organ at Bethesda Chapel there. The first thing that she did was to secure an accompanist, Alwen Enston of nearby Treuddyn, who was a teacher at Bryn Coch School in Mold and a skilful pianist. This was a good choice because Alwen had her own very good children's school choir, and when they left her, Marian would 'persuade' them to join her choir at Mold Alyn School. Later in life they would join Côr Meibion Cymau. 'She would absolutely chase them'. Recalling events now Alwen (still the accompanist after thirty-six years) says that Marian Jones was a very determined person and no-one dared spurn her demands, her word was law. Her approach had been direct : 'You're a good pianist, you've got to play,' Alwen had protested, 'I haven't played for a male voice choir in my life, but I'll give it a try for a week or two till you find someone else – she didn't bother looking for anybody else, and I'm still there!'

'If Marian as much as asked the men folk, "Come to my choir", they would come. And there was one man there – he's passed away now – Alan Roberts, a fantastic second tenor: when, during the practice, he wanted to know anything, his hand would go up, "Miss Jones" – no-one ever called her Marian – "Can I ask you something?" She was **still** his teacher!'

'Everyone listened to what she had to say, she had a way with the choir. She didn't want the *cythraul canu* to come into the choir – she'd sort them all out. They respected her, and to Marian, they were 'my boys'. Her Christmas Cards were always, 'from me and the boys'. There was no quarrelling, no disagreement. In the beginning there was no secretary, no treasurer, no nothing – Marion did the lot and she didn't get a penny for it! When we joined the Association in 1981, of course, we had to change and elect a treasurer, secretary and so on, but before that, Marion's word was law.' Under her direction the choir grew to a respectable thirty-six and took part in all of the Association's Royal Albert Hall Concerts, and also performed in various parts of England, Scotland and twice at the Celtic Festival in Tralee, Ireland.

The choir is a generous supporter of charities, usually donating their performing fee at concerts to such worthy causes as Hope House, who in 2007 received a cheque for six thousand six hundred pounds (and four thousand pounds in 2006).

Marian Jones was actively conducting the choir well into her eighties, when a fall precipitated her death in 2002. Her remains were interred in Bethesda Chapel Cemetery near the Schoolroom were for thirty years Marian had rehearsed her 'choir boys' every Monday night. That's where they still have their practices, and secretly the choir is still aware of her presence. Sometimes when things go wrong with the choir, they may hear noises outside – someone walking past, and a wit will say, 'That's Marian coming back to sort things out!'

When she died it was their accompanist Alwen Enston who stepped into the breach 'as best I could, playing and conducting at the same time'. Born in nearby Pont y Bodkin, Alwen grew up in the Welsh competitive tradition, singing solo at the Urdd Eisteddfodau and later learning to play the piano. In fact it was as competing at the last Leeswood eisteddfod, held in a big marquee on July 8th, 1948, that she first met her husband Bernard, a Treuddyn chartered surveyor. 'So music brought us together,' she says. Bernard is the long standing President of the Cymau Choir. Their son is the Wokingham based organist maestro and Director of Music at Bearwood College, Christopher Enston.

In 2003 Christine Williams who formerly conducted the Wrexham Police Choir and the Gresford Ladies Choir, through recommendation, became their musical director. She brought her own expertise into her role as conductor, and her ability to transpose pieces from old notation to sol-fa, or even to change the key was much appreciated. As well as their Monday night rehearsals at the chapel, they perform Thursday night concert performances in the Beaufort Park Hotel near Mold from March to December. The latter being part of their routine since 1994, a component together with harp music of the hotel's Welsh night entertainment, for an international clientele. Christine however moved from Wrexham to live in Cwmbrân in 2007, but still made the 135 mile trek to be with the choir. But in 2008 the weekly trek could not be sustained and by mutual agreement she left the choir. She was replaced *pro tem* by Dewi Hughes, a second tenor in the choir. In the locality of Coed Talwrn where he grew up and Pontybodkin where he now lives

Dewi is a well known choir devotee. He grew up in pre-TV days where a sing-song around the piano with teen-age friends after chapel and supper on Sunday night was part of the week-end fun. When still a youngster he had joined the Mold Male Voice Choir conducted by John Henry Lloyd, and later Leeswood Male Voice which was directed by Wilfred Roberts. Although this is Dewi's first experience at conducting a male voice choir, it's not a totally new experience for him because he's conducted small cymanfaoedd and congregational carol singing at Nercwys Chapel were he's a member and at other places. Now retired since 2001 after over forty years as a mechanic with the GPO, Hugh is secretly enjoying his role with the choir, happily drawing on a lifetime's choir experience. Is he nervous? 'Oh no, so long as the choir is enjoying it, it comes back to me then,' he says.

Like many male voice choirs Cymau has seen a reduction in choristers, now down to 19 and failing to attract younger members. But there's no denying their commitment and the satisfaction in their ability to provide good quality musical entertainment. They come from Treuddyn, Mold, Cymau, Little Sutton and Great Sutton and from various callings/professions: teachers, bus drivers, a social worker, and surveyor.

The Choir

Catchment: Treuddyn, Mold, Cymau, Little Sutton and Great Sutton
Officials
President: Bernard Enston
Chairman: Aubrey Green
Vice Chairman: Ken Salter
Secretary: Mair Williams, Rhoslyn, Ffordd y Llan, Treuddyn, Mold, Flints CH7 4LN. Tel. 01352 771442
Treasurer: Phillip Owen
Conductor and Musical Director: Dewi Hughes
Accompanists: Alwen Lloyd Enston and Rosemary Nicholls (Deputy)
Compere: Malcolm Edge

Rehearsals are held every Monday night 7.00-9.00
in the Bethesda Chapel Schoolroom, Cymau.

Côr Meibion Dinbych a'r Cylch
Denbigh and District Male Voice Choir

'She had this attitude, "that anybody can sing unless they're tone deaf! And it's my job to teach you to sing", she used to say. And fair play, she took a lot of us off the street and made us into some sort of singers. She was marvellous.' That's Paul Harrison, a long service police officer and chairman of Côr Meibion Dinbych, holding forth about Phyllis Dryhurst-Dodd, the choir's first conductor. 'She adjudicated at eisteddfodau and was highly regarded by the North Wales Association of Male Voice Choirs as well as amongst other choirs. And she was a fantastic organist, she could almost make it talk.' Mrs Dodd was a Denbigh girl, her father a keen musician, was a well-known butcher in the town. Paul Harrison recalls how Mrs Dodd would relate that she was encouraged or coerced by her father to play the organ as a child. And in the way of a child, skiving her practices when his back was turned, but he had his way of finding her out by placing a hair on the organ cover so he could soon see on his return, if it hadn't moved, whether she'd been obedient. That was the grounding for her prowess, never better shown than when she accompanied the hymns on Sundays at Capel Mawr.

Mrs Dodd's career as a probation officer took her, with her husband an insurance man, to Llanfair Caereinion where she conducted the male voice choir. And on her return to Denbigh, followed her inclinations by conducting the mixed choir at the North Wales Hospital. The hospital's impending closure brought that choir to an end, but as one door closed another opened, which is how in 1988, the Denbigh Male Voice Choir was born. It was formed from a nucleus of the old hospital choir plus a few men from the locality, making a total of twenty voices! Within a year or so, Mrs Dodd had taken her 'choir' to sing in the Albert Hall in the massed choir of a thousand voices at the St David's Day concert. They may have felt lost and bewildered in such surroundings, but it was to trigger their enthusiasm and there was no looking back. Soon the twenty became forty and the Albert Hall an ever more familiar destination for them. At the Albert Hall she was assistant accompanist to John Tudor Davies from Rhos. Paul Harrison chuckles at those London recollections and how backstage they would pin up a celebrity notice – a great star with her name Phyllis Dryhurst Dodd underneath – on her dressing room door! And how she'd see the funny side 'she was really made up'.

Mrs Dodd secured Dorothy Kirk LRAM, formerly a Director of Music in Liverpool, to be the choir's accompanist. Totally reliable she never let the choir down and was always immaculately turned out; a marvellous pianist, she was in constant demand by both soloists and other choirs too. Her playing was very sympathetic, 'she was not one to thump things out'. So the choir was doubly blessed by having two very musically talented people at the helm.

Dorothy Kirk retired as their pianist in 2005, while some three years earlier due to ill health, Phyllis Dryhurst-Dodd too had relinquished her role.

It was the choir's good fortune to have had a deputy from within their numbers. Arwyn Roberts, gifted with a fine voice and pleasing personality, had benefitted from understudying Mrs Dodd. He was also a founder member of Cantorion Colin Jones, the North Wales choir whose members are considered to be the elite, because of Colin's 'hand picked' policy of only enrolling singers of the highest quality. Paul Harrison reckons that Arwyn 'has learnt a lot from Colin Jones and he's doing us the world of good'. That's a sentiment Arwyn readily accepts. 'Although I've sung with several choirs, and learnt something from each conductor – it's with Colin Jones that I've learnt the most, especially about music and voice production, and that's what I try to get across in the Denbigh Choir,' he says. Arwyn himself a fine soloist, is by profession an undertaker in Denbigh, his native town, and his interest in choral singing goes back to his childhood days at Caledfryn as a member of the school choir. Later he joined the mixed choir at the North Wales Hospital, which was composed of the staff and their friends. Notable conductors that he remembers there, are Trefor Holywell, and R.T. (Bob) Roberts from Henllan who took them to success at the National Eisteddfod. Apart from Denbigh Male Voice Choir as an understudy for Mrs Dodd, he was formerly a member of Colwyn Male Voice Choir when Neville Owen was conductor.

Finding an accompanist wasn't easy. For eighteen months they were fortunate in having the services of Sioned Jones a young music teacher from Betws-yn-Rhos, daughter of the Betws Choir's conductor, Nerys Jones. But due to her later being appointed head of music in Holyhead 'we lost Sioned'. Now however the sun shines once more because they have Joyce Davies who was deputy accompanist with Colwyn Male Voice Choir, and Ann Edwards as her deputy, whilst the deputy conductor is Nia Wyn Jones, formerly a teacher at Denbigh High School, now Head of Music at Ysgol Maes Garmon in Mold.

The Choir has had moments of sheer magic. Paul Harrison remembers with a particular glow 'The Glory of Wales Festival' on the lawn in Howells School Denbigh which was a charity extravaganza in September 2005 to celebrate Michael Cunningham's term as High Sheriff. Major

Michael Parker, organiser of Her Majesty the Queen's Celebrations in London, masterminded it all with a massed assembly of Brass Bands which included bands from Holywell, Northop and Rhyl conducted by the conductor of Northop. While the singing was by the Denbigh Male Voice Choir and the Howell School Choir. It was a celebration of Welsh history from St David to Shirley Bassey, set to music and fireworks, and co-ordinated by Professor Robert Sells Conductor of Crosby Philharmonic Orchestra. 'We didn't think our voices would be heard above the furore,' says Mr Harrison, 'but thanks to the sound engineers it all went well, although when the rockets exploded we jumped that high on the stage.' And for the portrayal of The Falklands War, *Mars* from The Planets Suite, a stunning piece by Gustav Holst. 'You can imagine, with all the fireworks going off at the same time – it was out of this world.'

The choir has toured extensively; with Denbigh's twin town in Germany being Bierbertal near Frankfurt, they have established a happy relationship and the respective choirs have enjoyed exchange visits and performances. Ireland too, at the Celtic Festivals, has been a pleasurable stomping ground, and on one occasion when crossing on the ferry, they were invited by the mayor of Sudbury near London who happened to be on the same boat, to come down to perform in her Mayor's Charity Concert. This they did at the Church there in April 2006, then arranged to go to the big London Welsh Chapel in Clapham on the Sunday morning for their Gymanfa Ganu Service (Hymn Singing Festival). There they felt very honoured to be accompanied on the organ by the television newsreader Huw Edwards. 'He's a lovely guy and his children were there too – and he's just great on the organ,' says Paul Harrison.

So what is the kick that Paul gets when he goes to the Eirianfa Community Centre by half seven for the Choir's two hour practice session every Tuesday night? 'I just love singing,' he says 'and whenever I go to choir, it doesn't matter how stressful my day has been, whatever has happened – once Arwyn Roberts or Mrs Dodd before him taps the music stand and it starts, I can literally feel all the stress going – nothing else matters, you're doing something you absolutely love . . . '

The Choir

Tapes and CDs
Denbigh and District Male Voice Choir – *Craig yr Oesoedd and Other Songs* (Tape – Black Mountain Records))
Denbigh and District Male Voice Choir – *Music from the Vale* (CD 7 Tape – Black Mountain Records)
Catchment: Denbigh, Ruthin and surrounding villages and towns including Prestatyn, Cilcain, Llangernyw, Llangynhafal, Bodfari and Colwyn Bay.
Officers
President: Mr Gwyn Dryhurst-Dodd
Chairman: Paul Harrison
Secretary: David Hards, Seler, Llangynhafal, Nr Denbigh.
Tel: 01824 790524
Treasurer: Glyn Edwards
Musical Director and Conductor: Arwyn Roberts
Accompanist: Joyce Davies and Ann Edwards
Compere: Clwyd Wynne

Rehearsals are held at the Eirianfa Community Centre
every Tuesday evening from 7.30 until 9.30.

Côr Mebion Dwyfor

'We're a fair way behind "Only Men Aloud",' laughs Buddug Roberts. 'They dance with sticks, move about, wear fancy waistcoats and sing with a big band don't they. I don't think we're ready for that! No, that's a bridge too far,' she muses. Not that they haven't tried a bit of movement and clever footwork with their singing. One of their numbers, a Gospel song – quite rhythmic, lends itself to that. 'We've given it a try,' she says, but admits, 'it can be a bit of a disaster, with some members going one way, some the other and bumping into each other!'

With a musical director like the youthful forty-two year old Buddug, it's easy to see that there's a great deal of laughter and good humour with Côr Meibion Dwyfor. But she has her serious side too. 'We're a traditional choir and my aim is to keep it true to it's up-country character,' she says.

Buddug Roberts, who is Deputy Head Teacher at Ysgol y Gelli Primary School in Caernarfon and lives at Bontnewydd, first came to the choir in 1990 as their piano accompanist. The choir was conducted then by Blue Ribband Winner, John Eifion, who is now Musical Director of Côr Meibion Y Brythoniaid. When he left Côr Meibion Dwyfor in 1994, Buddug was invited to take over the baton. That was her first experience of conducting a male voice choir and readily admits to a degree of nervousness at the start. Choir members confirm that she was rather shy at first. 'The fact was, I didn't want to be too hard on the choir for fear of upsetting them,' she says. 'I now feel better able to speak my mind, and conducting is very enjoyable. They come from a variety of different callings, and although their ages range from mid twenties to seventies they all get on well together.'

But conducting choirs was not totally new for her, at the school where she teaches, Buddug had her own children's choir. And at teacher's training college, music, at which she took her ALCM qualification, was a primary course subject for her. Added to that she feels that her years as choir accompanist with John Eifion was a kind of understudy experience. She has a fine collaborator at the piano in Alison Edwards from Rhostryfan, a close personal friend since college days. 'We bounce ideas off each other, and understand one another well enough, so that there's no need for elaborate instructions,' says Alison, 'often Buddug's facial expression is enough!'

The compere at their concert engagements is Philip George, a grand nephew of David Lloyd George, son of W.R.P. George (the Cricieth solicitor and former Archdruid of Wales). Philip, who now heads his late father's company, has a natural ability to create a warm friendly relationship with an audience, through what amounts to a conversation with them, so in that way they too become part of the performance. Phillip joined the choir very soon after it was founded in 1975. Three members from that original choir, which was formed as a cerdd dant party in February of that year to sing in the 1975 National Eisteddfod at Criccieth, are still regular choir members. They are Robin Jones, of Siop Eifionydd; Gwilym Meirion Jones of Tremadoc whose son is the tenor of international fame Rhys Meirion; and Melfyn Jones father of John Eifion, a singer of great repute and present conductor of Côr Meibion Y Brythoniaid. Hefin Jones a farmer at Pant Glas whose son is the world famous baritone Bryn Terfel is also a long serving choir member.

Melfyn Jones has vivid memories of the early days. 'The first thing I knew about the idea of a choir was when I went to Rhostryfan Eisteddfod, in the Spring of 1974 to compete as a soloist,' he says. 'As I was going in at the door, I was approached by Dafydd Griffith Jones, Selyf – a white robe member of the Gorsedd of Bards and nationally acclaimed authority on cerdd dant, who told me of his plans to get a party together to compete at the National Eisteddfod to be held at Cricieth, Bro Dwyfor, in the following year. Would I like to join?'

'But it was May 20th, 1975 before we eventually came together as a group to practice with Selyf as conductor.' Melfyn recalls how the group sang from the Psalms, *Mor Hawddgar yw dy bebyll* . . . at the Sunday morning service of worship to open Eisteddfod week. Bringing them together was an act of blind faith because as Melfyn says: 'Previously we knew little about Cerdd Dant – Selyf taught us everything practically from scratch – he was a really wonderful conductor.'

Selyf – Dafydd Griffith Jones – still with us and with it – his mind needle sharp, formerly an official with Llŷn Council then later with Dwyfor, still lives at Garndolbenmaen, his home village for over fifty years. Although a nationally recognized Cerdd Dant adjudicator he is totally self taught, but admits that he may have inherited some of his mother's musical talent. Aled Lloyd Davies, the cerdd dant doyen says in his book *Canrif o Gân* that 'Selyf has been taught by no-one but himself!' 'At first I sang cerdd dant at the Chwilog Eisteddfod and did some home study about how to arrange the music and so on,' he says, 'in fact I learnt a lot from my mistakes.' Now, when Buddug needs reliable cerdd dant advice, Selyf is her first port of call. But as he explains: 'Cerdd dant parties must sing without a conductor, and therefore members need to have a good understanding of each other. Additionally while the tune is played, the choir must come in on the wing – without pause.'

The National Eisteddfod competition rules at that time specified that Cerdd Dant Parties would consist of no more than sixteen singers, so the Bro Dwyfor Choir at that time was relatively small. Practices were held in the Vestry at 'Capel Isa' (Lower Chapel) in Garndolbenmaen with Vera, Selyf's wife, as musical accompanist. Their first National Eisteddfod effort, gave them no award save the satisfaction of performing on stage at Wales's premier festival, although since then they have taken the top prize at several of the major eisteddfodau.

So for the first years it was a mainly Cerdd Dant Party who also sang in Folk Group festivals, and Selyf has a thick sheaf of Eisteddfod Certificates, proof positive of their successes. Gerallt, Selyf's eldest son, later followed his father as musical director and later still Alun, his other son, also took hold of the reins. So the choir got going with a fine flourish thanks to this very remarkable family. Gerallt was the one to tilt them towards Welsh Folk music, another dimension in the choral scene where the choir sing without musical accompaniment.

John Eifion was the next to take the rostrum and we see a further musical impetus. He was to steer the choir to be a main stream male voice choir, its portfolio, more versatile would still include cerdd dant but now they would broaden to include the familiar stirring male voice choruses as well as numbers from the shows and Robert Arwyn pieces. The Chapel Vestry soon became too small as the choir grew in strength and drew its members beyond the immediate locality of Garn to include much of Llŷn and Eifionydd. This was when they moved to the 'much larger' village school for their weekly rehearsals.

Now with Buddug Roberts at the helm the choir numbering forty-six still pursues a vigorous programme. They have a 'Noson Lawen', typically an echo of old style Welsh home-spun entertainment, which is held annually at the nearby Bryncir Livestock Market. The shed with its livestock selling ring, for one summer evening becomes an amphitheatre where the choir performs and delights a huge audience. They usually have celebrity guest artistes such as a section of the· now famous Glanaethwy Youth Choir there too. 'It's an event which helps to provide the choir with funds to meet its running expenses – and if there's anything left over, a sub towards the cost of overseas concert tours which we aim to arrange on alternate years,' says choir secretary Ifan Hughes. 'These have included Reims in France, Cork, Killarney Ireland, and Tuscany when we performed in a Church in Lucca followed by an open-air sing-along in the main square.'

Melfyn Jones adds: 'Competing at eisteddfodau is particularly important to us; it helps us to maintain high musical standards and also focuses us on new set pieces. Competing sets a target and so prevents us resting on our laurels.' And he's keen on maintaining the National Eisteddfod as a roving festival located in a different region of Wales each year. 'After all Côr Meibion Dwyfor owes its existence to the Eisteddfod coming to Cricieth in 1975,' he says.

The Choir

Catchment: Garndolbenmaen, Porthmadog, Pwllheli, Morfa Nefyn, Cricieth.
CDs/Tapes: *Hwyr o Haf* – Published Fflach 2007
Choir Officials
Honorary President: D.G.Jones (Selyf)
Chairman: Twm Prys Jones
Vice Chairman: John Gwynant Hughes
Secretary: Ifan Hughes, Ceiri Garage, Llanaelhaearn, Caernarfon. Tel. 01758 750238
Treasurer: Phillip George
Musical Director and Conductor: Buddug Roberts B.ed, ALCM
Deputy Director: Myrddin Owen
Accompanist: Alison Edwards
Compere: Phillip George

*Rehearsals are held in Garndolbenmaen Junior School
every Wednesday evening from 8 until 10pm.*

Côr Meibion Dyffryn Ceiriog

The choir was established in 1973 when the important Eisteddfod Powys came to Glyn Ceiriog. True there had been a mixed choir of long standing there before this, conducted by the celebrity Blue Ribband winner A.O. Thomas which flourished until 1983.

The coming of the Powys event, one of the main provincial eisteddfodau in the north, was however to stimulate the men into action. It is evident that the time was ripe and soon a choir of fifty singers conducted by R. (Richie) E. Davies from Oswestry went into rehearsal. Mr Davies, a well known musician and singer, was very well acquainted with this farming community because he was the rep for 'Days', the company which specialised in farm animal medicines and was a native of Llanrhaiadr ym Mochnant.

After Powys they did some further competing, even emboldened to go to the National Eisteddfod at Llanrwst but 'we didn't come into the frame, let's put it like that', while at the Butlins Eisteddfod they scored, pushing rivals Glyndŵr Choir into second place.

Richie Davies conducted the choir for over twenty years and on his retirement was followed by Peter Simpson Davies, a site manager with the civil engineering company Pochins, who was regarded as 'a good self taught musician and tenor soloist'. Peter held the choir together well for many years; in his time going into a concert routine rather than the competing mode. When failing health obliged him to retire in 2006, the role of conductor was taken up by Gareth Thomas the present occupant of the rostrum.

Mr Thomas is a son of the eminent singer A.O. Thomas referred to earlier. When his father retired from conducting, the mixed voice choir having run its course, Gareth joined the Rhos Male Voice Choir. Here he benefited from the influence of Colin Jones the choirmaster, who remains a role model. Gareth Thomas later joined Cantorion Colin Jones, The North Wales Choir. He joined Côr Meibion Dyffryn Ceiriog in 1997 and is now conductor of that choir as well as being a baritone with the North Wales Choir.

This has been to the ultimate benefit of his local choir because of what experience has taught him. He remembers as a child listening to his father practising at the piano; imperceptibly he picked up the vibes, learning how to bring out the vowels, becoming aware of the difference between 'crooning and proper singing'. He now has residual regrets about not taking in more from his father's rehearsal sessions. 'But I was far too shy to sing on my own in front of my father, I could never do that,' he says, 'although I'd sing in a group with others.' Shyness doesn't now best describe Gareth Thomas. Singing in choirs, absorbing what Colin Jones has taught him about breathing and voice production, has boosted his confidence. He now knows what a good male voice choir should really sound like and how it can be achieved.

Gareth Thomas has other plusses too. His ancestry going back to 1911 when grandfather Alun Thomas first came with his bride to Tyn y Groes Farm on the edge of Glyn Ceiriog have all had musical inclinations, so singing is plainly in the blood. Now Gareth's grandsons down in the village, through their Urdd (Welsh League of Youth) involvement, are singing too 'and they're not a bit shy'.

All this has given him authority; at practice sessions he knows what he wants from the choir and he transmits that with eagerness and urgency. But he faces the problem of singers who are unable to read music, so inevitably note bashing is a feature of rehearsals, learning new pieces is a very hard slog. Gareth often reads the riot act, stressing the need for choir members to spend time on their copies in between the weekly rehearsals, 'if only for five minutes a day, surely they could manage that'. His style is robust, his talk straight from the shoulder in the manner of up country people, one senses an impatience. He enjoys the experience of conducting and learning new pieces. Always there's a striving for a higher standard of performance.

He's fortunate in his excellent accompanist Sarah Morris, a schools accompanist.

Membership of the choir come from Chirk, Oswestry, Llansilin, Rhyd y Croesau, Llanarmon and Glyn Ceiriog and now number around twenty-five. Most are retired, their average age 'about sixty-five' with quite a few well into their eighties. He wishes more from the village – there are only four – would join the choir. 'They say that almost everyone in Llangwm is a Llangwm choir member, and if they're not, there's something seriously wrong with them! Here in Glyn Ceiriog it's the total reverse, it's choir members who are regarded as the really odd bods!'

Charity concerts, mainly in local villages and towns, are a strong feature of their activities programme with an annual celebrity event at Neuadd Dolywern in August. At the latter events they've had stars like Tom Gwannas and Trebor Evans to join them. One day they'll invite David Kempster, 'he was one of my son Gavin's best school mates. The audiences are drawn more by the celebrities than the choir,' he adds, tongue firmly in cheek.

The Choir

Catchment: Chirk, Oswestry, Rhyd y Croesau, Llansilin and Llanarmon
CDs/Tapes: Côr Meibion Dyffryn Ceiriog
Officials:
Chairman: Eifion Davies
Vice Chairman: Brian Eadon
Secretary: Peter Wilks. Tel. 01691 791288
Treasurer: David Cassidy
Conductor: Gareth Thomas
Accompanist: Sarah Morris
Deputy Accompanist: Brenda Cassidy

Rehearsals are held at the Ceiriog Memorial Hall
every Wednesday eveningp from 8 until 9.30.

Hogia'r Ddwylan

Bont y Borth is an important part of the background to Hogia'r Ddwylan, 'Fellows from the Two Shores'. The bridge in question is the beautiful Menai Suspension Bridge which links Anglesey with mainland Britain. 'It isn't symmetrical, there are four arches at the Anglesey end, three on the Bangor side,' explains Gwilym Williams the choir's archivist, 'this gives it strength.' So the bridge, their unique crest, is a symbol of their power to create bridges and through their music reach out to different places. It is also inspirational, and tells the world outside about their geographical base.

It all started as a cerdd dant group of six young men in 1966 who met in the house of Elwyn Edwards, a member of the party, living in Menai Bridge, the village at the Anglesey end of the bridge. Their conductor and founder was Prydderch Williams from Penmon, a highly regarded person in the world of cerdd dant, harp music, who had learnt the craft at the feet of Telynores Maldwyn and Telynores Eryri who frequently visited his home, while Elwyn's wife played the piano for them. They found early success too with a win at Llandegfan Eisteddfod. Two years later, Menai Williams a young music student and harpist at Bangor became their accompanist and conductor: the party was now growing in strength. The archives reveal a group which was quickly becoming a choir with popular appeal, and a concert appearance is noted for the Welsh Society in Manchester during 1969, their first performance outside Wales. Their first real breakthrough at the National Eisteddfod of Wales came in Bangor in 1971 when they were placed second in the competition for cerdd dant choirs. 1973 proved even better, coming in first at both the National Eisteddfod and at the Gŵyl Cerdd Dant, the National Festival of Harp Music, which was that year held in Llangefni. It was a busy time for the choristers as they fulfilled several concert performances throughout Wales; during one such event at Portmeirion in 1974 meeting a German millionaire holidaying there, who instantly besotted, invited them over to his luxury villas on the Luneberg Heath. And there on a fourteen day 'working' holiday they wowed further audiences with a brand of music which was gradually encompassing traditional male voice as well, with guest soloists Leah Owen and Nora Jones. It was to start a close association with their host which resulted in further visits. The choir also visited the town of Eschelbronn near Heidlberg in 1983 and have kept a close relationship with the Eschelbronn Male Voice Choir ever since. In the intervening years there had been a visit in 1976 to Lorient (Brittany) to sing in their World famous Celtic Festival. Recalling the event Elwyn Edwards said the choir could hardly believe that the venue for one of their concerts was a football pitch, 'we were in the middle and the huge audience were all around in the stands'. While in Brittany they went to the nearby village of Doelan to record a performance for television and shared the stage with the local Doelan Choir, appropriately since the Celtic French 'Doelan' equates with the Welsh 'Ddwylan' in meaning.

In 1988 Menai Williams left after 21 years; during her time she had seen the choir grow, they had toured extensively, their name was now synonymous with choral music at the highest level, sharing the stage with the likes of Hogiau'r Wyddfa, Wales' leading quartet and the inimitable Charles Williams, and had produced their second tape and LP. They had played an honourable part in their concerts supporting Ysgol y Bont, Llangefni a school for pupils with special educational needs.

Mary Stevens Jones, head of the music department at Llangefni Comprehensive, temporarily conducted the choir pending the appointment of Sioned Webb head of the music department at Ysgol Tryfan, Bangor as director. Sioned brought her own stamp on the choir; their emphasis would now be 'folk'. And once more they would enter the competing arena, a practice left in abeyance since 1973. In 1995 achieving a creditable second prize in the Choral 'folk' category at the National Eisteddfod, then in the following year, a double at Yr Ŵyl Pan Geltaidd, the Irish Arts Festival for Celtic Nations, where they were adjudged best in their class as well as the best choir over all in the festival.

In 1996 Sioned left and the baton was passed briefly to Mary Price followed by Margaret Jones (Head of Music at Bodedern) who revived the ancient Hen Galan tradition of a new year vigil on the fourteenth of January with a celebratory concert. 1997 saw Ilid Anne Jones, a music graduate, taking the director's role and imperceptibly we see a change of emphasis. The choir had begun as a cerdd dant group but each succeeding conductor had tilted the tiller to their own strengths. It had gone from cerdd dant, creating music to harp accompaniment, to 'folk', now came another spin as Ilid Anne took the choir traditional, fair and square onto the classical middle ground. There would be further forays abroad, Eschelbronn in Germany again in 1999, but there would be competitive excursions too. At Llangollen International in 2001 coming fifth against the World's best in a field of eighteen, but at the Denbigh National Eisteddfod in the same year taking the top honours. Winning again at the Meifod National Eisteddfod in 2003 where they also performed in *Rhaglen Goffa i Leila Megane*, a tribute to the singer of legendary fame on which Ilid Anne had done her M.Phil. thesis.

And linking up with Côr Godre'r Aran and Côr Meibion y Rhos to perform Y Pren Planedig based on the Biblical concept. Kilkenny in the same year scored another 'first' for the choir at the Irish festival 'Gŵyl Pan Geltaidd'. 2003 saw Hogia'r Ddwylan winning at 'Y Gŵyl Gorawl', the Choral Festival held in Llandudno's North Wales Theatre. Also taking part in major concerts at Llangollen and the New Pavilion in Rhyl as well as establishing their own annual Celebrity Charity Concerts.

Spurring the home team before their game against the All Blacks at the Millennium Stadium in Cardiff was another milestone for the choir in 2005; and in 2006 releasing another CD as part of a special Fortieth Birthday Celebration when they all sailed down the Menai Straits underneath the two all-important bridges followed by an evening of social jollification! And at the end of 2008 winning the BBC Wales Male Voice Choir of the Year Trophy.

* * *

Ilid Anne Jones is surely a true example of musical genius. Born in Talysarn, she claims that her musical ability was inherited from her mother Eurgain Eames, the long serving conductor of Côr Meibion Dyffryn Nantlle. Musicianship flows strongly in that side of the family, branches of which flourish in several directions – Cefyn Roberts of the famous Glanaethwy Children's Choir is a member of the clan.

Seated at the organ in Seion Chapel in Talysarn as an eight year old, to accompany the congregation spurred on her musical inclination. She remembers going as an eight year old to the Thousand Voices Concert in London in 1971, and witnessing for the first time the repertoire of such a momentous occasion. That was probably a moment of destiny. Soon guided by her music teacher, the legendary George Peleg Williams, she started playing at rehearsals for Côr Meibion Dyffryn Nantlle where conductor C.H. Leonard, a moving spirit, gave her every encouragement. When only a fifth form schoolgirl at Ysgol Dyffryn Nantlle she was already a deputy accompanist for Côr Meibion Caernarfon. Soon she was in demand at other places too; number one with Côr Meibion Y Brythoniaid, then with Côr Meibion Yr Eifl and for a short while Glannau Llyfnwy.

Alongside all this there had been her junior school education at Waunfawr before going on to Ysgol Uwchradd Dyffryn Nantlle, the local high school, and then on to the University College of North Wales at Bangor for her B.Mus. degree, a treatise on Meirion Williams and M.Phil. degree, a highly researched thesis on the Life and Achievements of Leila

Megane, the Welsh singer of legendary international fame. Her line of inquiry had led her to Paris and New York as well as the Albert Hall, where Leila Megane was the first to sing *Land of Hope and Glory* for Sir Henry Wood. The resulting voluminous tome, now regarded as the standard work on Leila Megane, is lodged at the National Library of Wales Aberystwyth, but a much shorter version of it was published for the National Eisteddfod of Wales at Denbigh in 2001 entitled *Leila Megane 1891-1960, Anwylyn Cenedl.*

Conducting Côr Meibion y Ddwylan was her first foray as a musical director back in 1997, which she admits was hugely different to being an accompanist. 'As a pianist I simply followed the conductor's directions, but swapping roles meant I had to think all that out for myself; I had to think about the repertoire and the technique of voice production – matters which hadn't occurred to me before.' But her experience with so many leading choirs, learning by watching how other maestros work has perfected her skill. 'Now standing conducting in front of forty men is not so scary,' she says.

The Choir

Tapes and CDs: See Website: hogiarddwylan.co.uk
Catchment Area: Arfon and Ynys Môn – both sides of the Menai Straits
President: Trefor Selway
Chairman: Rhys Jones
Secretary: Edward Evans. Tel. 01248 810646
Treasurer: David Ellis Jones
Musical Director and Conductor: Ilid Anne Jones, B.Mus., M.Phil
Accompanist: Rhian Roberts B.Mus.
Compere: Hywel Wyn Owen, Gwilym Williams, Lyn Davies
and Emlyn Thomas

Rehearsals are held at Capel Mawr, Menai Bridge (Anglesey)
every Thursday evening 7.30-9.30

Côr Meibion Dyfi
Dyfi Male Voice Choir

A few of us came together on the Thursday evening of January 17th, 1980, to consider raising a party to sing Cerdd Dant, Music to Harp Accompaniment. After some discussion it was decided to go ahead and Mr Iwan Morgan of Corris was invited to take us in hand with Mrs Gwyneth Morgan (Iwan's mother) as accompanist: starting date Sunday night January 27th.

27th January: A good number turned up and the first piece to be rehearsed was Eloise, a work set to music by Iwan Morgan, the second being Cynhaeaf by Dic Jones, again set by Iwan Morgan.

28th January: The numbers had now increased to 17, all working hard on the set pieces. It was decided to elect officials:

> *Chairman: Mr Edward Lloyd.*
> *Secretary: Mr Ellis W. Jones.*
> *Treasurer. Mr Tom Pugh.*

It was decided to have a 'Soup and Song' evening together with a Disco as a St David Celebration on Friday evening March 7th, to raise funds to cover our costs. Individual items to be provided by Iwan Morgan, John Francis, Ieuan Griffiths, and Edward Lloyd who would also act as compere. And it was announced that a further concert would be held on March 16th towards the costs of the National Eisteddfod to be held at Machynlleth in 1981.

Those are the brief notes signaling the origins of Meibion Dyfi, the Pantperthog (near Machynlleth) based male voice choir. Although it started as a Cerdd Dant party under the inspired leadership of Iwan Morgan, a school teacher from Corris, and competed in the National Eisteddfod at Machynlleth in 1981, it was as a conventional male voice party that it ultimately became established.

It was when Iwan Morgan moved away from the area that the change took place. Later Mr Morgan became headteacher at Cefncoch Primary School, Penrhyndeudraeth and also the Musical Director of Meibion Prysor. Finding a replacement was difficult; cerdd dant as a particular musical art form is quite different to the customary choral harmony. At this point it was decided to concentrate on male voice choral singing and thus the present choir was formed. Tom Pugh, a farmer from Ffriddgate, Machynlleth, himself a member of the choir, took over for many successful years until he had to retire due to ill-health.

It was their good fortune to have as a member, Gwilym Bryniog Davies, of the eminently musical family from Melin-y-coed, near Llanrwst, and it was he who was persuaded to pick up the baton in 1988. Back in Melin-y-coed there had been a lot of music and Gwilym remembers the communal involvement, but on his part, there had been no wish ever to be a conductor. True there had been times when he'd helped children with their singing for a Christmas concert or eisteddfod, and there had always been music in the home. In Melin-y-coed there was a choir party similar to Meibion Dyfi; and in Llanrwst a mixed choir of which he was a member and another in the Conwy Valley at Tal-y-bont, Côr Bodnod, learning classical works in aid of charity. Gwilym Bryniog had come to the area as a farm bailiff to Maespandy, Talyllyn, Tywyn. A man of great natural talent, Gwilym might easily have made a distinguished career as a baritone soloist on the concert platform. He often sings at various concerts and conducts the Gymanfa Ganu at different venues.

'It's difficult when your choir members ask you to be the conductor,' he says, 'because they're all your friends and it's difficult to impose discipline, and you have to live with them tomorrow, don't you?' That's why he rates lots of patience and a sense of humour as the prime virtues that he needs. 'Few people have the good fortune to be able to read music these days let alone knowing what music should sound like.' This makes learning new songs all the more arduous. 'Good musicians who can sing are scarce, even among youngsters,' he says. 'Yes, they can press the right keys on an instrument in front of them, a "G" for instance, but when it comes to learning something to sing in a short time, it's another matter.' 'Ours is a small choir drawing people out who simply enjoy singing; many with fine voices who never once realised they could sing, come and join us after a conversation with friends.'

'Gwilym is doing a fine job of work with the choir,' says Dei Pugh, the choir's enthusiastic secretary since 1998 and a first tenor in the choir. Dei is a native of Abergynolwyn where he did farm work on leaving school before moving to Machynlleth as a 21 year old where he drove buses for Crosville but now lives in comparative retirement. His passion for the choir is both positive and infectious.

'I enjoy the company of the lads, we're very good friends and of course I enjoy the singing,' he says.

The majority of the 30 members live locally in the Dyfi Valley community and they enjoy performing at numerous concerts each year covering the length and breadth of the country.

The pinnacle of the choir's achievements was winning the Male Voice

Choir competition (under 40 voices) at the well known Pontrhydfendigaid Eisteddfod in 1993, and also recording their first compact disc and cassette in March 1999 which was a tremendous success. The CD programme features a selection of traditional and contemporary music.

The choir have travelled to Bournemouth to entertain at the Liberal Democrat Conference in response to an invitation by the late Lord Geraint Howells of Ponterwyd; they hold a triennial event at Colchester, Essex, and in September 2008 the choir sang at two concerts in Dumfries, Scotland. They also perform 10 concerts annually at the Plas Talgarth Holiday Complex in Pennal, Machynlleth, together with numerous performances locally.

Their honorary President is Dafydd Wyn Jones, a farmer and poet from Blaenplwyf Uchaf, Aberangell, who is a well known member of the Bro Ddyfi Talwrn y Beirdd team. While the choir's Chairman, Robert Edwards, a farmer from Bryn Sion Farm, Abercowarch, Dinas Mawddwy, a second tenor, 'is a compere at all our concerts'.

Their loyal accompanist since 1986 is Catrin Jones, from Mallwyd, a schoolteacher and a native of Rhoshirwaun who is also involved with numerous organisations throughout the Dyfi Valley as an accompanist.

The Choir

Tapes and CDs: Parti Meibion Dyfi – CD produced by Cwmni Sain (1999)
Choir Officials
President: Dafydd Wyn Jones, Aberangell
Chairman: Robert Edwards, Abercywarch, Dinas Mawddw
Secretary: David Pugh, Cefn Coed, Machynlleth, Powys SY20 8EG. Tel. 01654 702604
Treasurer: Ifor Davies, Braichithel, Aberhosan
Musical Director: Gwilym Bryniog Davies
Accompanist: Mrs Catrin Jones
Compere: Robert Edwards

Choir Practices are held at The Old School, Pantperthog, Machynlleth,
every Tuesday evening: 7.30-9.00 Winter months
8.00-9.30 Summer months

Côr Meibion Dyffryn Nantlle
Dyffryn Nantlle Male Voice Choir

Côr Meibion Dyffryn Nantlle was reborn in 1932. Many years before that, the busy quarrying area centred on Pen y Groes, six miles south west of Caernarfon, had long been a hive of culture and song. Indeed the archives show that Côr Meibion Dyffryn Nantlle competed at the National Eisteddfod of Wales in 1884, but the choir's history may go back further than that. Taking Pen-y-groes as the pivotal point, it can be claimed that here was a centre of intense choral activity at the end of the nineteenth century. The vale could boast a ladies choir of 150 members at Carmel; at the small village of Nebo a choir of 50, at Tal-y-sarn a thriving children's choir and in Pen-y-groes itself, a mixed choir of 100 as well as the male voice choir of 150.

This was at the time of the great slate quarrying days in the vale: the Dorothea, Penyrorsedd and Cilgwyn quarries employed thousands of men, added to that there were over 30 small scale ones, many of which were owned by farming folk. The 'barracks', billets for the quarry workers, were often centres of earnest cultural discussion and song, the 'cabannau' vying in friendly rivalry. While the chapels built as a result of tides of religious revivals in the nineteenth and early twentieth centuries, fostered the choral culture, in their services of worship, hymn singing festivals and inter chapel eisteddfodau.

But a very long and bitter strike in the quarries and, in 1914, the onset of a dreadful war was to change many things.

The man who singularly re-launched the choir was C.H. Leonard the head of science at Pen-y-groes Grammar School. He had come there in 1930 from South Wales fired with an interest in selecting 'twenty chosen men' for the Choir's re-birth. Myfyr Williams, the present secretary of the choir, a former pupil at Pen-y-groes, has vivid recollections of the impact this man had on the school. He was evidently charismatic in his influence, and among those 'chosen men' there were three or four fellow members of staff, including the flamboyant Peleg Williams, head of music there. 'Precise in appearance, always dressed in a morning suit and stiffly starched collar, his teacher's cloak flowing, C.H. Leonard looked for all the world like Batman,' says Myfyr, 'while Peleg Williams bow tied, hair flowing – a sheer maestro at the piano, was nick-named Beethoven the Second.' Many Pen-y-groes pupils in those halcyon days are the male voice choir torch bearers of today, such was his profound influence, not only with his after-school children's choir but also his re-invented Côr Meibion Dyffryn Nantlle.

But it was never a competing choir, 'Leonard was never a one for that', it was always on the concert platform that they excelled, appearing at such places as the Manchester Free Trade Hall and the Philharmonic Hall in Liverpool. He was innovative too, C.H. Leonard got local bard J. Llywelyn Roberts to write a piece to sing to Sibelius's *Finlandia*, a long time before Lewis Valentine's now famous hymn. The words spoke of the Summer season merging into Autumn and was sent to Finland for the great composer's approval.

Then came a commission from the BBC to appear on 'Noson Lawen', one of the most popular series ever devised for radio. Myfyr Williams well remembers going as a child with his father, who was a choir member, to Bangor and sitting next to Sam Jones in the producer's box for the rehearsals. 'It was a privilege to sit next to the great man, and watch him stage managing. Often the programme would over-run and he would say, "Now then lads, we must shorten this piece".' Whereupon C.H. Leonard and Peleg Williams would have to re-score on the spot 'It was wonderful to see them at it, achieving the impossible in next to no time'! The programme format was a re-creation of traditionally Welsh homespun fireside entertainment, with musical items from the Choir, Sassie Rees, Triawd y Coleg (The College Threesome), and comedy turns by Richard Hughes (Co Bach), Charles Williams and Huw Jones.

C.H. Leonard, who died in the early seventies, was by far the longest serving conductor the choir ever had when he retired in 1960. Many have wielded the baton since, but the standard had been set, the choir enthused and there was no looking back. Alwyn Hughes Jones came next followed by Maldwyn Parry a fine baritone Blue Ribband Eisteddfod Winner, and a notable soloist. Anwen Rowlands, a native of the vale – again a C.H. Leonard protégé – succeeded him, followed by Deio Morgan from Portmeirion. For a period the choir was conducted by the conductor of the Dyffryn Nantlle Silver Band.

Presently Mrs Eurgain Eames is director, a role she has fulfilled since 1998, establishing yet again a Leonard link – she was a member and soloist in his children's choir at Pen-y-groes. Born in Carmel of a long line of quarry people with a natural love of music, she had gone on to Cartrefle Teachers Training College in Wrexham and a career in teaching. Marriage and two daughters later, Ilid and Meinir, were both to excel in the world of music. Ilid Ann Jones as the conductor of 'Hogia'r Ddwylan', while Ilid's daughter Angharad is a harpist in such West End shows as *Carousel* starring Leslie Garret. Eurgain's other daughter Meinir, head of mental health at Bangor, while more into literature is also a competent pianist and plays the fiddle. Eurgain meantime had done her share of conducting before the call to Côr Meibion Dyffryn Nantlle. In the 1970s she had taken over Maldwyn Parry's mixed voice choir which had been formed after the National Eisteddfod at Cricieth, and later known as Côr Glannau Llyfnwy. Later as a Merched y Wawr member, her local branch asked her to form a singing party: result Lleisiau Rhyn, a young ladies choir which flourished for many years. By 1997 it was coming to a natural end. By then Deio Morgan, Dyffryn Nantlle's conductor, had passed away and the call to Eurgain Eames: Would she fill the breach? She was reluctant, not having conducted a male voice choir before, at the same time humbled at the thought of conducting a choir originally formed by her arch mentor of years ago, Mr C.H. Leonard. She remembers Leonard as a man rigid in his expectations, and although his role in the school was as a science master, no-one dared cross swords with him in matters musical. His word was law! He was held in awe, not a man to be crossed or confronted: 'no one would ever say, he's a jolly fine fellow'. Little to wonder then at Eurgain's hesitation before agreeing to be the choir's conductor. Decision taken however she feels immensely privileged, it seems as if much of Leonard's vision is being fulfilled under her watch. She still remembers what she learnt at his feet as a child; how he gloried in her talent. He called her 'Aur Gân' (My Golden Voice), and how he gave her much good advice in its production and what songs she should sing. He knew about singing, its discipline and interpretation. At rehearsal in the lunch hour with his children's choir, he would walk along listening intently to each one. Often he would admonish, 'the singing is flat, you've eaten too much pudding, that's not good for your singing'. 'Honestly, I still tell my choir not to have pudding before we sing in a concert,' says Eurgain. The choir still true to its original aims excels on the concert platform, its size hardly changed nor its singing portfolio. Myfyr Williams, scanning through old programmes smiles knowingly: *Arwelfa, Speed your Journey, Cymru Fach, Walking in the Air, Pan fo'r Nos yn Hir, Africa Prayer, Soldiers Chorus, O Isis, Babylon's Way, Gwahoddiad, Amen, Danny Boy* and B*attle Hymn of the Republic* are still firmly on our agenda,' he says. The choir's membership catchment area includes Pen-y-groes, Bethel, Pont Llyfni, Clynnog Fawr, and Bontnewydd, and they are of varied professions: 'We have a Caernarfon garage manager, a National Grid engineer, farmers, teachers, Water Board employees and retired men amongst our choristers,' says Myfyr. 'It's a small choir with a lot of good humour and we all know each other, but it also means that everyone must know their part – there's no room for passengers.'

The Choir

Catchment Area of Choristers: Pen-y-groes, Bethel, Pont Llyfni, Clynnog Fawr, Bontnewydd, Caernarfon, Llanberis and Llanrug.
Chairman: John Shorney
Secretary: Myfyr Williams, 13 Ffordd Glasgoed, Caernarfon, Gwynedd LL55 4LG. Tel: 01286 675412
Treasurer: Eric Pritchard
Musical Director and Conductor: Eurgain Eames
Accompanist: Alun Rhys Williams
Compere: Dafydd Ellis/Richard Jones

Rehearsals are held at Capel Brynrodyn
every Monday evening from 7.30 to 9.30

Côr Meibion Dyffryn Peris

'White hair, bald heads – and false teeth'. There's always a good dose of humour in the terraced house in Llanberis which is the home of Elwyn Jones and his wife Hefina.

Describing male voice choirs in those banterous terms contains an element of truth. Elwyn wonders whether there will still be male voice choirs in fifteen or twenty years. But the Llanberis choir, of which they are both leading members, Hefina as accompanist and secretary, Elwyn always the morale booster, has remarkable powers of survival.

That is not surprising, both are rooted in a tradition where a sing-song around the piano on Sunday nights after Chapel 'and mam made plates of butties' was part of their childhood. Hefina at Llanfaglan near Caernarfon, playing the piano for her teenage friends; Elwyn in Llanberis crossing the road to his mate Arwel Jones' house to be joined by Myrddin who lived further along. Those were the days when the modulator hanging on the wall was part of the fun thing in many homes and chapel vestries, where children were taught and challenged to do their sol-fa scales. 'Once mastered, you never forget them,' says Elwyn.

Later Elwyn, Arwel and Myrddin, over forty years ago, gained international fame as Hogia'r Wyddfa – The Snowdon Lads – a folk group still guaranteed to fill any Welsh concert hall.

'There's always been music here in Llanberis,' says Elwyn, 'the slate quarry bands and choirs at Dinorwic and Blaenau have made certain of that.' He goes on to expand about the mini eisteddfodau once held in the 'cabans', where the men ate their mid day 'snack', and how each quarry level vied with the other in cultural attainment.

That was all part of the industrial custom where both Elwyn, starting as an apprentice fitter in 1953, and his father Hugh Richard Jones worked until the quarry closed in 1969. Elwyn has no personal recollections of the halcyon caban days – but the echoes live on.

It was Ifor Jones of the hardware shop in the village who got the idea in February 1990 of forming a male voice choir and printed some membership flyers. Hefina inevitably got involved in their distribution. So Elwyn and Hefina were in at the start and remember how about twelve local men showed a positive interest.

The first practices were held in the vestry at Capel Coch in the village and 'we had John Huw Hughes headmaster of Ysgol Dolbadarn as conductor'. He'd been a member of the Dyffryn Nantlle Silver Band and was also an experienced solo singing performer and readily agreed to help get them off to a good start. Hefina, who had played the piano since her Sunday School days and still plays the organ in rota at Jerusalem chapel, was a natural choice to accompany the choir. Monday night at 7.30 is still their practice time, but they now meet in the Electric Mountain.

The Electric Mountain is a state of the art visitor centre, the terminus where the buses pick-up for the unique Dinorwic Power Station experience. It also has a wonderful space upstairs which doubles as an exhibition area and gallery. This is the choir's rehearsal room. It's an ideal facility where they have their own piano, gifted to them by the ladies committee in memory of choir member Ieuan Ellis Jones, who was the chemist in Llanberis. 'The Electric Mountain Centre is much better than the Capel Coch vestry,' says Elwyn, 'because in winter it was so cold there that we had to practice in our overcoats.' The ground floor in mid December becomes the venue at which they are joined by the Deiniolen Silver Band in a grand concert in aid of local charities.

When they do a concert away from their home base, they have their own portable electric keyboard. Hefina is particularly pleased with it because 'you can never be sure that the place we go to has a piano of concert pitch available'. Concerts are very much in favour with the choir, some being on a regular monthly seasonal basis as at the Royal Victoria Hotel Llanberis where they entertain holiday makers.

They do many charity concerts, a particular favourite with the 'lads' being the one held annually at the Rhosgadfan Mountain Rangers Club where they usually raise six hundred pounds for the Ysbyty Glan Clwyd Cancer Unit. This gives them great satisfaction because Ann Thompson who runs the club with her husband has set this up as her own designated fund in recognition of her own treatment for throat cancer. The aim being to provide funds to secure more voice transponders for the hospital. The concert which is a mix of homespun Noson Lawen entertainment of choir items, solos, duets, community singing and sketches is always a sell out. For the choir it is an enjoyable night out They have a good friend at Express Motors, Bontnewydd who gets them to the club free of charge, 'and of course we give our services free – so all the proceeds go to the fund, and its nice to know that we're supporting a local project'.

They've done some foreign travel too, specifically to Trier, the oldest city in Germany. This came about as the result of a local connection with the Llanberis born composer with an international reputation, Dafydd Bullock, who is a teacher at the Luxembourg School of Music. It's a friendship which has resulted in two visits to Germany and one to an isolated Netherlandic island. The latter being quite remarkable since the main transport for island sightseeing was on bikes, and the church in which they sang was mainly constructed of the hulks of shipwrecks washed ashore. And their musical accompaniment was provided by an accordion band of sea faring whalers!

Their conductor since 2007 is Dafydd Roberts, of Llawr yr Hafod, a Llithfaen sheep farmer, county councillor and builder. He's an experienced musician who with his sister Ann Williams sings duets and solos at concerts. Of a musical family Dafydd has been singing since childhood and was educated at the local Ysgol Pentre Uchaf, then went on to Ysgol Glan y Môr Pwllheli. Part of his musical learning he received from Gwyneth Sol Owen, Pwllheli, a notable voice trainer and accompanist. The possessor of a fine baritone voice, choral singing has been an abiding interest. He also sings with Côr Cymysg Yr Eifl (The Eifl Mixed Choir) who meet at Rhos Fawr near Y Ffôr and is deputy to their conductor Elenna Hughes, Pwllheli. He has a great deal of respect for her musical ability and is gleaning a lot from her conducting style. 'She's ever ready to help me over a piece I'm rehearsing with Côr Dyffryn Peris. I really enjoy conducting but I'm still a learner,' he says. Elwyn adds, 'He has what is essential for a conductor, which is the right kind of personality.'

Since its formation there have been other conductors. Following John Huw Hughes, their first – they've had Mair Hughes the head teacher at Cwm y Glo, who was succeeded by Arwel Jones a school master latterly at Bontnewydd – a capable raconteur and musician. Arwel is now deputy to Dafydd Roberts, accommodating his need for time off in March and April during the lambing season. During all this time the accompanist has been the ever present Hefina, while Elwyn has been ever ready to deputise at the rostrum.

The Choir

Tapes/CDs: Côr Meibion Dyffryn Peris (2001), Recordiau Sain.
Catchment: Llanberis,Betws-y-coed, Llanrwst, Bangor, Capel Garmon, and villages within the *Eco'r Wyddfa* (Welsh Community Paper) circulation area
Officials
Chairman: Eifion Roberts
Vice Chairman: Gwilym Evans
Secretary: Hefina Jones, 2 Blaen Ddôl, Llanberis, Gwynedd LL55 4TL. Tel. 01286 871006
Treasurer: Emerson Hughes
Conductor and Musical Director: Dafydd Roberts
Deputy Conductor: Arwel Jones
Stage Managers: John Pritchard and Medwyn Roberts
Compere: Arwel Jones and Cyril Jones
Accompanist: Hefina Jones

Rehearsals are held every Monday night at 7.30
in the Electric Mountain Visitor Centre, Llanberis.

Côr Meibion Bro Dysynni

Mair Eleri Jones's involvement with Côr Meibion Bro Dysynni came about around the turn of the century, when she heard that they were looking for an accompanist. She reckoned that it would be a nice change at the end of her busy day as manager of the Ty'n y Gornel, a beautifully located hotel on the edge of Tal-y-llyn in the Dyfi Valley. 'So I went along and gave it a go,' she says 'and thoroughly enjoyed it.' She makes little of her evident talent. 'I haven't any degrees or anything like that, I just do it for pleasure,' she says. Now she's a key person there. For three months at the end of 2007 she also conducted the choir pending the appointment of Jim Chugg, a native of Kent who lives at Llwyngwril to the post. He's a man with experience in mixed choirs and is the organist at Llwyngwril and Fairborne Churches.

So Mair has seen choir practices from two perspectives and knows full well how the choir, the accompanist, and conductor must gel. 'The understanding between the accompanist and the conductor is paramount,' she says 'because the music must be played to his interpretation.'

'In essence it's team work, the conductor directs the choir and the accompanist, so that the performance finally works out in complete harmony. That means I must keep my eyes on him and on the score all the time.'

Practices are held every Wednesday evening at Llys Cadfan, the old folks home in Tywyn. Often, if dad is working, she will bring her two boys who are five and eight along with her. They enjoy it too 'because they're usually humming the tunes on the way home.' The people at the home look forward to the weekly practices, in fact one of them, Lewis Lewis (over a hundred), is the father of one of the choir members and really savours every moment.

The choir was established in 1967 with Gwynorydd Davies, a shopkeeper at Abergynolwyn and brass band enthusiast in the village, as conductor. Under his stewardship it grew to thirty members, competed in local eisteddfodau and on the sixteenth of October 1969 joined the 'Second Festival of One Thousand Welsh Male Voices', a celebration in the Albert Hall London. It was composed of one thousand choristers from eighteen choirs united under the baton of Roy Bohana.

Gwynorydd continued through the 70's, mainly as a concert choir with Gwenda Hunter Graham, who had been with him from the start, as accompanist. By the early 80's we see a Mr Kennard from Abergynolwyn on the rostrum with Margaret Price Evans at the piano. The Albert Hall Concerts were still on the agenda at this time with all the preparation and practices which they involved. But as so often happens choristers dwindled in number to less than ten. Mr Kennard was ailing in health.

For some years as there was no conductor, the choir ceased to exist. But in the late 80's we see Gwynorydd Davies back as conductor with Gwenda Hunter Graham as pianist. This was the time when Bryan Davies joined and became choir secretary. Recalling those days, he says numbers remained around the ten mark, 'but the choir gave us great pleasure, and there was a lot of hwyl'. It was the choir's good fortune at that time to get a regular slot every three weeks at Plas Talgarth near Machynlleth, a time-share complex, 'at a hundred pounds a session'. It was an arrangement which continued for years and was an invaluable boost to their funds.

By the late 90's Gwynorydd Davies decided to leave the rostrum and his place was taken by Aled Williams from Abergynolwyn, a talented young musician – conductor of the Brass Band there, while Val Jordan took piano duties. She of the musically famous Gwanas family was a good choice. After a while Aled found that he was unable to continue in a dual role and decided to give up his choir involvement. He was followed at the turn of the century by Eirian Lloyd Owen, a graduate of the Royal Welsh College of Music and Drama in Cardiff, and a fine solo singer in her own right. She proved to be an inspirational choice, with Mair Eleri Jones at the piano, the choir was once again growing in stature with further Albert Hall appearances in the massed choirs conducted by Alwyn Humphreys MBE. She left the choir after six years at the end of September 2007 as Eirian Lloyd Evans, having married one of the first tenors.

The significance of the Albert Hall concerts meant that the choir would meet with other North Wales choirs for rigorous practice sessions with the maestro before hand. Alwyn Humphreys demands the highest possible standards, even the sight of a copy will elicit a threat of instant dismissal! For a small choir like Dysynni, the musical pieces to be sung in London by a massed choir of hundreds, were not ones best suited for their local repertoire. But balanced against this however was the chance for small choirs to experience singing powerful pieces such as *Arwelfa* or *Llef*, where the effect is pure electric. That was the challenge.

Other venues have included churches, hotels, village halls, British Legion Clubs and the station platform at Abergynolwyn on the Tal-y-Llyn Railway. The choir is now set fair for the future, and their numbers have increased to fifteen. All drawn, as secretary Bryan Davies emphasises, from the beautiful Vale of Dysynni. Amongst their members they have a paper-shop proprietor, a council worker, an Arriva bus driver, a retired warehouse man at the local farmers co-operative and quite a few like Bryan himself retired (after forty years with Barclays Bank), others comprise a former hospital porter in Tywyn, farmer, a railway worker, engine driver and a BBC man from Cardiff. 'With Jim Chugg now on the rostrum and Mair Eleri Jones at the piano we have a lot of hwyl!' says Bryan, 'and that's most important.'

Jim Chugg, a native of Kent, first came to the Vale of Dysynni in 1990 when he caravanned in the area, later buying a property to live there in 2000. He was educated at Gillingham Grammar School and later Exeter University where he studied Geography and Economics. Since which he's been a teacher, first in Harvey Grammar School Folkstone and then, for 28 years, at Wolverhampton Grammar School, from which he retired as Director of Studies and moved to Llwyngwril. But throughout his life music has been a passion, starting when he learnt to play the piano and the violin. This led to playing in dance bands and performing solo, as well as conducting symphony orchestras in the South of England and the Midlands. Although he's never taught music in his teaching career, Jim has done a fair bit of conducting in his school work and conducted the Newport (Shropshire) Choral Society mixed choir when he worked in Wolverhampton. And here in Wales he's also a piano accompanist for the Aberdovey pantomime, 'a really big one'. 'Music has always been a main sideline in my life rather than a professional one,' he says. 'I've done a lot of piano work with many people for solos and in shows.' This means he can switch with Mair in brief role reversals taking over on the piano occasionally at choir practice. Although conducting a male voice choir is a new experience for him, there's no doubting that he's enjoying every moment. And he enthuses about the cameradery amongst choristers and his fellow North Wales conductors. 'It's a kind of brotherhood,' he says. Amongst his other interests is the Tal-y-Llyn narrow gauge railway where he's a guard and station master, and long distance walking. 'The choir is improving, we're doing more and more concerts and we're getting new members.' He's done quite a bit of learning Welsh. 'I'm very, very, Welsh in my feelings,' he says 'and I just love how the male voice culture carries on here.'

The Choir

Catchment: Aberdyfi, Abergynolwyn, Bryn-crug, Dolgoch, Dolgellau, Llanegryn, Llwyngwril and Tywyn.
Choir Officials
President: Paul Ducros
Chairman: Gareth Evans.
Secretary: Bryan Davies, 106C Plas Edwards, Tywyn, Gwynedd LL36 0AS. Tel. 01654 711524
Treasurer: Graeme Cox
Musical Director and Conductor: Jim Chugg BA, FRGS
Accompanist: Mair Eleri Jones
Compere: John Meirion Richards

Rehearsals are held at Llys Cadfan Tywyn
on Wednesday evenings from 7.00 to 9.00.

Flint Male Voice Choir

For dedication, enthusiasm and commitment look no further than John Bevan. Eighty years old and retired from running his Mr Bevan chain of hardware stores in North Wales, he's still bursting with excitement about Flint Male Voice Choir. Crusading for new members, spreading the word, at Asda in Queensferry singing and recruiting, or likewise on the street in Mold with fellow choristers. Car stickers and posters around Holywell, John Bevan's zeal is incredible. He's been on Radio Wales alerting the nation to the crisis in choirs and the need for new members. The average age of the choristers is sixty-five, several are over eighty, their knees creaking, their hips are going and the clock is ticking. 'So we're looking ahead for younger men to join us.' Mr Bevan grew up when the chapels were very strong and 'families learnt the sol-fa, that's where the pleasure is, when you can sing the part'.

'Once you get hold of that thing and you want to sing and come part of the music, you get that feeling – the *hwyl* if you like, to sing your part.' Getting people to the rehearsal, to the starting gate is the objective. 'People in the depths of Wales have had it since they were that high, they've grown up with it and understand it.' His enthusiasm is boundless and highly infectious! 'Can you pitch a note? All that's necessary is to decide if you're a tenor, baritone or bass. Once you've done that, you come into the choir and stand next to an established member – that's what most do – that's how easy it is. I've known men coming in knowing nothing, picking it up and in the end they're criticising the conductor!'

'You try to get it: for weeks you can't get away from the soprano line, then suddenly you get it – a eureka moment! From then on you can't wait for the next rehearsal – like a boozer who can't wait for the pub to open, he's got to have his fix. If the rehearsal is cancelled or there's a holiday break, you feel deprived and get withdrawal symptoms.'

That's John Bevan in full flight extolling the joys, sharing his thoughts of pure ecstasy. For him Flint is a choir like no other, always up for the big occasion. When the Millennium Dome was opened they were there representing Welsh Choirs, sharing the stage with the Covent Garden Opera Chorus and Orchestra singing in front of the Queen, Tony Blair, the Prime Minister and 10,000 people. They had 'spent a week rehearsing for a marvellous day staying in a posh hotel and bussed in daily. Beautiful girls plied champagne. Then they sang *Speed You're Journey* from Nabucco, quietly at first then louder and the rockets were going off – fantastic'.

Or Lorient in Brittany for the Inter-Celtic Festival in early August, where they have represented Wales four times since first invited there in 1997. 'Lorient is a coastal town about the size of Chester,' John explains, 'where all the Celtic nations meet in a huge celebration of their native cultures: singing and dancing to pipe bands.'

'We start singing at the quay near the caravans and boats – wonderful! There's a large stadium and arena and a big cathedral where we sing with Breton and Spanish dancers and pipe bands from Ireland and Scotland. On four nights in the week there's a pop concert followed by a great big firework display. During the week we do a spot in one of the marquees which is usually packed out – and the welcome they give us is terrific!'

* * *

Setting up Flint Male Voice Choir back in 1975 was a great act of faith in an area considered by many people to be a 'land of Philistines' as far as music was concerned, a cultural desert. The moving spirit was Tom Williams, a native of Pen-y-cae, near Wrexham, and therefore well accustomed to the choral tradition. He set about finding like minded people and in September of that year, with the help of the Mayor of Flint, Councillor Neville Meese and the Town Clerk, Len Baker, a public meeting was called. This was the catalyst which was needed; the Mayor became the Choir's first president, Dai Williams chairman, Mrs D. Thomas vice chairman with Tom Williams as secretary and Len Baker treasurer. Mrs Eirlys Turvey agreed to be accompanist. Thus was the 'Flint Choral Society' established, all that was now required was a conductor.

John Bevan recalls that the first rehearsal was taken by Rowland Jones, Music Co-ordinator for Flintshire County Council, 'a wonderful musician who had conducted at the 1000 Voices Concert at the Albert Hall'. It was on his recommendation that Eifion Tudno Jones, a native of South Wales, a trained musician and excellent organist who was a peripatetic music teacher in Flintshire, would be a suitable choir conductor. Len Baker through his involvement with the County Music Department at Mold and the 'Quality of Life Experiment' had also come into contact with Eifion Tudno Jones, and when contacted by Tom Williams, Eifion agreed to be their musical director.

And so the rehearsals took place at the Flint High School, but as time went on fewer women were attending so that inevitably it became a male voice choir, meantime numbers increased to a regular 30 choristers. The choir was gradually taking root and concerts were held.

When Eifion Jones left they were again in search of a conductor, for a time John Bevan and Dick Jones held the fort. Then John Stone who was a teacher of music and drama at Flint High School and a choir member, stepped into the breach as a 'temporary' measure, and with new ideas improved the choir and stayed on for fifteen years. With John Bevan as his deputy they began competing and won the 'Butlins Challenge Cup'. While at the National and International Eisteddfodau level against the male voice superstars they were taught humility and a desire to match their sound. 'I would teach the choir the notes, John Stone would then take over for the final polish,' says Mr Bevan. 'I was reading the map, if you like, John was looking at the scenery to make it into something beautiful. That's what music is, you've got dots on telegraph wires – someone has to take that and make it into scenery.'

When John Stone left the area to pursue his career in Edinburgh, another conductor had to be found, and again they secured one from their own ranks. Rodney T. Jones had but recently joined the choir from Colwyn Bay, and held an executive position with a national company which had shop outlets throughout the United Kingdom. He was a most remarkable young man who was self-taught in both musical theory and piano playing, and directing a choir, for him, was fulfilling a lifetime's ambition. During his first year he took the choir to a win at the Ellesmere Port Music Festival and in 1989 demonstrated real progress by winning at the National Eisteddfod at Llanrwst, again repeated at Mold in 1991. Flint was now a front line choir with further wins at the Powys Provincial Eisteddfod and the like.

The choir made its first trip abroad in 1985 when the town of Flint was twinned with Menden in Germany, and were invited to sing with the Menden Police Choir. Since then both choirs have exchanged visits and long lasting friendships created. Foreign tours are now a regular arrangement every two years and have included visits to Austria, Czech Republic, France, Germany and Malta. Their appearances representing Wales at Lorient in Brittany for the Inter-Celtic Festival date from 1997 and have led to their performing *Nuits Magique* at the Stade De France in Paris for two nights to capacity audiences of 45,000, receiving standing ovations on both occasions.

Rodney Jones retired as conductor in 2006 – after twenty years he had taken the choir to new heights of achievement 'but new pastures beckoned for both'. Huw Dunley, the deputy conductor, a well qualified music teacher, excellent singer and communicator from Chester, was appointed as his successor.

To help fund a music degree course Huw Dunley had auditioned for a Choral Scholarship at Chester Cathedral but was appointed Lay-Clerk instead, a post he held for 18 years. While studying, he also taught French

Horn both privately and for Clwyd, becoming French Horn Tutor to Clwyd Youth Orchestra. On graduating (Liverpool Uni BA Music) he attended Bretton Hall College near Wakefield qualifying with a PGCE in Music and Drama. He then taught secondary school music at various schools in Cheshire, Wirral and Clwyd, 8 years as head of Dept. Continued as Lay-Clerk at Chester Cathedral until 2000.

During this time he ran and conducted numerous school music groups, founded and conducted Halton Youth Choir, conducted Waverton Singers (Chester), Grosvenor Choir (Southport) and Liverpool Metropolitan Opera, sang in Vale Royal Singers and BBC Northern Singers. He also frequently appeared as soloist throughout Wales and the North, including many recordings and live broadcasts. He also composed and arranged music, including some for BBC's Songs of Praise.

He was invited to join Côr Meibion y Fflint as assistant MD in 2001, taking specific responsibility for choral training and voice production. In January 2006 he was appointed Music Director of the choir. Highlights have been winning the Male Voice section of S4Cs Côr Cymru competition, 3rd at Llangollen and frequent Celtic Festivals in France. Currently in Final of Male Voice section of Côr Cymru 2009 (February 22, 2009).

His regime of voice training exercises as a regular feature of rehearsal night soon paid dividends when they won S4C's 2007 Côr Cymru Male Voice Choir Section Competition. 'He's taking us on and on, and he's doing great,' says John Bevan.

A particular feature of the Flint Choir's vision for the future is their Young Musician competition held annually since 1988. Promoted and organised by the choir, the winner stands to win a First Prize Cup and substantial cash prize plus suitable awards for the runners-up. Also a prize for the most promising newcomer. Contenders perform before a panel of professional judges. The winners will perform at the Choir's Annual Festival at the Pavilion in the Flint Leisure Centre in April, a grand concert with the Flint Choir and guest soloists from the Manchester College of Music.

The Choir

CDs/Tapes: *Songs Across the Dee*
Catchment: North East Wales, Cheshire and Merseyside
Officers
President: Terry Renshaw Mayor of Flint. The presidency is conferred on the current Mayor of Flint each year.
Chairman: Gwyn Lloyd Hughes
Secretary: John Bevan, 13 Northop Road, Flint, Flintshire CH6 5LG.
Tel. 01352 732122
Treasurer: Michael Stenhouse
Musical Director and Conductor: Huw Dunley BA, PGCE, ATCL, ALCM
Deputy Conductor: Aled Wyn Edwards ALCM, LLCM, DAR, P.Dip
Accompanist: Eirlys Haf Jones B.Ed and Aled Wyn Edwards
Compere: Gwyn Lloyd Hughes

*Rehearsals are held at Emaus Methodist Chapel Flint
on Sunday and Wednesday evenings at 7.15.*

Côr Meibion Y Foel

'Eyeballing,' says Grês Pritchard, 'is the secret of my success with Meibion Y Foel.' She needs to see each one of her choristers eye to eye. That is some achievement, because as well as conducting the choir, she also provides the piano accompaniment. Normally she stands at the piano for her weekly rehearsals in the village school at Llannerch-y-medd, so as well as eye contact, when a mere glance or grimace means 'watch out', her head movements also indicate a message for the lads. She has an extremely sensitive musical ear and is quick to identify a discordant note. 'They've come to understand me now,' she says.

Her dexterity is drawing plaudits. Over at St Johns Church Llandudno 'next to Marks', where they occasionally perform, there is a gentleman who comes all the way from Holmes Chapel in Cheshire just to see and hear Meibion Y Foel and their conductor perform. This has developed into some kind of a fan-club following, which has led to the choir responding to an invitation to go to Holmes Chapel to take part in a concert with their choir over there.

The Church in Llandudno is evidently one of their favourite places because 'the acoustics are very good', and Grês likes the staging arrangements which enables her to see the choir very well. Her husband Don, who acts as master of ceremonies, says that the three hundred or so people who come to the concerts at Llandudno 'really appreciate good male voice choral singing'. So here then is a couple who work in tandem totally aware of the other's needs on stage. He sees his part as putting the choir at ease and preparing the audience for a satisfying evening's entertainment. His presentation will vary with each musical item, aware always that an over-long introduction can easily bore the audience and tire the choir which is standing on stage ready to sing. Often the programme will include a guest soloist such as National Eisteddfod winner Marion Roberts, up and coming youngsters like twelve year old Lucy Kelly who collected a bundle of awards at the National Eisteddfod in Cardiff (2008), or may be one or more of the choristers, variously in solo, duet or threesome performances. Grês is always keen to provide an opportunity to develop young musical talent of promise.

Don's introductions have evolved from his experience as a naturally extrovert compere in local chapel eisteddfodau, which has progressed to regional and National Urdd events and Nosweithiau Llawen entertainment.

Grês Pritchard, musician extraordinary, who is also the Deputy

Conductor and accompanist of Côr Meibion Y Traeth since 1970, formed Côr Meibion Y Foel in 2000. 'It came about,' she explains, 'when we decided at Capel Ifan, our chapel in Llannerch-y-medd, together with a few friends, to form a small group to sing a couple of carols to celebrate the Millennium year.' This was all that was needed to fire local enthusiasm: after the Christmas celebration, they wanted to carry on. Eisteddfod Môn, Anglesey's premier regional event was due to take place at Llannerch-y-medd in 2001 and the 'party', now growing in number and confidence wanted to go for it!

But alas 2001 brought with it the dreaded 'Foot and Mouth Disease' and a clamp-down on communal activities in Anglesey; inevitably the Eisteddfod was postponed until 2002. But the choir was still eager and competed in the 'open choir' event. 'They got second prize,' Grês says rather mischievously. 'The first prize went to the Llannerch-y-medd Ladies Choir which I also conduct!' From that beginning they have grown in esteem and their fame is spreading; they have sung in concerts with opera stars like Rhys Meirion, David Kempster, Gwyn Hughes Jones and Mary Lloyd Davies. And are increasingly in demand at weddings, mayoral services and gymanfaoedd ganu. Various charities, such as Air Ambulance, have benefitted from their performances. Often Grês's two choirs share a concert platform, the singing rivalry is quite benign! At Christmas-time they come together at Capel Ifan for a Charity Concert with guest celebrities (in 2008 David Kempster and Glenys Roberts) 'which is always a sell out'. And usually there's also a night of revelry, song and Yuletide celebration over a meal at the 'Alastra' in Amlwch.

How Grês Pritchard finds time for everything defies explanation. For most of her life she's been a full time teacher and for two years was assigned to the Musical Department at the University of Wales Bangor. On top of all that she fulfils a heavy engagements schedule as a piano accompanist, National Eisteddfod of Wales included, who in 2006 honoured her with a White Robe Bardic Order, a signal recognition of her service to music. Often artistes request her services for her ability to bring out the best in their performances, playing in a key higher or lower is never a problem for Grês. And whenever there's a free moment she's setting musical arrangements to get the very best from her choirs. Little wonder that she's known far and wide as 'Amazing Grês'.

Grês Pritchard was born on the lower slopes of Parys Mountain in the north of Anglesey and later went to Pen y Sarn Junior School. The family moved to Pentre Felin near Amlwch when she was still small; her earliest recollections are of 'always wanting to play the piano', probably influenced by what she'd seen in chapel. At home there was a dining table with two drawers, and oh how she loved playing with that, the drawer knobs were the organ stops, and in her make-believe world she strummed away. She still remembers how her parents bought a tiny piano and how her mother taught her to play 'Gentle Jesus'. There was no holding her back, this was evidently her destiny.

Piano lessons with Elizabeth Lemin were soaked up like a sponge. Not content with one exercise, Grês with great abandon would go through the whole book! Her teacher's plea to do 'one at a time' fell on deaf ears. Such talent was not to be thwarted, soon up a stage, she went to Jones Owen in Bangor for lessons. Walking to the bus in Amlwch, she would then take the twenty mile journey to Bangor.

She confesses her debt to the chapel influence, and fulfilling a childhood dream of playing the organ there. Her teacher's course at Bangor Normal College availed her while there with further piano tuition by Maimie Noel Jones. This resulted in her twice winning the pianoforte competition at the Royal National Eisteddfod. Her teaching career began in Amlwch, and while there indulging her musical passion with the school choir, she went on to win the 'All Wales Shield' at the Urdd National Eisteddfod in Pont y Pridd.

She taught at Amlwch for thirteen years and whilst there met and married Don, a native of Pentreberw, who was a teacher there. The chemistry between them is sheer magic, their common wavelength very finely tuned. It's a partnership that is spelling success for Meibion Y Foel.

In October 2008, a landmark month for the choir, they visited Falkirk in Scotland and gave a concert at the Alowa Town Hall; and also released their first compact disk *Croesi'r Bont* (Crossing the Bridge), the name of a song especially written for Grês by Richard Jones, the headmaster where she taught. A particularly relevant title because the choir was now making a statement. It was metaphorically crossing Pont y Borth, the island's link with the mainland: the bridge beckoned and out there the world was theirs to captivate.

The Choir

CDs/Tapes: *Croesi'r Bont* (Sain 2008)
Catchment: Holyhead, Amlwch, Cemaes, Rhos-y-bol, Porthaethwy, Llannerch-y-medd, Llanfechell, Benllech, Bodedern, Bryn Gwran, Valley.
Officers
Chairman: Arfon Jones
Secretary: Emlyn Parry, Hiraethog, Rhos-y-bol, Amlwch, Anglesey LL68 9PT. Tel. 01407 830815
Treasurer: Emrys Hughes
Musical Director and Accompanist: Grês Pritchard, LLCM, ALCM
Compere: Donald Glyn Pritchard

Rehearsals are held in Llanerch y Medd Junior School
every Tuesday evening at 8 o'clock.

Côr Meibion y Fron
Fron Male Voice Choir

Founder member, Vice Chairman and former Chairman,
Dennis Williams tells the story.

"Our first concert was at Black Park Chapel only a mile up the road, but it was a very big event for us back in 1948.

I remember going to London for the first time down the A5 in a Bryn Melyn Coach to sing in a competition at the Westminster Central Hall. Finally the adjudicator Dr Woods called all six choirs back on stage to sing the set piece, *Martyrs of the Arena*, together. It's an experience I'll always remember. The hairs on my neck stood up on end as I was caught in the sensation of the occasion. Singing there as a seventeen year old first tenor standing in the front row, I really felt as if I were a martyr in the arena!

The village of Froncysyllte had a fine tradition of singing with 5 Chapels and a Church but it was not until 1947 that this Choir was formed. The first International Eisteddfod at Llangollen was held in 1947 and many of the village men had attended the event and were so impressed that they decided to form a Choir to compete at the 1948 Eisteddfod. They called a meeting and a Choir was formed from the men of the village and the Youth Club Choir, which was quite unique to have so many fifteen and sixteen year old choristers.

So we went along to the first choir meeting and appointed Lloyd Edwards, who just happened to be the local piano teacher, as conductor. I knew him because I'd been for lessons; he was a lovely man and lived across the valley in Garth. Having fixed up the conductor we appointed Menna Hughes, a pupil of his as accompanist

So off we went, the first piece was *Laudamus* which we sung for the first time at the cenotaph in the village on November 11th. The test pieces for Llangollen were quite alien to us. There was always one early religious piece and another unfamiliar piece from Europe, the sort of music which choirs in Wales were not familiar with. But we chugged away and learned the pieces well enough to enter at the Llangollen International in July 1948.

We were up against the Moravian Teachers Choir from Czechoslovakia, all smartly dressed up in their long tail coats standing in a large semi-circle. The sound they produced was beautiful – they were all singers of a very high standard. That was a bench mark of what singing should really sound like. The Eisteddfod was good at bringing these choirs from all over the world, setting standards we never dreamt of.

So we went to Llangollen every year and set ourselves up as a competitive choir. We had no trouble getting 60 voices because of the singing tradition in the village. When it came to travelling to places like Butlins Eisteddfod in Pwllheli, where we had our first major win, it was just a matter of picking everyone up in Fron and we were off in a couple of Bryn Melyn Coaches. Now we're over seventy strong and the membership is spread out from Wrexham to Welshpool as well as the immediate locality. Many of them, from the more distant parts, have strong family links with Fron.

Lloyd Edwards died when still quite young. He'd been a wonderful conductor for 20 years, he was very persuasive, never got agitated, and therefore got what he wanted. He had worked tirelessly to improve the quality of the Choir and was justifiably proud of the second position that the Choir achieved under his baton at Llangollen. So we had to appoint another conductor, and took a gamble with John Daniel, a twenty-one year old student at the Manchester School of Music, who possessed a good bass voice and was an excellent pianist. So what John learned in Manchester about voice production came back to our benefit as a choir. The gamble paid off handsomely, he took us to our first and second wins at Llangollen and the choir started touring. John had an international outlook, he took us to Germany and Canada with Vancouver being a popular place to visit. But Llangollen remained firmly on our agenda, it was our competitive base. In one year, John took the choir to honours at both Llangollen and the National Eisteddfod in the same year. Eventually after about twenty years John moved on, he was married with children and had a teaching career to pursue.

That was when we appointed our first lady conductor, a graduate of the London School of Music. Val Jones from Berriew near Welshpool, was an excellent pianist and musician. We were extremely lucky to have such a well qualified person of her calibre. But to my surprise the appointment brought on a mini crisis, some of the choristers were not happy with a lady conductor and left the choir! However we survived and Val took us to further success at Llangollen, Athens and Malta. We went on very successful tours to the USA, Canada, Spain, Holland and Germany. After eleven years Val decided she needed to spend more time with her family.

In 2002 we appointed our next conductor, Ann Atkinson from up the valley in Corwen, a very musically talented person with a fine singing voice. Ann had graduated from the University of Wales as a teacher and then went on to the Royal Academy of Music, London and sung with all the leading Opera Companies. Ann soon got the Choir competing again and we went on successful tours to Germany, Cyprus and Barcelona.

In 2006 everything changed for the Choir, the former manager of boyband Blue, Daniel Glatman heard the Choir singing at a wedding in Trevor Hall and was so impressed that he negotiated a deal with Universal Music for 3 CD's.

We were packaged as the Oldest Boy Band in the World and Universal moved very quickly to start recording the first CD which they called *Voices of the Valley*.

The Producer Jon Cohen and our Musical Director Ann Atkinson were a formable team who encouraged the choristers through very demanding and highly technical recording sessions.

In preparation for the launch of the CD, we were involved in the production of the TV commercials. The Film Company requested that the Choir assemble on top of Dinas Bran Castle, Llangollen at sunrise for a film shoot! I eventually convinced the Film Director after a colourful sharing of opinions that it was not a good idea to expect the Oldest Boy Band to clamber up to the Castle in the dark for sunrise, even to capture the special morning light.

We reached a compromise with six of the younger choristers volunteering to do the sunrise film shoot while the main body of the Choir assembled below the Froncysyllte Aqueduct for a 10.00am shoot.

The Film Shoot was a success and the cover of our first CD has a beautiful picture of six choristers in silhouette on the Castle.

The Choir's debut album, *Voices of the Valley*, exceeded all expectations and became not only the Best Selling Classical Album of 2006 but also the Fastest Selling Classical Album ever, beating the professionals such as Russell Watson, Charlotte Church and The Three Tenors. The choir's manager, Daniel Glatman said that 'the music and sound of the choir had captured the hearts of people across the UK and beyond'.

The choir has completed two tours of the UK singing in all the prestigious venues.

They appeared at the Classical Brit Awards alongside Sting, Juan Diego Florez and Katherine Jenkins. Sir Paul McCartney referred to the choir in his award acceptance speech. The choir has sung at the Wales v Ireland rugby match at the Millennium Stadium, Cardiff.

They have appeared on numerous radio and TV programmes including Breakfast Special, This Morning, Ready Steady Cook, Country File, Parkinson and Paul O'Grady Shows, Prince of Wales Birthday Show and a never ending list.

I went on a short PR Tour of Australia with David L. Jones and Allan Smith.

We were persuaded to participate in a nude calendar for 2008 in aid of Help the Aged.

We have Busked in Chester main street for the Culture Show and the celebrity trip just goes on and on.

A script has been produced for a possible Hollywood Film of the choir's rise to fame, there is much humour amongst the choir on which filmstars will be involved.

The choir have been filmed for a one hour documentary which has been shown in the UK and Canada.

A DVD of a live concert at St Jude's Church, London was released in 2008.

Our 2nd CD *Encore* and 3rd CD *Home* have been very successful and we have been requested by Universal to record a 4th CD in 2009.

Whatever we do, it keeps the spotlight on choirs and it shows what enjoyment you can get out of being a member of a choir, a wonderful leisure activity that I can thoroughly recommend."

The Choir

Catchment: Immediate Froncysyllte area and from Wrexham to Welshpool
CDs/Tapes: See Website – www fronchoir.com
Choir Officials
President: Louise Parker
Vice President: Gethin Davies
Chairman: D.L. Jones
Vice Chairman: Dennis Williams
Secretary: B.J. Clark, 3 Taliesin, Marchwiel, Wrexham LL13 0RF. Tel. 01978 361722
Treasurer: A.D. Smith
Musical Director and Conductor: Ann Atkinson B.Ed.,LRAM, Dip Adv RAM
Deputy Director: Owen Roberts
Musical Support Team: Owen Roberts, Alwenna Nutting and Bryan Evans
Accompanist: Caroline Morris

Rehearsals are held in Acrefair School
every Monday and Thursday from 7 until 9

Côr Meibion Bro Glyndwr

Ask Len Atkinson what he thinks of the Corwen Choir, and you'll get an unexpected reply. 'Which one?' he responds. Because this eighty-three year old retired farmer, of a family which originally came from Yorkshire to settle at Groes Efa, Llandyrnog in the Vale of Clwyd in 1831, becoming thoroughly Welsh in the process, has a very long choral memory. Great-grandfather Atkinson had come as a carter to one of the stately homes in the Vale.

Len's father, Price Atkinson, was one of a family of nine children, all of whom were 'very good singers'. Price was particularly good, always technically correct. His mother's family too possessed very fine voices and while very proficient 'they were never as good as father's'. He recalls one hour Sunday night sessions with his Auntie Nelly being drilled in voice production. She would play notes on the organ in Seion Chapel Corwen for exercises, with a stern warning 'No slurring, no shouting and strict production of vowels – breathing and phrasing also very important'. So Len now heads a musically orientated family reaching back at least to Grandfather Atkinson.

At his home near Corwen he has all the memorabilia of a life enriched by music: books, documents and an illustrated picture album (which his daughter Ann gave him on his eightieth birthday). His thoughts gravitate back to a time when every village had a choir, many had an annual eisteddfod too. 'And the standards were much higher then,' he says. 'I first joined a choir soon after my voice broke. Choirs refined their yardstick in the competitive melee of the eisteddfod.'

'Some of today's singers would be unable to attain those high standards.' He goes on to demonstrate his point: 'Many sing vowels like this' and intones the open, rather flat way that he despises. 'The sound should come from the top of the mouth, like this,' and he pitches accordingly. Point made, you can't quarrel with the old warrior.

So there you have it: where do you start comparing the old days when choirs reigned supreme, against the present day Corwen choir, Côr Meibion Bro Glyndŵr? It was formed in 1973 to compete at the Powys Eisteddfod, and as founder member Phillip Green who in 2008 is Choir chairman recalls, the first conductor was Robin Williams from Corwen. He was known locally as Robin yr Exchange from the time he ran the family's grocer's shop and a delivery van which served the needs of the country district. By 1973 however Robin is remembered as a postman in the town and, like his father, a very good musician. Robin had previously conducted a ladies choir in the town with some success, frequenting such challenging eisteddfodau as the one held annually at Butlin's Holiday Camp at Pwllheli. And later, for some years, conducting Côr Dyffryn Iâl, a choir which had earlier been directed by the Rev. Roger Hughes, vicar of Bryneglwys. Robin Williams also played the violin, being professionally trained in Liverpool. Len Atkinson says, 'as a choir master, he was an excellent noter with a fine ear for music and knew exactly what he wanted from his choristers.' Their first accompanist was Manon Easter Ellis who was a teacher at Ysgol y Berwyn and a fine pianist, also organist at the Welsh Congregational Chapel in Corwen (later she was to establish and conduct a ladies choir, Côr Merched Edeyrnion). Under Robin's direction, Côr Meibion Glyndŵr was the first Welsh one to compete in 1978 at the Highland Gaelic Mod Festival, the Scottish musical and literary festival held at Oban, where they gifted a Challenge Cup. Widely travelled both in the UK and in Europe, the Choir have established a close link with the Maasbre Male Voice Choir in the Netherlands, a connection renewed in 2006 when they took part in the remembrance service held annually at 's-Hertogenbosch to commemorate the liberation of the city in 1944 by the 53rd Welsh Division.

The Choir has made several television appearances in both musical programmes and competitive events organised by the BBC, as well as on the Bargain Hunt programme with David Dickinson. Meanwhile the Choir works hard within the community for local and national charities, and in collaboration with other local choirs, notably the Froncysyllte Male Voice Choir and Côr Merched Edeyrnion have raised sixteen thousand, five hundred pounds for MS, Cancer and Parkinson's research.

Following the retirement of Robin Williams, Ann Atkinson (Len's daughter) who had been Robin's deputy, became the Musical Director. At this time the Choir was invited to compete in the prestigious Gŵyl Gorawl Cymru. In 1990 when Ann left the choir to study at the Royal Academy of Music in London, Gwerfyl Williams the Choir's accompanist became the Musical Director, also briefly, Paul Johns, a particularly gifted musician who with his wife gave piano, violin and recorder lessons and kept a shop at Gwyddelwern.

In 1998 Ann returned to the Choir as MD with Gwerfyl Williams as Assistant Musical Director. Ann who is also Musical Director of Froncysyllte Male Voice Choir, the Artistic Director of the North Wales International Music Festival, and the St Asaph City of Music Initiative, was born in Corwen and educated at Ysgol y Berwyn in Bala. She went on from there to gain her B.Ed. Hons degree at the University of Wales. After graduating she started a teaching career at Ysgol y Berwyn, but her fine

Mezzo Soprano voice won her a scholarship at the Royal Academy of Music in London. Since finishing her studies at the Royal Academy she has performed with many of Britain's leading Opera Companies.

The Choir

CDs/Disks: See Website: WWW.broglyndwrmalevoicechoir.co.uk
Catchment: Corwen and Bala Area – and St Helens!
Officials
President: Lord Newborough
Chairman: Philip Green
Secretary: Keith Jones, Tŷ Ucha, Bethel, Llandderfel, Bala.
Tel. 01678 530278
Treasurer: Malcom Wynne
Musical Director: Ann Atkinson B.Ed., LRAM, Dip Adv RAM
Assistant Musical Director: Gwerfyl Williams
Accompanist: Alice V. Evans and Ann Jones

*Choir rehearsals are held at Neuadd Edeyrnion, Corwen
every Wednesday night at 8 o'clock.*

Ann Atkinson is Musical Director of both Y Fron and Bro Glyndwr Male Voice Choirs.

Ann Atkinson is a whirlwind living the enchanted life lesser mortals can only dream of. Born in Corwen, after junior school she went to Ysgol y Berwyn in Bala. Then on to Cartrefle College Wrexham, part of the University of Wales, for of a B.Ed. teaching degree. 'It suited me very well, being fairly near my home, and what is more Cartrefle had a strong Musical Section,' she says. This was an obvious bonus for a young lady with a fine singing voice who was already achieving eisteddfodic success. Cartrefle was a treasure chest of musical talent, and Ann, like a sponge, was receptive to all that was on offer. From Roland Jones the distinguished tenor and Colin Jones she had voice training, breathing exercises and piano lessons. Mair Carrington Roberts was to enrich her appreciation of sound, while the composer Raymond Williams was to extend her history of music, the organ, as well as improvisation and composing. Ann was in her element, savouring every moment.

Then it was back to Ysgol y Berwyn, the school she had left only four years earlier as head girl, but now on the teaching staff. This was to be her life for the next few years in tandem with a course of voice training by the vocalist composer Brian Hughes from Rhos. Meantime refining her stage performances and doing the eisteddfod rounds with some success, including many firsts at both the National Eisteddfod and the International Eisteddfod at Llangollen. Brian could see that here was a talent with great potential. What of the future? was a recurring refrain. The answer was quite evident: she would go to the Northern College of Music in Manchester, Ann thought. This would allow her to continue as conductor of Côr Meibion Glyndŵr, the Corwen Choir, in a role she had taken up. She reckoned the weekly rehearsals were manageable if she was based in Manchester. These were her thoughts by way of progressing her musical destiny. Before making a final decision she decided to go to see Kenneth Bowen at the Royal Academy of Music in London. His advice was very positive, perhaps more a command: 'You must come down here to London as soon as possible,' he said. That was a turning point. 'I went there for an audition, then immediately on to a second hearing. I didn't realise at the time that success at these sessions would provide me with a two year scholarship to the Royal Academy,' she says. 'I got the scholarship,' she whoops, 'my feet hardly touched the ground.'

Then an audition for an opera course, which was what she really wanted. 'And I was lucky with that too,' she says. This led her into the lead role in *Dido and Anias* at the academy. For the whole of the time she was at the academy this continued: one lead role after the other: 'It was fantastic, I was getting good stage experience, acting, absorbing languages – the lot. I tried to be the biggest sponge ever created to soak up this lovely knowledge.' Her time at the Academy finished at the end of July, by early August she was in Glasgow rehearsing her first professional part as Innes in *Il Trovatore* – Verdi and understudying the main mezzo soprano. Singing with the likes of Lisa Gasteen (winner of Singer of the World in Cardiff) and Dennis O'Neil was all part of her wow factor experience.

After Scottish Opera came four years with Glyndebourne Festival Opera. 'I was lucky enough to sing at the new theatre at Glyndebourne on its opening night in 1994,' she says, 'that was a particularly exhilarating experience.' Engagements with other Opera Companies have taken her all over the world, to places ranging from the Sydney Opera House to Vietnam!

'What I missed most after leaving home was the seductive sound of Welsh male voice choirs,' she says. That was 1998 and although her husband the baritone Kevin Sharp whom she met in Royal Academy days and sang with at Glyndebourne, at first had serious reservations about coming back to Wales, he too is enjoying the tranquillity of Corwen and the mountain scenery. 'He's even a member of the Corwen cricket team,' she says.

But tranquil may hardly describe Ann's work schedule: two choirs – Y Fron and Bro Glyndŵr – umpteen countrywide choir concerts in which she also sings, regular rehearsals, her own singing engagements as well as being Musical Director of the North Wales Music Festival at St Asaph takes very good care of that.

Côr Meibion Godre'r Aran

Tom Jones Llanuwchllyn, one of the village's famous sons (by adoption at least – he was born in Shrewsbury in 1910 and moved to the Bala area as a youngster) was the founder of Côr Godre'r Aran. His career was multifaceted. The son of a railwayman, he initially went into farming and later made a significant impact on Welsh life. However he left practical farming for an appointment as local NFU (National Farmers Union) secretary. A born organiser he became actively involved in local government and spent an influential lifetime as a Meirionnydd (later Gwynedd) county councillor. People who remember him recall a person of tremendous charisma and influence. He was a powerful public speaker with great presence and persuasive charm. He was a public spirited gentleman whose work and interests touched many people. Fairly late in life he studied to become a qualified chartered surveyor and valuer. He was a dynamic personality in the Farmer's Co-operative movement and a key figure in establishing 'Hufenfa Meirion' a farmers' co-operative dairy at Rhyd-y-Main near Dolgellau and 'Farmers' Marts', a co-operative farmers' auctioneers' group. He gained wide respect for his part in negotiating the purchase of the 69,000 acre Glanllyn Estate from the government on behalf of a tenant-farmers' co-operative.

When the National Eisteddfod came to Dolgellau in 1949 Tom Jones is seen in the driving seat as honorary secretary of that important event. He took a keen interest in poetry and traditional folk songs. During the years of his youth at Llanuwchllyn he was influenced by the increasingly popular Cerdd Dant culture. He was a faithful deacon and Sunday School teacher in his local Congregational Church where the renowned Whit Monday Annual Chair Eisteddfod had established a musical buzz in the village. It somewhat naturally followed that in 1949, the first green shoots of a choir, which Tom had encouraged were preparing to go for it at Dolgellau. The prime members then being Geraint and Trefor Edwards with their sister Heulwen providing the harp accompaniment. They were given a good adjudication by Gwyndaf Evans, but not placed among the top three to appear on stage!

1950 saw another group brought together by Tom, with Arthur D. Jones as conductor, this time to entertain at an NFU Dinner at the Dorchester Hotel. A fusion of the two parties was to form 'Côr Godre'r Aran', their target being another National Eisteddfod effort, this time at Llanrwst in 1951. Another valiant effort, but they were again unplaced! However in 1952 at Aberystwyth they scored top placing. And again at

Aberystwyth in the King's Hall for the National Cerdd Dant Festival with their rendering of the 23rd Psalm, the audience went wild and called them back for an encore.

At the National at Llandudno 1963 a repeat performance of a hymn by Ehedydd Iâl, *Er nad yw 'nghnawd ond gwellt*, electrified the occasion. Such were the heady days under the direction of Tom Jones, always with a frisson of excitement as he led them to ever greater achievement. He was to take them on several concert tours abroad. He was a prominent member of a group from Wales that visited Patagonia, Argentina in 1965 for the Welsh Community's First Centenary Celebrations. His dream to take his choir to Patagonia was fulfilled in 1977. That was the first ever visit there by a Welsh choir. Several subsequently followed and Côr Godre'r Aran made the return visit 30 years later in 2007. Over the past 40 years the Choir have made frequent visits to America and Australasia. Tom seemed to have contacts all over the world – many through his National Eisteddfod involvement, with its practice of keeping in touch with expat Welsh people through 'Undeb y Cymru ar Wasgar' now renamed 'Undeb Cymru a'r Byd'.

Tom Jones decided to retire as conductor in 1972. Appointing a successor was no problem. He knew exactly who that person should be. Eirian Owen, a local music teacher – an extremely talented musician – was their accompanist. Without hesitation as he bowed out Tom Jones, referring to Eirian, declared, 'This is your next conductor!' That was it! He had spoken – there was to be no argument! Eirian at the time was head of the music department at Ysgol y Gader, Dolgellau.

A native of Llanuwchllyn she had via the Bala Grammar School for Girls and Ysgol y Berwyn gone to the University of Wales Bangor to study music under Harry Williams, William Matthias and Reginald Smith Brindle. Leaving there having done her post grad she had been appointed to Ysgol y Gader as Head of Music, a position she held for thirteen years. Then came an urge to further refine her skills at the piano, so to promote this desire she was placed on a year's secondment to the Manchester Royal College of Music. This led to her becoming staff accompanist at the renowned Chethams School of Music in Manchester, the nursery for gifted young musicians. 'It meant that I was in Manchester three days a week and back home for four days, which allowed me time with the choir and other pursuits,' she explains. During this time she discovered another ideal niche for her talent: many people were approaching her regarding piano lessons for their children. So in January 2006 she made a career adjustment and left Chethams in favour of life as a freelance piano teacher and accompanist as well as her continuing work with Côr Godre'r Aran.

Looking back now she admits that following Tom Jones was a rather terrifying undertaking: he was a colossus in the area, a councillor, chairman of the County Council, member of countless committees and a mainstay of Welsh culture. 'And here was I, young with no experience of public service and lacking in confidence.'

She had come to the choir about five years earlier as an accompanist in response to his invitation, 'And I suppose the crafty old devil had spotted me and thought to himself, here's a young lady who given five years – when I'm ready to retire, could take over as conductor. He was very astute like that'.

'It took me about ten years before I could feel that I had made my mark on the choir,' she says, 'I tried continuing the choir in Cerdd Dant mode as Tom Jones had done; it was quite a struggle because this was not my first choice of music.' In the late eighties she decided to make the switch and decided that the choir would compete as a male voice choir in the 1989 National Eisteddfod at Llanrwst. 'We won,' she says, 'at last, after fourteen years I was standing on my own two feet. This was the stamp of approval that I needed, it gave me self belief.'

Laying the mantle on Eirian Owen was a good decision. Under her direction the choir has gained further kudos and acclaim. She was to take the choir away from the Cerdd Dant mode which had been Tom's chosen medium. They are now a traditional male voice choir, competing at national and international levels, with upwards of 12 major concerts a year and very well travelled. In 2008 they won the Llangollen International Eisteddfod Male Voice Section for the fourth time, currently a record. And following their National Eisteddfod win at Llanrwst they've gone on to win four times more – winning at each visit. To date their touring tally includes North America three times, Patagonia twice, Australia eight times plus New Zealand, Singapore, Hong Kong, Portugal and Ireland. Their numerous British concerts have included events at The National Eisteddfod Pavilion, The Royal Albert Hall, The New Globe Theatre and Earls Court in London, the Birmingham Symphony Hall, the Royal Northern College of Music Manchester, the Sage Gateshead, Llangollen International Eisteddfod Pavilion, and the Royal Highland Show-ground Edinburgh.

And a flagship performance each year end at the Bala Leisure Centre when they invite stars like Rebecca Evans and Willard White to join them in a celebrity concert to crown each year's achievements.

In 1985 Tom Jones tragically died in a car accident near Rhaeadr. He had been on a business mission abroad on behalf of the National Eisteddfod and had then attended a meeting of the Eisteddfod Court at

Cardiff before that fateful journey home. A commemorative biography of his life, edited by Guto Roberts, was published in 1991. The book which contains forty-three written tributes by people who knew him well is called simply, *Tom Jones Llanuwchllyn*.

The Choir

Catchment: Llanuwchllyn, Bala, Sarnau, Rhyd-y-main, Dolgellau, Llanferres, Ruthin, St Asaph, Machynlleth, Aberdyfi, Aberystwyth, Barmouth, Ardudwy, Caeathro, Llandegfan.
Officials
Musical Director, Conductor, Accompanist: Eirian Owen BA, ARCM
Secretary: Arwel Lloyd Jones. Tel. 01678 540465
Treasurer: Irwyn M. Jones
Comperes: Penri Jones and Hywel Jones
CDs/Tapes: See choir website for full list, concert dates, venues, etc.
Website: corgodreraran.org.uk

Rehearsals held Thursday evenings 8.00-10.00 at the
Village Hall, Llanuwchllyn, near Bala. Visitors are welcome.

Gobowen Orthopaedic Hospital Male Voice Choir

It was decision time for David Stainsby when he came out of sixth form college. The choice of career before him was unusual, to go for music at which he was particularly gifted, or for orthopaedic surgery. Ultimately the way ahead for him amounted to a combination of both options. And so we see him at Gobowen Orthopaedic Hospital, near Oswestry in 1968 progressing his life as a young surgeon and at the same time enthusing his colleagues about music.

Forty years later present chairman of the choir Griff Evans, then a theatre technician at the hospital, remembers those halcyon days. How Stainsby got all the staff together to form a mixed choir to do concert versions of Gilbert and Sullivan. Griff recalls how, 'Under his direction he had us doing what Stainsby called the three Ps – *Pirates of Penzance, and Pinafore*'. His term at the hospital done, promotion beckoned and Dr Stainsby moved on; he had inspired the hospital workers and they wanted more.

This wasn't easy because nurses kept changing. That's when a decision was taken to form a male voice choir and the moving spirits were three members of staff: Griff Evans, Humphrey Jones and Gwyn Jones. The three had been to school and grown up together. It was an unlikely mix, Griff wasn't a singer at the time – his only claim to musical flair was that he used to be a trombonist in the Porthywaen Brass Band, Humphrey was at the mortuary, a man with a robust sense of humour, while Gwyn Jones, a mechanic who serviced the hospital's after care cars sang in the Llansilin Choir.

They invited all the male members of staff to come, the original intention being to have two practices a week – on a Monday and a Thursday. 'On the first Monday ten turned up, on the Thursday we had eight,' says Griff. Two practices a week was obviously not an option, which is why they resolved to meet on Thursday evenings only. It was a wise decision because the numbers went up to eighteen. This remains to this day their practice night.

But they felt that they could do with more choristers, which is why they decided to open choir membership to their friends. 'The choir went up to over sixty,' says Griff Evans, 'which included soldiers from Park Hall Army Camp in Oswestry.' When the camp went (it was sited on what is now the Oswestry Show Ground), numbers came down to a steady thirty.

Their first conductor was Gwyn Jones, the mechanic, with weekly practice sessions in the theatre cum chapel within the hospital where they're still held. This is a spacious 350 capacity main hall with sliding doors at one end which admits to the hospital chapel. The chapel has an organ and altar, but as needed can be opened up to increase audience space for big occasions.

The theatre evidently plays a key role in much of what they do, and the hospital too benefits from the choir's existence. In fact there is a close working relationship between the League of Friends at the hospital and the choir. The League of Friends raises funds to enhance the facilities there; likewise the choir; through their annual concert in the theatre at the beginning of December raises upwards of six hundred pounds. Moreover patients are encouraged to come to the practices, sometimes members of other choirs at the hospital for treatment, come in on their crutches and are delighted to join in with the songsters. Christmas is a busy time for the choir, as they bring seasonal cheer to the wards with a spirited rendering of carols.

On balance it's a concert choir with a penchant towards charity fund raising. For example their link with the North Staffordshire Special Schools Annual Concert at the Victoria Hall, Hanley (Stoke on Trent), is one that is firmly on their calendar. There, with two or three like minded choirs and a brass band, they are happy to play their part.

And when Gobowen Church was burnt down by a feckless arsonist some years ago, the choir was first off the mark fund raising for the rebuilding, with a concert at the Oswestry Leisure Centre that raised two thousand pounds.

Gwyn Jones continued as conductor for many years, and even when his health deteriorated stood in as deputy. His successor was John Owen of Bwlch y Cibau, an extremely good soloist, a blacksmith – of a family of blacksmiths, who traditionally sang in the smithy workshop.

At the beginning of 2008 John was unable to continue through illness and had to resign as conductor. 'He was a very good conductor and we were very sad to see him go.'

During John's incapacity, Isobel Clare an accomplished musician, who recently celebrated fifty years in music at a special event in Oswestry School and also had Covent Garden experience, deputised. Educated at the Guild Hall in London Isobel taught in schools, then did further education piano classes for adults with the Rochdale Education Authority. In 1989, responding to a request from her classes, she established a choir for older people in Rochdale, which she ran for five years. Conducting and piano playing is evidently her forte: she was conducting a choir when in her twenties. Her connection with the choir came about when Isobel attended one of the choir's concerts and offered her services as an accompanist. 'She asked if she could accompany us – we said, my gosh yes please!' says Griff. Isobel says introduction to the choir came about indirectly through the Women's Institute at Selatyn which she joined soon after moving with her husband to Hengoed in 2003. At the WI she played piano duets with a fellow musical enthusiast: word gets around, soon her name was brought to the attention of the Gobowen Male Voice Choir. While their accompanist Catherine Wilson was away nursing her ailing mother, Isobel chipped in. When Catherine returned following her mother's demise, came a sideways move for Isobel covering at the rostrum during John's illness. At the Choir's 2008 Annual General Meeting she was officially appointed conductor. Preparing the choir for the rounds of charity concert performances and consolidating are her current priorities.

The Choir

Catchment: Members come from Ellesmere, Baschurch, Llanymynech, Welshpool, Oswestry, Gobowen.
Officials
President: Gwyn Evans FRCS
Chairman: Griff Evans
Vice-Chairman: Ian Faulkner.
Secretary: Colin Law, Hampton Road, Oswestry, Shropshire SY11 1SJ. Tel. 01691 791255
Treasurer: Roger Tanner
PRO: John Hanmer
Compere: Griff Evans
Conductor and Musical Director: Isobel Clare LGSM, LRAM
Accompanists: Catherine Wilson B.Ed

Rehearsals are held at the Theatre/Chapel
in Gobowen Orthopaedic Hospital
every Thursday evening 7.30-9.30.

Llanddulas Male Voice Choir

It was after a concert they had given at St John's Church in Llandudno that the Llanddulas Male Voice Choir had an invitation from an Australian clergyman to come to give a concert at his church in the Blue Mountains outside Sydney. 'It would be great if you could come,' he had said. Secretary Ted Francis and Director of Music Meirion Davies told him that if it was a serious invitation, would he please send them a formal letter of invitation. He agreed, but warned them not to expect anything for three months because he was mid way through a world tour.

Ted and Meirion scarcely believed anything would come of it, it was probably something caught up in the euphoria of the moment! But to their surprise the letter from Australia **did** come through the letter box of Ted's home in Abergele! Now came the challenge: were they up for it? The Llanddulas choir formed of a nucleus of local quarry workers in 1954 was never a big one, a fairly constant thirty-two in number. The cost of an Australian visit with a concert tour was rather daunting. Recalling those times now, Ted Francis said that if we went 'we would have to sing for our supper', code for saying 'fund raising'.

Treasurer Glyn Jones negotiated a loan facility for the choir at the bank. And then they began a Summer season of weekly choir concerts at Seilo Chapel and the Emanuel Christian Centre in Llandudno, now really 'singing for their supper'. It was a successful ruse and in the event precluded the need for a bank loan.

The Choir had previously visited the USA so yes, 'we were on,' says Ted 'on to our second big long haul trip outside the United Kingdom to a place called Springwood near Sydney.' During their visit they did a number of concerts in the area. On the way there they had stopped in Singapore 'and sang with the Dewi Sant Singapore Welsh Society Mixed Choir in a joint concert'.

Since then they have toured Canada and many European countries as well as to several locations in Britain and perform regular Summer Tuesday night concerts at the Gloddaeth United Chapel in Llandudno, which continues to delight thousands of visitors every year.

This leads to ever more requests to perform; they have forty engagements for the year ahead. 'A lot of our concerts come about in this way. Can you come to sing in our chapel? I don't know how many church roofs we've helped to repair!' says Ted. 'So off we go, in 2006 we were invited to Marple in Cheshire by the Dovedale Singers to join them on stage in a mixed concert.' The breezy way he tells the Llanddulas Choir's story reflects their spirit of bonhomie, fun and adventure. 'Many choirs present seriously straight faces on stage, that's not our style,' he says. 'Although their ages range from forty-seven years to well over eighty, their singing enjoyment is reflected in their happy appearance whilst always striving for the highest standard of musical performance.'

Early in 2007 they were invited to Ireland to lead the United Reform Church in Bray with their 150th Anniversary Celebrations. Later in the year they were in Italy on the banks of Lake Garda and received a standing ovation in Malcesine's glorious Town Hall with its timber ceiling and mosaic marble floor. That tour also incorporated visits to Verona, Venice and the Dolomites. 'It's quite nice visiting different places and raise money for those less fortunate. We're quite happy doing that,' says Ted.

The Llanddulas Male Voice Choir with its reputedly wide portfolio, ranging from operas to the musicals, presented with verve and style, strives to entertain. And with the added benefit of a good master of ceremonies, Derek Roberts from Llandudno, a guides trainer with the Welsh Tourist Board, provides the audience 'and us' with a nice bit of background information.

The Llanddulas Male Voice Choir's founder and first conductor was J. Meirion Davies of nearby Rhyd-y-foel who graduated at Bangor, the Royal Northern College of Music College and then studied at The Royal Academy under Sir Adrian Bolt, before becoming Head of Music at Prestatyn High School. He ran the choir in his own particular way for almost fifty years, up to the time of his death from cancer in 2003.

Ted Francis, the choir secretary since 1987, remembers him as an exceptionally good pianist but of a rather shy personality. He remembers how Meirion conducted the choir and played the piano, both at the same time. The choir would be positioned in a semi circle with the piano placed where the conductor normally stands, and it was from this position, seated at the piano, that Meirion conducted.

The Choir was extremely fortunate in securing the services of Eirlys Dwyryd following Meirion's demise. A native of Llangollen, she had been trained for a career in music by Lottie Williams Parry at Wrexham and although she had married Sion Dwyryd (also now a choir member), son of Telynores Dwyryd (Elinor Dwyryd) and therefore into the harp tradition, her first love was classical music. So this was an ideal choice for Llanddulas because she too was a devotee of the harp as well as main stream choral music. Often she's called upon to provide harp accompaniment for the Gorsedd Ceremony in the National Eisteddfod (where she is a white robe Gorsedd member) and for a period conducted her own ladies cerdd dant choir in Ruthin where she lives. Up to her retirement from full time teaching Eirlys was responsible for the music instruction unit to children with special needs at Ysgol Twm o'r Nant in Denbigh, and during her career had taught them to sing in children's choirs and with musical recorder instruments. She was also piano accompanist for the recently disbanded Pwllglas (near Ruthin) mixed voice choir for eighteen years and often called on to serve at village eisteddfodau in the region. Her experience with the therapeutic value of music involves her nowadays in quite a lot of hospital work.

So how did it feel taking on a male voice choir, especially after Meirion's fifty years as conductor? 'There were no problems, the choir co-operated perfectly – although I have to say, I probably work them harder than he did. That's down to my experience preparing people for an eisteddfod performance where the standards are very exacting,' she says. And did she like the custom at Llanddulas where the conductor also provided the piano accompaniment? 'That's not at all difficult,' she says, 'that's what I've always done, and because of my piano experience I can provide the accompaniment in exactly the way I want it.'

'She's accompanying the choir, and controlling us with facial gestures and smiles – and it works,' says Ted Francis. 'Sometimes she accompanies us on the harp, and audiences really go for that.'

The Choir

Tapes/CDs: Côr Llanddulas Choir 2005 (CD) and Sept 2008 (CD)
Catchment: Llanddulas, Colwyn Bay, Llandudno, Abergele and Ruthin.
Officials
Chairman: Trevor Williams
Vice Chairman: Tommy Morris
Secretary: T.E. Francis, Hill Top, 16 Trem y Môr, Abergele LL22 7DZ.
Tel. 01745 823791
Treasurer: Glyn Jones
Conductor and Musical Director. Eirlys Dwyryd
Accompanist: Eirlys Dwyryd
Compere: Derek Roberts and Noel Payne

*Rehearsals are held in the Winter on Sunday and
Tuesday evenings at Gloddaeth United Chapel.*

Côr Meibion Llanrwst
Llanrwst Male Voice Choir

'They don't sing in pubs now do they,' George Jones remembers the old days at the 'Pen y Bryn' when suddenly the whole place would erupt. And although they were in different rooms, the singing was in perfect harmony.

At Llanrwst there's a long singing tradition. Just before the war and continuing up to 1966 there was a fine stock of great musicians. People like Arthur Vaughan Williams in great demand as an Eisteddfod adjudicator; George Lloyd head of music at Llanrwst; John Griffith Evans; T.J. Williams adjudicator and Gymanfa conductor and Richie Thomas (Penmachno) all part of the standards who sustained the choral tradition. George remembers the last years of the old choir, coming along as an eight year old with his father and elder brother to the practices at the temperance hotel in the 'King's Head': an experience which he now values beyond price in his present role as conductor of the revived choir.

The renewal came in 1986 when Ian Woolford, a young policeman in the town, while out fishing with his friends broached the idea of a choir and they decided to put an advert in the paper. This resulted in a meeting in the now demolished Victoria Hotel, which led to the choir's rebirth. Ian became the choir master and saw the choir grow to almost forty members during his five year tenure. A native of Rhosllannerchrugog, Ian Woolford the possessor of a very fine baritone voice, had on a Roland Jones Scholarship attended the Royal College of Music for two years and benefited from a course of voice training with Colin Jones. He had then decided to join the police force which was to ultimately benefit Llanrwst. Now living in Colwyn Bay, he later became involved with other local choirs. As a matter of interest, his sister Eleri Woolford was the award winning soprano in the Welsh National Eisteddfod held at Mold in 2007.

He was followed by Gwen Grench who had retired with her husband to the area from Southend, where she was head of music at a college. Her husband, formerly a headmaster, was also a choir member. Mrs Grench was the musical director until she had to give up on health grounds in 2001. That was when George Jones was drawn in on a 'temporary' basis. He wasn't a choir member from the outset in 1986, but had joined later when the pressure of running his garage/bus company had eased up. But always there had been a passionate love of singing. That's what he now misses most of all, because as conductor he has to remain silent. 'I've never been taught how to conduct a choir,' he says, 'that's something that I'm still picking up.'

'I don't suppose that I'm conducting like anyone else,' he says, 'but at least the lads understand my commands and they know what I want them to do.' In 2004 Colin Jones invited him to join his choir, the Côr Colin Jones. To get such an invitation is a unique privilege, because the Colin Jones choristers are hand-picked and vetted by Colin himself. George had to make a big decision: could he take on that added undertaking in addition to conducting his own Llanrwst Choir? Although Llanrwst will always come first, his decision to accept is one that he's never regretted. 'Since I've joined I believe the Llanrwst Choir has benefited from what I've learnt and passed on; being with Colin Jones has been a terrific education.' 'And there's a lot rubbing off on me,' he adds.

The Llanrwst Male Voice Choir now numbers 24 members, but although quite a bit down from its peak, it's as busy as ever. Concerts are their speciality, singing lighter pieces better suited to their voice power like Gwin Beaujolais, Lleucu Llwyd, Gogoniant Duw and Jacob's Ladder. Pieces by Robert Arwyn and Dafydd Iwan too are choir favourites. Although they have been to festivals such as the one in Coleraine in Northern Ireland, generally competitive events have little appeal for George Jones. He reckons the test pieces are often works that have very little concert attraction, and so, once performed, are promptly forgotten!

He enjoys the challenge of finding new works for the choir, often songs from the London Shows which are adapted for male voice by Richard Thomas, George's mate from school days, 'who's an excellent singer and a whiz-kid on the computer.' George likes to select songs which the lads will enjoy singing; with a small choir he'll very soon get feed back on that score and 'if they're singing or whistling the tune on the way out from practice,' he knows that he's picked a winner.

And whether it's a concert in one of the villages up the Conwy Valley, at St Johns Church in Llandudno or even further afield in Keswick, they have four top class soloists from their number to entertain. They are Merfyn Rogers Jones a retired school master, twenty-eight year old John Hughes, the extra deep bass Richard Thomas and John Kennerley who often doubles as an accompanist, while the compere is Jon Richmond a tourist board worker. Their regular accompanist is Gwyneth McDonald, a graduate of The Royal College of Music, who lives in Llandudno Junction.

They are increasingly popular at weddings too where they can swell the congregational hymn singing, as well as sing appropriately during the registrar signing and 'they sound good on the video too'!

The Choir

Catchment area of Choir members: Llanrwst, Penmachno, Trefriw, Dolgarrog, Abergele, Llandudno and Llandudno Junction.
Choir Officials
Chairman: Charles Griffiths
Secretary: Andrew Davies,Y Berllan, Glan Dulyn, Tal-y-bont, Conwy. Tel. 01492 660530
Treasurer: Joyce Roberts
Compere: Jon Richmond
Musical Director and Conductor: George Jones
Deputy Conductor: Richard Thomas
Accompanist: Gwyneth McDonald

Rehearsals are held every Sunday evening in the
Church Hall Llanrwst from 7.30-9.00

Côr Meibion Llywarch
Sons of Llywarch Choir

What if Dan Puw had made different choices? Gone on to University for instance, as he could well have done, because in all subjects at school he was always top of the class. That was due to his phenomenal memory. 'But it was parrot fashion and wouldn't be much use now because children are these days expected to remember and work things out for themselves,' he says. 'And I couldn't see myself as an academic anyway.' His inclinations lay in other directions 'carpentry and engineering and things like that'. There was also a feeling of obligation, being the only son in a family of girls, that he should come home to help his father on the farm.

But there were other doors. When Dan was eighteen he joined the Bala Brass Band as a trombonist. This might ultimately have offered him further options because it widened his musical horizons beyond the classical Cerdd Dant, which from childhood, had been his food and drink. He makes little of any talk of inherited talent, and rather speaks of how the constant strum of the harp in the home meant 'I couldn't be anything else but musical, could I?' But the beat of the drum was to broaden his talent. 'I once won a first prize in the National Eisteddfod as an instrumentalist,' he says. Even offered an audition with one of the big brass bands from the North of England. 'Can you just imagine,' he says feigning mock horror, 'if I followed that up, I might have married an English girl and had a house-full of English kiddies by now!' Talking to Dan at seventy something, it's hard to imagine the consequence of those possibilities.

He'd also once had the yen to go to Patagonia, influenced probably by the tales of heroism of the early Welsh settlers as told by the Welsh master, Ellis Evans, and the fact that two of his ancestors made the voyage there rather later than Michael D Jones. Choices! Choices!

At his farmhouse home in Y Parc, a village three miles off the Bala to Dolgellau main road, Dan Puw is happy in his world – a combination of farming, music and homespun philosophising.

Looking back now, that was inevitable. Life in Y Parc with its country traditions were to impose that. There were expectations too – that his parents, Gwilym and Gwen's influence, should continue. They had been part of the nurture, immersed in village life with their musical enthusiasm rubbing off on all they knew. Choir parties and singing practices was all that Dan had ever known. He has quite a few silver cups and other eisteddfod trophies in his cupboard, which are an indication of family and personal achievements.

In 1929 Gwilym and Gwen Puw had competed as cerdd dant duetists in the National Eisteddfod held in Liverpool. Even though they were adjudged second prize, their performance was greeted with stupendous applause, a glowing report in the Daily Mail headlined: '10,000 PEOPLE SPELLBOUND. GREAT OVATION FOR FARMER AND HIS WIFE' and a recording contract by the Dominion Record Company in London 'which sold very well'.

When Gwilym and Gwen retired from farming 'to their new home over the hill', Dan took on the farming responsibilities as well as their musical legacy. Teaching the art of cerdd dant and folk music as well as doing harp arrangements. Local people had said 'You must do it now'. It also took in an over view of 'Parti'r Parc', a cerdd dant party of eight which his father had taken to success at the 1947 National Eisteddfod in Colwyn Bay.

Later, a group known by the name 'Meibion Llafar' (Llafar being the name of the river at Parc) was formed to compete at the annual Gŵyl yr Ysgol Sul (Sunday School Festival) at Bala in 1974. Following success there they went on to win many prizes at local and national festivals. Dan already had a ladies choir, Parti'r Brenig from the Cerrigydrudion area, under his supervision, so after that first victory in Bala he declined the invitation to continue with Meibion Llafar except as an ordinary vocalist, and his good friend Trefor Edwards, another Cerdd Dant expert took over as a very successful conductor.

All that is the outline to what led ultimately to the formation of the Meibion Llywarch Choir in 1986. It began with calling a meeting of all who were interested. 'Thirteen turned up,' says Dan, 'and three of those were my own sons!' He laughs heartily at the recollection. 'But we managed to recruit three more and decided to compete at the National Eisteddfod held in Porthmadog in 1987. We would start in the top,' he says with an air of defiance. Before Porthmadog they did a dry run of four local eisteddfodau. Llanuwchllyn, Llandderfel, Tal-y-bont and Llangwm – all with rather mediocre degrees of success. Porthmadog, here we come! Did they strike gold? 'Nothing like it, we didn't even make the short list to appear on the stage. But we weren't broken hearted – and we'd enjoyed the experience,' he says.

1987/1988 saw them doing concerts and once more setting their sights on the Welsh National Eisteddfod at Newport where they were placed third. And third again at Cwm Rhymni in 1990. By 1991 they had made it to second place in the folk section. In the National Eisteddfod of 1995, they struck gold for Cerdd Dant and Folk Groups – repeated again when the festival came to Bala in 1997. Now they could walk very tall! Invited to go to the Irish Folk festival in Dingle in 1998 and performing in ten separate events. And what's more, one of the members found a wife there!!

2002: A fourteen day concert tour of Alberta to celebrate the Welsh Society in Ponoka's 60th anniversary, was crowned with a Welsh style Hymn Singing Festival, Cymanfa Ganu.

2007: Northern Spain with a mix of folk and Cerdd Dant performances as well as the traditional choral renderings. So this is a choir with a great wow factor.

Rehearsals are held in the school hall at Y Parc each Wednesday night. Getting ready for the National Eisteddfod needs special preparation so that the choir can get accustomed to the size of a large stage. 'The National Eisteddfod stage is enormous, as big as some of the fields here in Parc,' says Dan. 'For such occasions the piano is moved out into the school yard and the practice held in the open air.'

The Choir

Catchment: The Bala area known as Penllyn (not to be confused with Caernarfonshire's Pen Llŷn!)
Officials
Secretary: Geraint R. Davies, Cerist, Bala. 01678 520863
Treasurer: Iwan Jones
Conductor and Musical Director: Dan Puw
Deputy Conductor: Arfon Williams
Compere: Dan Puw
Accompanists: Bethan M. Jones and Eirian Jones

Rehearsals are held every Wednesday night at 8.30p.m.
in the school hall at Parc, near Bala.

Côr Meibion Llangollen
Llangollen Male Voice Choir

'I'd love to have a choir of my own,' was a sentiment expressed by Peter Denis Jones to the right people in the right place, which triggered the formation of Llangollen Male Voice choir. That was back in 1982, a wish confided to Denis Roberts of Llangollen and later passed on to two of his friends, Leslie Wilson and Arthur Bailey. It was in Leslie Wilson's front room that this was first discussed: the tinder spark needed to get things moving. It was no idle dream because Peter trained at the Manchester School of Music, possessed a fine tenor voice and was already deputy conductor of the Police Choir in Wrexham. So what was to be done? They decided to put an advert in the local paper requesting anyone interested to go along to The Hand Hotel in Llangollen on a given date. Leslie Wilson, 84, the only surviving member of that small band of enthusiasts, former long time Chairman and now President of the choir, takes up the story. 'Only six turned up and that included the pianist and conductor,' he says, 'but we didn't lose heart, and at our second session there were 12 – by the end of the year we had 40. Pete brought us out something great, when you consider that most of us couldn't read music.' Within a short time Peter was teaching them tonic sol-fa to get to competition level. 'Their first "concert", if you can call it that,' says Leslie, 'was at the Lager Club in Wrexham. We had no uniform. We just managed black trousers and white shirts so that we looked something like a choir.' Their first competition was in Morecambe where they came in third.

A big break came in a letter inviting the choir to sing at Holy Trinity Church, Llandudno, during their summer season of evening concerts. Fulfilling this engagement led, later, to an overseas tour, because there was a party of Dutch people that night in the Llandudno audience. 'After the concert, they chatted with our members saying how much they had enjoyed the performance,' says Mr Wilson, 'then told us of their own choir, the Christelyke Mannenkoor from Deventer, (a town near Arnhem), which was shortly celebrating its 45th Anniversary. For that special occasion they were looking for a small choir to join them.' That chance meeting led to a close bond between the choirs with several exchange visits. Rima Lap, the Dutch choir's secretary, and his wife Trienke, came to the Llangollen choir's 25th Anniversary.

A memorable occasion in Deventer was when Llangollen's choir had learned an old Dutch song, 'Piet Hein,' without telling the Dutch people, and at a concert in the Cathedral, when the first notes of the melody were played, the Dutch congregation looked at each other in amazement. At the end of the piece the choir was given a standing ovation. It was a very moving experience.

Overseas trips followed, the first to Malta. Leslie remembers a particularly moving occasion there when the choir sang in St Mary's Church, Mosta, which had received a direct bomb hit in 1942. Amazingly it did not explode and the bomb is now on display in this beautiful church. The hole in the roof had been suitably glazed, the whole providing evidence of an amazing escape. Appropriately the choir sang *O Iesu Mawr rho danian bur*. 'The acoustics in that church were perfect,' Mr Wilson comments. Over the years there were to be more overseas visits – Holland, France, Canada, and Germany.

Peter Denis Jones served the choir long and well, and even when he was ill and weak he remained a true friend. A high stool with a back was found for him, since standing too long became difficult. Eventually he had to give up but still came along to practices to give moral support to his successor. Peter Denis Jones died in 2006. Mr Wilson says he was an amazing conductor who 'could teach anyone straight off the street to sing! He had us exactly where he wanted us, and instantly recognised a discordant voice – even threatened to name and shame – but he never did! He was brilliant, spot on'! In the early days, if he was away, his sister-in-law, Mary Hughes, would conduct and 'she was every bit as good, in a different way'.

The person who succeeded him was Paul Young, a marvellous pianist, organist and flautist. This was his first experience as conductor of a male voice choir so that having Peter's briefing was invaluable. Unfortunately after a year, Paul's other work meant he had to leave the choir.

It was difficult to find a replacement; for the interim period they were helped out by Silian Evans, originally from the Wrexham Police Choir. A former member of Llangollen Choir he was happy to stand in pending the arrival of Rhonwen Jones, a farmer's daughter from Llandderfel near Bala, a very young lady with excellent musical qualifications and a fine mezzo soprano voice, as conductor. Educated at Ysgol y Berwyn where she passed with high marks in Welsh, History and Music, she plays the piano, harp and violin. When fifteen she conducted the school choir and orchestra while vocally she's had eisteddfod successes, notably in a duet with Rhian Arwel Rowlands, a soprano, at the 2008 National Cerdd Dant Festival held in Rhyl.

She admits that her first experience with the Llangollen Male Voice Choir left her with a feeling of inadequacy. 'I was a bit timid at first,' she says, 'didn't know what to do properly, not having faced a male voice choir as a conductor before. I had only twelve men then; once I got the feel myself, got the experience under my skin, it came natural to me. In less than a year the numbers had increased to thirty.' Her father is a member of Côr Meibion Glyndŵr, the Corwen based choir which is conducted by Ann Atkinson. Often she will go with him to rehearsals to watch how Ann conducts. 'I like to study people like that to see how they have control, and how they make the choir come together rather than each person singing as an individual.' Colin Jones is her idol, 'He has so much control, he hardly moves his finger for the desired effect. I think he has about fifteen single voices in the choir yet they blend, I like the way he uses his hands and how he puts a song over. He mesmerises me.' All these ideas she brings to bear at her workouts with the choir at Llangollen. When learning new pieces she will bring her tenors together for the first half-hour at rehearsals and the basses for the second half hour to ensure note purity before finally bringing both sections together. 'They learn more that way, it's the best way to learn. That's what Alwyn Humphreys has passed to me,' she says.

The choir is warming to her style, a young twenty-three year old, married with two young children she may be, but it is evident she has a natural talent, is ever ready to learn from any reliable quarter and is destined to go places with the choir.

The Choir's motto is 'Cyfeillgarwch trwy Gân', (Friendship through Song), which is very appropriate given the joy they convey through their performances at The Hand Hotel where they still practice. The choir takes up engagements at many different places in Wales and England, often in support of local churches, chapels, and homes for the elderly. Occasionally they do weddings and birthdays, sometimes joining with mixed choirs at events in Hanley (Stoke-on- Trent) and Rhyl. They have appeared several times at The Royal Albert Hall massed choir concerts, which is a particularly exhilarating experience for a small choir, especially when singing The Creation, when the dimmed lights are turned fully on for the amazing finale. The choir has also been on television on the Welsh 'Dechrau Canu Dechrau Canmol' programme.

Regulars and visitors are welcome to listen to the choir practising on a Friday evening. In the choir's archives they have an Australian magazine with advice to anyone visiting Llangollen to 'go and listen to the choir singing in The Hand Hotel on a Friday night'. The choir is very proud of that. The sing-songs in the bar after the practice attracts many visitors, who often return, even from abroad, especially for the friendly feeling the music offers.

The ladies, a kind of official choir supporters' club, are very supportive with fund raising, arranging raffles and sales tables – so necessary for a choir, which gives generously to local and national charities. The choir's secretary is a lady, Lesley Willis, who regularly attends practices and organises the choir's business, a task she has undertaken since 1997. The treasurer Glyn Davies is also the librarian, keeping track of all the music.

The Choir

CDs and Tapes:
The first recording was an LP called *Passing By*
Tape: *O'r Dyffryn i'r Byd* (From the Valley to the World)
Memories
CD *Friendship through Song*
Catchment: Apart from Llangollen, choristers come from as far as Formby, Deganwy, Abergele, Congleton, Sychdyn, Treuddyn, Corwen and Llandrillo.
Choir officials
President: Leslie Wilson
Chairman: Alf Bluck
Secretary: Mrs Lesley Willis, Tŷ Gwyn, I Abbey Terrace, Llantysilio, Llangollen LL20 8DF. Tel. 01978 861482
Treasurer: Mr Glyn Davies
Musical Director/Conductor: Rhonwen Jones
Accompanist: Mrs Alwen Enston

Practices are held in The Hand Hotel, Llangollen
every Friday 7.30pm-9.30pm

Côr Meibion Llangwm

Bethan Smallwood gained her B.Mus. degree at the University of North Wales, Bangor. 'But you need more than a qualification in music to conduct Côr Meibion Llangwm,' she asserts. 'You need stamina and good humour! And the ability to persevere whatever the difficulty.' She's been hard at it since 1973, when her predecessor Ifor Hughes persuaded her to take it on. 'I had then left Bangor and started my career as a music teacher at Ysgol y Berwyn in Bala,' she says. 'As I had always admired the sonorous and beautiful tone of male voice choirs in the National Eisteddfod I immediately agreed to have a go. After all, my father sang bottom bass, I knew every member personally as I was born and bred here and I suppose I slotted in well.' She remembers it back then as a small choir of twenty members. 'They were all keen to learn, very enthusiastic and quite patient with me!' she states.

The valuable experience she gained as a soprano in the University choir, Cantorion Seiriol, (under the baton of John Hywel and Sebastian Forbes) would be put to immediate good use.

'I don't come from a particularly musical background,' she says, 'my mother, Gwyneth Jones played the piano and organ, while my father's brother, Medwyn Jones, was the founder of the cerdd dant group, Meibion Menlli.' Her mother played from sol-fa only, and taught her daughters to read it fluently, an attribute which Bethan also embraces. Llangwm is a rural village, where the Urdd Welsh League of Youth – both Adran and Aelwyd are strong – and the choir, take up most of Bethan's spare time. 'It's a big part of my life.'

Her enthusiasm is highly infectious, her love for the Llangwm Male Voice Choir evident – they're part of her own extended family. Many are inter related, several like herself, are of a farming background. She understands their concerns and knows how farming and country life has changed, many now do other jobs as well and they have to work long hours. The weather often finds them late into the night still harvesting hay or silage.

It's a Monday in early July, the weather has been patchy lately – but today the sun is shining. She will make allowances, there will be a few still hard at work in the fields, absent from choir practice at Y Gorlan Ddiwylliant, the centre where they meet.

So what are the difficulties? When she first took over, almost all could read sol-fa to perfection, 'it was the ideal situation, every member could read the notes,' but since those days there has been a general decline, 'in the chapels as well as the schools; in some schools there's no singing at all.' She continues: 'There's a great flaw in our educational system. If children were taught to read music like their ABC, things would be greatly enhanced. That is the nub of the problem, that's where we should start putting things right.'

The present situation has seriously affected Llangwm Choir as well as many choirs throughout Wales. 'It means that there's a tendency for us, and other male voice choirs, to sing the old familiar pieces rather than to learn new work. She talks of the long arduous note-bashing sessions which now forms part of the process of embarking on new set pieces. It's a tedious experience which requires infinite patience and stamina. 'But we must move on,' she says defiantly, 'I am not interested in singing old repertoire and love the challenge of learning new pieces although in our concerts we do of course include some of the old favourites.'

Her first experience with the choir was to prepare them for the Powys Eisteddfod, held that year in the Ceiriog Valley, with the set piece – Schubert's arrangement of the Twenty Third Psalm. Since then there have been several notable eisteddfod successes including three times winners at the Royal National Eisteddfod: Abergwaun (1986), Rhymni Valley (1990) and at Neath (1994). Her first stab at the National was at Wrexham in 1977 where she was presented with a major problem: persuading the choir, all strong willed individuals, that for the great public occasion they would have to wear a uniform suit. 'That nearly caused a riot amongst them, one or two members just couldn't see any sense in it, and they all eventually agreed to appear wearing white shirts and purple ties!' she says.

Nowadays they're very competitive; preparing for the National Eisteddfod brings their adrenaline up to fever pitch and a near hundred percent attendance at rehearsals. And even, if perchance their numbers are exceeded for a given competition, finding one or two to voluntarily drop out is next to impossible. So it's not surprising to discover that Bethan Smallwood is a committed Eisteddfod person. 'There should be an opportunity for every choir to compete whatever their size, experience or attainments: competition categories should be extended to encourage local small choirs to participate without the fear of harsh adjudication!' At the Cardiff National of 2008 she will be initiated into the Bardic Circle to wear the Green Robe, a very distinguished Welsh honour bestowed by the Royal Welsh National Eisteddfod Council to the country's great achievers. Bethan thinks the choir may well be behind all this, already they're giving her a friendly ribbing by offering her suitable bardic names!

The Choir has a membership of forty-five with a catchment centred mainly on the upland villages of Uwchaled in Denbighshire – Cerrigydrudion, Pentrefoelas, Cwmpenanner and Llangwm and the towns of Ruthin and Bala, with an age range from thirty to eighty – 'their average, 51 years precisely'. Her own outlook is that Choir membership should be an enjoyable experience, and she will quickly dispel any evidence of discord. Many people have said that she treats them too gently, 'that may be true, but they know when it comes to the crunch exactly who's the boss!' That comes down to her experience as a teacher which she sees as 'an advantage for any conductor'.

Being broadly country based has meant that Llangwm Choir has done relatively few overseas tours. In 1988 and the 90s they visited Bavaria in Germany three times, the result of an invitation to Mittich near Passau by that district's Sangerrunde Choir. 'We're on very good terms with them, they have an up-country sense of humour and outlook on life which is similar to ours.'

Scotland seems to have held their particular affection too, the Isle of Arran especially, when in 1995 they shared the stage with the Gaelic diva Mairi Mac Innes. This led to a great bond of friendship and many joint concert appearances with the Choir. Also, famously, the haunting 'Ysbryd y Gael' best selling CD they made together. Scotland, just a weekend away, has been an irresistible destination and has included Festivals in Fife and Dundee.

The Llangwm Male Voice Choir was first established in 1930 to compete in the local Llangwm Chair Eisteddfod, in its heyday one of the finest in the country. They went on to compete in the other local eisteddfodau as well as the bigger regional events and eventually at the National Eisteddfod where they gained significant kudos. Their first conductor was David Jones (father of Emrys Jones) a great exponent of Cerdd Dant, later the baton was passed on to William Jones, a relative of Bethan Smallwood (in 2008 she was given three of his ornately decorated batons, which she regards among her most treasured possessions); next in line was Ifor Hughes, he who persuaded Bethan to take on the Choir's destiny. Bethan's deputy is Rhian Jones, who also accompanies the choir occasionally. Their accompanist for well over forty years was Ellen Ellis from Cerrigydrudion until her retirement in recent years – a long track record, and invaluable contribution! Their present accompanist is Gwerfyl Williams, a HSBC employee, from Bala.

The Choir

CDs/Tapes: *Clychau'r Gôg* (Sain)
Ysbryd y Gael with Mairi Mac Innes (Sain)
Dilyn y Fflam with Mairi Mac Innes (Sain)
Catchment: Uwchaled in Denbighshire including Cerrigydrudion,
Cwmpenanner, Pentrefoelas, Llangwm, Ruthin and Bala.
Officials
Chairman: Ifor Thomas, Cae Haidd, Pentrefoelas, Betws-y-coed
Vice Chairman: Dewi S. Jones, Disgarth Isa, Tŷ Nant, Corwen
Secretary: Arwel Jones, Arddwyfaen, Llangwm, Corwen,
Denbighshire LL21 0RA. Tel. 01490 420256
Treasurer: Trebor Bryn Jones, Is y Coed, Tŷ Nant, Corwen
Musical Director and Conductor: Bethan Smallwood, B. Mus.
Deputy Conductor: Rhian Jones
Accompanist: Gwerfyl Williams
Compere: Aerwyn G Jones, Garth Gwyn, Llangwm

The Choir meet for rehearsals every Monday night
in Gorlan Ddiwylliant, Llangwm at eight o'clock.

Côr Meibion Llansannan
Llansannan Male Voice Choir
Côr Meibion Bro Aled

It was an invitation to Mair Selway to address the Gentlemen's Fellowship known as Cylch yr Aled at Llansannan that started it all. The reason for the call was her expertise as a harpist and her mastery of the uniquely Welsh way of singing to harp accompaniment. Would she please explain to them the intricacies of this particular musical art form? She was well endowed to do so. She was born in Goginan, a village seven miles outside Aberystwyth, and as a child had done the eisteddfodic rounds singing to harp accompaniment. By the time she was eighteen Mair possessed her own harp and was receiving lessons, which was not at all surprising, since she could claim descent on her father's side from the doyen of Welsh harpists, 'Telynores Maldwyn', Nansi Richards. As a young adult her destiny had taken her home to help at her father's busy garage/shop in the village astride the 'A44 main road that in the Summer led to Birmingham'. Here was the centre of his multifarious activities: in modern lingo he was an entrepreneur, well able to spot a business opportunity. A house for sale, he'd be up for it and its contents too, or even a farm: 'anything for sale, he'd have a go at, self drive cars or whatever'. Later she was accepted to study at the Welsh College of Music and Drama, but she had to decline due to her father's illness. Mair received harp lessons from 'Telynores Iâl', Alwenna Roberts, Aberystwyth and became a member of the 'Gorsedd of Bards' in 1957 with the bardic name Telynores Rheidol.

When she married Alwyn Selway in 1963 they lived in Colwyn Bay, and while he taught at Penmaenmawr she became a part time roving schools instructor giving harp lessons.

So it was little wonder that when Alwyn was appointed headmaster at Llansannan, the lively rural community nine miles inland from Abergele where they went to live in 1966, that the 'Cylch yr Aled Fellowship' soon became aware of her talent. Giving the up-country lads lessons in Cerdd Dant was a bold if foolhardy exercise, but she persevered. Starting with simple Welsh Folk songs and discussing the works of the maestros they progressed to forming a Cerdd Dant Party to compete at the National Cerdd Dant Festival which was to be held at Llansannan in 1976. She sees the funny side of it all now, but knocking the local party into shape made her sick with worry – 'I'd been straining my voice with them, my throat was really sore,' she says 'and on top of all that it was to be broadcast live!'

As the fateful day drew closer she realised the enormity of the challenge because cerdd dant singing is like no other, such singing doesn't begin at the first chord and an uncertain start would ruin the rendering. A last minute rehearsal an hour before going on stage, to make sure that their performance would succeed, confirmed her worst fears. Nothing seemed to go right – she braced herself for disaster. Perhaps she had set her sights too high, whatever – the adjudicator gave them a reasonable score and placed them second from the bottom in their class! 'I went home rather happier, at least it was not a total calamity,' she says. It was a salutary experience which showed the men of Llansannan that 'cerdd dant' perhaps was not quite their forte.

That's how the Llansannan Male Voice Choir (Côr Meibion Bro Aled) took root from the embers of a 'cerdd dant' group. Thus in 1976 with a membership which gradually grew from 32 to its present 47 (in 2007) with the dynamic Mair Selway at the helm, here was a choir growing in stature. And although Alwyn and Mair Selway have retired to Mold since 2004, where they now live, the choir still binds them warmly to Llansannan which was their home for 38 years. And come hell or high water she and Alwyn, a choir stalwart, make the 40 minute drive back to the Community Centre every Thursday evening for Choir practice. And however stressful her day has been, once at her rostrum she's unstoppable. For most of the formative years its been a learning curve for the choir and their conductor. She realises that for this mainly farming community, singing takes second place to their seasonal work on the land. 'Often, when I lived in Llansannan, as I went to choir practice by half past seven I would see some members still in their overalls hard at work in the fields, but bless them, slightly late, but still eager to sing, they'd be there in the hall.'

Its now a very well balanced choir despite the fact that she doesn't go out canvassing for members, 'some even come in as tenors and ultimately find their true place as bottom bass! Some don't even know if they can sing'. The wonder of it all is that the sound they make is so good. And she's delighted with how they respond to her very individual conducting technique: its taken long and arduous practice to get them relaxed in their singing, sometimes to smile joyously, at others sombre faced, reflecting the mood of the song. The way she does it now is, she smiles her infectious smile at them – they smile back, in turn the audience sees this too and reflect the happy mood. Similarly if the piece is more serious, she will express that in her face and they will pick it up. And with all songs she will mime the words while conducting. One particular difficulty she had when rehearsing a Negro Spiritual was to get them to click their fingers whilst singing. She very nearly had a revolt on her hands, they just weren't going to have any of that! But perseverance and her boisterous charm won them over, and by now they have conquered their inhibitions. The choir's highlight in 2007 was coming second in the male-voice competition at the National Eisteddfod, held in Mold.

It's a very friendly choir with a nice cross section of ages ranging from eighteen year olds to late seventies drawn from Llansannan itself and a ten mile radius of the village. 'And apart from the farming people we have members from many professions and retired people as choristers.'

They usually do about twelve concerts a year and also perform at five local residential homes for the elderly over Christmas. They've toured too in Brittany, Austria, Paris, and in Enniskillen Northern Ireland were regarded as ambassadors for peace. In Killarney at the prestigious Inter Celtic Festival, Gŵyl Pan Geltaidd, in 1987, they were acclaimed to be the best choir. At the National Eisteddfod in 2007 they were invited to Pennsylvania – 'but we drew the line at that'.

The Choir

CDs/Tapes: Produced by Romani in Stiwdio Sain (1983)
Dewch am Dro, Stiwdio Sain (1990)
Lleisiau Bro a Bryn, Warren Studios, Hay on Wye (1995)
Gawn Ni Gwrdd, Stiwdio Sain (2004) – CD
Catchment: Llansannan, Llanrwst, Pandy Tudur, Gwytherin, Abergele, Henllan, Tremeirchion, Llandyrnog, Denbigh, Bylchau, Trefnant, Conwy and St Asaph
Officers
President: Bleddyn Hughes, Trefin, Ffordd Betws, Llanrwst
Vice-President: Berwyn Evans, Gelli, Llansannan.
Secretary: Elfed Morris, Argoed, Tremeirchion, Denbs. LL17 0AU.
Tel. 01745 812251
Treasurer: Alwyn Selway, Crud yr Awel, Mold
Musical Director and Conductor: Mair Selway, Crud yr Awel, Mold, Flints.
Assistant Musical Director and Conductor: Jac Davies, Bryniog Ucha, Melin-y-coed, Llanrwst, Conwy
Accompanists: Annwen Mair ALCM, Hen dŷ, Bylchau
Ann Evans, Gelli, Llansannan
Compere: Berwyn Evans and Bleddyn Hughes

Rehearsals are held every Thursday evening from 7.30 to 9.30
at the Community Centre/Y Ganolfan Llansannan.

When Alwyn Selway passed away suddenly at the close of 2007, his wife Mair Selway understandably gave up her position as conductor. The situation was resolved by the role of conductor being taken by Annwen Mair, the choir's accompanist of twenty years. She had come to the choir as a sixteen year old after a course of piano instruction firstly with Megan Williams of Denbigh, then by Mr Kruger who had taken her through to an ALCM qualification. She was educated in Rhydgaled School at Groes near Denbigh followed by Ysgol Glan Clwyd, the Welsh Comprehensive School at St Asaph. Following her fifteen years employ with Barclay's Bank Denbigh she made a career move in 2004 and is now employed in a supervisory teacher's assistant role at Ysgol y Llys, Prestatyn. Annwen, who also plays the harp, relies on her knowledge of the choir and her experience with Mair Selway to take the choir forward.

Gwyn Roberts was appointed treasurer when Alwyn Selway passed away.

Côr Meibion Llanfair Caereinion

Côr Meibion Llanfair Caereinion started off as an octet singing group for a small local eisteddfod and grew from there. Emlyn Evans remembers the early days: how a discussion led to its formation in 1956 with the formidable Mrs Dryhurst Dodd as conductor. For three years he was her deputy and stepped in on two occasions to lead the choir, when at different times, she broke her leg. When Mrs Dodd left the area to live in Denbigh, where she continued her musical flair, he became the choir's musical director. Emlyn is now ninety-two and still savours those bravado days.

Llanfair Caereinion had its musical tradition and he grew up in its echoes. Childhood days were at Rhiwhiriaeth, a small local country school, now no more ('closed on the day of the Aberfan disaster'), where Tom Hamer taught 'Tonic Sol-fa' on Curwen's Modulator. Emlyn reflects that 'years before my time', Tom Hamer's father-in-law had a male voice choir locally. 'He would go along the line of singers, and cupping his ear, would listen to each one – we need more of that now,' says Emlyn. By the age of twelve, Emlyn himself was conducting the singing at the chapel, where he had a choir.

'To be a good conductor, you need to have plenty of practice,' he says. So did he learn much shadowing Mrs Dodd? 'N . . . aw,' he drawls thoughtfully. 'She was very musical, mind you, had her standards and knew how to achieve them; no two ways about that. But she tended to be short tempered.'

So that's how Emlyn began his twelve year stint as choir master. 'It's what I've always enjoyed doing,' he says. So were there any passengers? 'Yes, there was the occasional one or two, who just came along to meet their friends,' he says, 'and if you'd listen very carefully you might just about hear them singing! And they'd come to a concert, particularly if there was a meal afterwards – that was really what they'd come for. They would eat enough to keep them going for a couple of days.'

What are the attributes of a good conductor? 'Often you have to know when to keep your mouth shut – in other words you have to be a bit of a diplomat, know how to handle people; that's very important.'

'In the beginning two or three members were agitating about a uniform for the choir. My view at that time was that it wasn't necessary,' he says. 'There were many then, like myself, without a lot of spare cash – buying a uniform could be an expensive item. Working on Tŷ Isa, the hundred acre family farm, meant that I never had wages; all I ever got in my hand was pocket money. When I got married at thirty-one, I managed to buy a ring for the wife with rabbit money! My view was that it would be better for members to buy dark suits for best, which they could also use for weddings and funerals. That's what I wanted and perhaps wear a red tie for concerts.' Now however they have smart uniforms; the jackets are purchased with choir funds while members pay for the trousers. If a member leaves the choir, the jacket is returned.

'Ah yes, but do they bring them back?'

'Oh yes,' says Emlyn Thomas the choir's secretary who is a Welshpool accountant, 'I have a cupboard full of them at home!'

Memories, memories – Emlyn has plenty of them. 'We had second at Aber and at Bridgend; once we had a first at the Powys Eisteddfod,' he says in his unique mid Wales dialect. 'It's the comradeship and enjoyment of singing that matters, if you don't get that – you stop going.' And the characters. Emlyn recalls, 'Dave Sidevalve, a tenor, so nicknamed by his mates because he sang from the side of his mouth.'

But twelve years on, balancing farm work against commitment to the choir, proved difficult. Arwyn Evans, Emlyn's son, now the choir's registrar, says: 'When a cow was showing signs of calving, Dad faced a difficult decision. To stay around until the calf was delivered, and provide assistance with a sometimes complicated birth, or leave it to Mam to keep an eye on things while he went to the weekly practice. In the end it was often one o'clock in the morning before the calf came! But how was he to know that? That was the reason why he eventually decided to give up conducting the choir.' Arwyn now farms Tŷ Isa, the hill farm with land above the 1100 foot contour, but Emlyn still drives the tractor at harvest time.

When Emlyn stepped down, the rostrum was taken over by Richie Jones followed by Hywel Rees and then by Val Jones, a music teacher. Then came Linda Gittins who was formerly the piano accompanist when Val was conducting. Linda came originally to Llanfair Caereinion as a teacher and was later to enhance her musical reputation, not only with the Choir, which increased in number to over fifty choristers under her watch, but also her work with Theatr Ieuenctid Maldwyn (The County Youth Theatre). Here she was part of a team which produced rock opera. A particularly successful production being 'Ann', which depicted the life and work of the Welsh Hymn Writer, Ann Griffiths for the Meifod National Eisteddfod. Her life is now devoted to youth theatre work within the county and her contribution to Music in Wales has been justifiably acknowledged with an MBE award.

She conducted the choir for fifteen years joined by Jane Lewis as accompanist, who was also an accomplished musician and for many years musical director of Buttington Amateur Opera. It was during Linda's tenure that Emlyn Thomas first joined the choir and became its secretary in 1988. He remembers Alex Carlisle (now Lord Carlisle) then the local Member of Parliament, who lived at nearby Berriew, as being for a short time an active choir member and elected president. But when he was elevated to the House of Lords and sold his Berriew home he left the area. Emlyn Thomas describes the choir as local with a strong country bias. This means that foreign travel has been out of the question for them since only half could make it due to their farm commitments. So concert tours have tended to be relatively local with the ocasional foray to Cornwall, Scotland (Dumfries), and London (for the Albert Hall Massed Choir Concert). But even London is losing its gloss for them, because 'when all the participating choirs are rehearsing the same pieces it means our own concerts are losing their individuality'.

Concerts are still a strong part of their retinue, usually limited to destinations a one and a half hour journey from their home base. Apart from the attraction of providing a fine evening's musical presentation they also hold an ace card in their compere, Geraint Peach. He does exactly what is expected, which is to quietly warm up the audience, putting everyone at ease. He has a fine voice for a solo turn and 'is quite a character; a bit of a comedian who is known to have the audience in tucks of uncontrollable laughter'. So a concert date inquiry usually has a special request: 'Can we please have Geraint?' – an assurance that there will be plenty of 'hwyl'.

When Linda stepped down in 2005, Nick Aston Smith, a mathematics teacher took over the baton. Surrey born he had first come to live at Llanfair Caereinion in 1989 when he took up a post in Welshpool. In a way he was coming back to the land of his grandfather who was born in Cefnmawr near Wrexham, while his wife also had relations in South Wales. Nick owes his love of music to having attended Trinity School Croydon which had an extremely strong musical tradition. 'That was the core of my musical education,' he says, siting David Squibb the Director of Music there as a particular influence. Nick had been to piano lessons since the age of six and when eleven years old had started learning to play the oboe. 'I also learnt percussion and for a while had organ lessons. And I was very fortunate in having singing lessons with Hervey Allen,' he continues.

So how come he ended up teaching the sciences? 'I had a big decision to make when I was eighteen,' he explains, 'because I'd passed my Grade A Exam with distinction on the oboe, and as a result had received an invitation to audition for a place at the Royal College of Music in London. I was also taking my Science A Levels, so I decided to go on with that.

Science would be my bread and butter while music would provide the jam!' So music 'has always been my predominant hobby'. Since then music has featured strongly in his life, playing in orchestras and singing in choirs. 'As a teacher I got involved in music ensembles, and while I was at Welshpool High School, because of the illness of the head of music, I took over conducting the orchestra for several years.' For many years he conducted Cantorion Llandrindod, a mixed choir in Llandrindod Wells.

He'd moved on from there, when a neighbour called asking him: 'What are you doing these days?' Followed by the invitation to be conductor of Llanfaircaereinion Male Voice Choir! Three or four successful bonding sessions later and the deal was sealed. So what sort of experience was it to follow the musically high profile Linda Gittins? 'It was really a luxury,' says Nick, 'because the choir was used to being rehearsed, making demands on them – someone else had already done all the hard work. She had established a lot of tradition which I'm trying to carry forward. Obviously, looking at a different repertoire, I've had them singing some Tudor Church Music and Italian Baroque as well as the standard fare of Welsh hymns and spirituals.'

He's been an ideal choice. 'He certainly knows his stuff and has the confidence of the choir,' says secretary Emlyn Thomas.

The Choir

CDs/Tapes: *Llanfair Caereinion Male Voice Choir In Concert*
(CD by Tryfan)
Catchment: Welshpool, Llanfair Caereinion, Llanymynech, Llanfyllin, Newtown, Telford.
Officials
President: Linda Gittins
Chairman: Martin Liddiart
Secretary: Emlyn Thomas, Cadwaladr & Co Accountants, 25 Severn Street, Welshpool, Powys SY21 7A. Tel. 01938 552625
Treasurer: Mike Rogers
Registrar: Arwyn Evans
Musical Director and Conductor: Nick Aston Smith
Accompanist and Deputy Conductor: Jane Lewis LRAM
Deputy Accompanist: Huw Davies

Rehearsals are held at Llanfair Caereinion High School
every Wednesday night from 8.00 until 10.00.

Côr Meibion Maelgwn
Maelgwn Male Voice Choir

William Lloyd was a Llandudno Junction based train driver in the age of steam, as well as a highly rated exponent of harp music, cerdd dant. And it was as a 'cerdd dant' party of 'a couple of dozen lads who were mainly railway workers' that Côr Meibion Maelgwn first saw the light of day; set up under William's guidance to compete in the 1963 National Eisteddfod at Llandudno. 'We sang "Seimon Mab Jonah",' recalls Gwyn Jones, who was to become their long serving secretary, 'and received an encouraging adjudication.' It was a promising start, within a short time the twenty-four had become eighty-eight!

When William died in 1970 the role of conductor was taken up by R. Davy Jones, up to the time of his illness in 2000 and of his death in 2005 possibly the best known pianist in Wales: the first choice at every Eisteddfod or Test Concert, for thirty years one of the chief accompanists at the National Eisteddfod. He is remembered as a mild mannered gentle sympathetic person who nailed Maelgwn as a first rate male voice concert choir. From then on came the change, no longer a cerdd dant group, Maelgwn entered the male voice first division. But not an Eisteddfodic competitive one; during Davy's time over 2000 concerts, many in support of charities, as well as others overseas were performed. Grand concerts at the old Arcadia Theatre or the Pier Pavilion Llandudno with stars like Russ Conway, Stuart Burrows, Frankie Vaughan and Moira Anderson became the norm. It was a choir for the great occasion, their first overseas was to Veldhovens in Holland, then entertaining the Dutch Choir back at Llandudno in a joint return concert. Likewise to Germany, an exchange with a German Police Choir. 1988, Israel on a tour organized by Roger Roberts, now Lord Roberts, and a memorable singing performance on the sea of Galilee; in Jerusalem a Welsh Gymanfa Ganu at a Scottish Church there, up to that time the first occasion for a Welsh Male Voice Choir to sing in that country. 1990 to Greece and Thesalonica; 1995 a concert tour to Canada and singing in a Gymanfa Ganu at the Dewi Sant Church in Toronto.

Trips to Wicklow in Ireland which began in 1978 have been very popular. 'We've been there fifteen times,' says Gwyn Jones, 'and we get a huge welcome each time.' It's usually a weekend visit 'when we're welcomed by a piped band and treated like royalty'. Then the choir does a Saturday night concert in the Rugby Club; on Sunday morning, singing in the ten o'clock Mass at the Catholic Church to a congregation of twelve hundred. 'Then it's to the Methodist Church by twelve for a concert, which is followed by a grand parade through the town. Each evening at eight o'clock, a concert in the Fatima Convent which goes on until about half past ten and continues in the Square into the early hours of the morning'. The local Wicklow newspaper said, 'The quality of their music was so good that several people were drawn out of bed to hear them, and could be seen standing around the audience in their dressing gowns'.

Davy suffered a stroke in 2000, and for a while his deputy Ifor Clwyd Jones, Gwyn's twin brother, an experienced musician and organist at Hermon Chapel Old Colwyn, took over. This was a temporary solution which Ifor bridged while the committee pondered the future. It was Ifor who prepared the choir for a Prague tour The answer to their prayers came from within their own ranks; while on their tour, a sub-committee decided to ask Trystan Lewis, a young bass singer in the choir, who was then a student at the University in Aberystwyth to be their musical director. It was an inspired choice.

He had joined the choir in 1995 as a sixteen year old schoolboy, most of the choristers were old enough to be his father, some even his grandfather! He was still a choir member when he later went to the University College at Aberystwyth, joining in the practices whenever he came home. He got the conducting bug early on, soon forming his own mixed choir, and later for two years, conducting the College choir, Côr Pantycelyn. For normal mortals that would be more than enough, but not for Trystan Lewis. He was clearly a young man obsessed, next he was forming a male voice choir for the Urdd, Welsh League of Youth, Eisteddfod and winning! In the meantime joining the Aberystwyth Male Voice Choir, while at the same time keeping up with Côr Meibion Maelgwn back in Llandudno Junction. 'Singing with Côr Meibion Maelgwn was fantastic,' he says, 'joining in with the older ones taught me a lot and deepened my experience.'

So in August 2001 came the call for this young student, midway through his college studies, to be the Maelgwn Choir's musical director. The choir's sub-committee could see the potential and pressed their case. For a young man this was a very great commitment. Yes he would give it a go. Looking back now he just doesn't know how he did it, for two years he travelled twice a week from Aberystwyth for the practices in the Junction, a weekly journey of 600 miles. 'I started from Aberyswyth at four o'clock and was back there, having done rehearsals, by midnight,' he says.

Up to that time Maelgwn was mainly a concert choir; Trystan had little sympathy with that emphasis, henceforth it would be a highly competitive one. 'It's the only way to raise standards' is one of his favourite maxims. His first target was to compete in the 'Sea-Link Competition for Male Voice Choirs' to be held at Llandudno in the following November – scarcely two months on. For most it was too ambitious an objective, but Trystan's zeal should never be underestimated, targets are made to be challenged. There were six choirs competing, and one of the adjudicators was George Guest. Trystan was delighted with the adjudication, and even more so when they were declared the winners. They were now ready to take on the National Eisteddfod, another mountain. But this young conductor is totally unfazed by mountains! In their first two stabs they came second before getting the top award when the festival came to Faenol Park near Bangor in 2005.

What of the future? Keeping up the competitive edge is definitely on his agenda. 'That's the only way to raise standards, and to maintain the quality of our performance,' he says. 'Programme building is important too, to please the audience, the judges and to be as musical as possible.' He then makes a telling observation: 'These days there's not enough importance placed on how to produce the voice and express it musically. Mozart said that the organ was the king of instruments, that is rubbish – man's voice is uniquely mysterious and wonderful, no two voices are the same, and no-one really knows how it's produced. When the great Italian singer Gigli died they opened him up expecting to find that he had a very special sound box, only to realise that it was no different to anyone else's. Man's voice excels.'

The Choir

Catchment Area: Conwy, Llandudno Junction, Llandudno, Llanrwst, Llanfairfechan, Abergele.
Tapes/CDs: See Website: www.maelgwn.co.uk
Officials
President: R.D.O. Williams
Chairman: Lloyd Williams
Secretary: Emyr Williams, 29 Llwyn Gwgan, Llanfairfechan, Conwy LL33 0UT. Tel. 01248 681159
Treasurer: John N. Williams
Conductor and Musical Director: Trystan Lewis BA
Deputy Conductor: Ifor Clwyd Jones
Accompanists: Mererid Mair B.Mus., M.Th. and Sian Louise Bratch BA
Organist: Rhys Roberts
Compere: Norman Roberts

Rehearsals are held every Monday and Wednesday night
7.30 – 9.00 in Ysgol Maelgwn, Llandudno Junction

Côr Meibion y Moelwyn
Moelwyn Male Voice Choir

The original Choir was formed in 1891 in the slate mining town of Blaenau Ffestiniog by Cadwaladr Roberts, a very talented musician from Tan y Grisiau. For many years the choir was known as the 'Oakley Male Voice Choir', after the area's slate quarry reputed in its day to be the largest in the world. Under the tenure of T.O. Thomas a local music teacher as conductor, some eighty years later, the name Moelwyn was adopted after the highest mountain in Blaenau.

In the summer of 1907 the choir was invited to entertain King Edward VII and Queen Alexandra on board the Royal Yacht, which was moored in the Irish Sea off Holyhead, during their visit to North Wales. In 1910 and 1911, two successful years for the choir, they toured America and Canada, both tours lasting three months. These were ostensibly fund raising tours to aid sufferers from the dreaded effects of slate dust. With a general decline in the slate industry and the coming of World War 2, the choir was disbanded in the late 30's.

Public demand for the restoration of Blaenau Ffestiniog's choral tradition led to the choir's revival in the early 1960's. Thus Moelwyn Male Voice Choir began a new successful phase, and tribute should be paid to the talented conductors who have been at the helm, T.O. Thomas (1960-1971), Harry Jones Williams from Penrhyndeudraeth, an experienced choir man (1971-75) and Glyn Bryfdir Jones (1975-81) an accomplished musician and raconteur who could claim direct descent from one of the ancient princes of Gwynedd. And father of the well known soprano from the world of opera, Marian Bryfdir.

In 1981, Sylvia Ann Jones a local schoolteacher, an accomplished pianist and organist, took over as their first woman conductor. A lady of exceptional musical talent, she studied music at Cardiff and Bangor universities, where she gained her BA, and LLCM degrees. Her future seemed already mapped out when, as a nine year old, she regularly played the organ at Salem Chapel. Her successful journey through college, left her in those days with a fairly limited career option, which was as a performer or a teacher. And since she favoured the piano, teaching was an obvious choice which took her to Maenofferen Junior School in Blaenau Ffestiniog. Her first big choir involvement was with Côr y Brythoniaid in the early sixties as a junior musical accompanist to Katie Pleming (her music teacher) and Meirion Jones choir master. 'Working with them provided good experience for me when I later became the accompanist for Côr Meibion y Moelwyn and later, their conductor,' she says. This was a bold appointment at the time 'because there were very few women conductors then'. The choir also has two very gifted accompanists Gwyn V. Jones, ALCM, a postal officer at Blaenau Ffestiniog, who is very accomplished on the piano, organ and harp. And Wenna Jones B.Ed., ALCM, a local schoolteacher, who graduated at Bangor University, and plays the piano, organ and clarinet. Sylvia has on two occasions taken the choir to success at the National Eisteddfod.

In 1983 the choir acquired the dilapidated Salem Chapel in the town, which with enthusiasm and hard work, voluntarily undertaken by the choir members, has been adapted for rehearsal and concert purposes. This was a costly undertaking financed mainly from choir funds, local authority grants and the goodwill of friends. It was officially declared open on May 26th, 1984, by Dr Meredydd Evans, a famous son of Blaenau Ffestiniog, and a very impressive pine framed collage by a choir member, the late Gilbert Griffiths of Porthmadog, is a worthy memorial of that occasion. Salem Chapel's restoration meant that Côr Meibion y Moelwyn now had a first rate rehearsal auditorium which can also be easily used as a hundred seater concert hall. It's a compact building with a gallery, which makes it ideally intimate in atmosphere and acoustically satisfactory. The work has been carried out very sympathetically using the pulpit area as a stage and the lectern nicely placed as a conductor's rostrum. A small anteroom doubles as a general office and kitchen suitable for providing hot interval drinks on the choir's Friday rehearsal night. Future ideas for the chapel are likely to include a display area for their extensive archive material. In short, as a rehearsal facility and choir base, Salem is first rate.

The choir has travelled extensively being the first Welsh choir to tour Iceland (1979); Spain (Alicante) 1995, and they've visited Brittany twice. They toured in Europe in 1981 and 1986 when they represented Wales and Great Britain at a 3 day International Festival in Ahrweiler, (Germany). It was during these tours on their visits to the Old Church in Oosterbeek (Holland), that a bond of friendship grew between the choir and the Dutch people. In fact out of the firm friendship with one of their Choir's Vice presidents, Henk Duinhoven of Oosterbeek grew a special invitation for the choir to travel once again to Holland to participate in the 75th Anniversary celebrations of the Etten choir in May 1988. It was during one of these sojourns that choir member and treasurer Meirion Ellis recalls a moving occasion when the choir sang 'through their tears' in the World War Cemetery at Arnhem.

In August 1990 the choir travelled again, a nine day tour this time, to

Norway, visiting Oslo, Fredrikstat, Voss and Bergen.

Moelwyn Male Voice Choir are seasoned travellers, but they nearly had to go on stage without their suits on a visit to the Bahamas in February 2000 because their luggage hadn't arrived. They were there as the guests of millionaire David Wynn Griffiths a native of Prenteg, who had invited the whole choir to the Bahamas, where he now lives, to celebrate his 60th birthday.

But after flying out, it looked like they would have to appear on stage in Tee shirt and shorts. But luckily they managed to get their suits just minutes before the concert began.

Needless to say, to their great credit, it didn't spoil their performance one bit in front of an audience which included members of the government and other important local dignitaries.

Proceeds from the $100 a ticket concert went to the Grand Bahamas Children's Home, which was established by Lady Henrietta St George. The Moelwyn Male Voice Choir as well as the Ffestiniog Town Council made generous donations and presented a framed picture of Blaenau Ffestiniog to Lady Henrietta to be hung up in the Children's Home as a memento of a very happy occasion.

The choir received a warm welcome from the island people. During their stay the local children saw the choir and soloists Glyn Williams and Trebor Evans rehearsing accompanied by Colin Jones on the piano, which ended happily with everyone singing *When the Saints Come Marching In*.

The Choir

CDs and Tapes: See Website.
Catchment area of choir members: Blaenau Ffestiniog, Manod, Ffestiniog, Penrhyndeudraeth, Porthmadog, Ysbyty Ifan, and Betws-y-coed.
Choir Officials
Chairman: Anthony Mc Nally
Secretary: Gwyn Jarman Tel. 01766 830799 and Eifion Morris Tel. 01690 710491
Treasurer: Meirion Ellis
Compere: Glyn Jones
Accompanist: Gwyn Vaughan Jones ALCM and Wenna Frances Jones B.Ed., ALCM
Conductor and Musical Director: Sylvia Ann Jones BA., LLCM
Deputy Conductor: Wenna Frances Jones B.Ed., ALCM
Compere: Glyn Jones

Rehearsals are held on Friday evenings at the Old Salem Chapel
Blaenau Ffestiniog from 7.30-9.30.

Newtown and District Male Voice Choir

'The rehearsals are held at the United Reform Church in Newtown, every Sunday night from 7.00 until 9.30,' says Meurig Jones, a Newtown Choir member for over 40 years, now into his third or fourth stint as chairman! Chairing events seem to come easy for this 65 year old local farmer who in 2009 is also leading the Welsh Ploughing Association, second time around, having recently stepped down as chairman of the 'Mid Wales Vintage Machinery Society'. 'He has a calming influence,' says Enid Morgan, the choir secretary since 1978. Her office background in accounts has channeled her talents into various roles, including St Asaph Diocesan Treasurer of the Mother's Union, Treasurer of her local church at nearby Mochdre (where she is also a Warden), and Secretary to local branches of 'The British Heart Foundation' and 'The Diabetic Foundation'. She became the choir secretary as the result of the then chairman asking her to do a joint programme for six choirs. A year later, when the secretary retired they asked if she would take it on. Enid explains that her late husband was a choir member and so she agreed to 'try being secretary for twelve months – and I'm still doing it'!

'We need a long practice session,' says Meurig 'because Christine Roberts our Musical Director comes from quite a distance – the other side of Shrewsbury – so we need to make the best use of her time and make it worth her while.'

So what goes on at rehearsal? 'First we do breathing exercises, going up and down the scales in one breath,' he says. Christine is strict on discipline and is 'not averse to calling us to order in no uncertain terms! But we think the world of her. At rehearsal or a concert we have to behave ourselves and do as we're told – she's in charge – but afterwards when its all over, she'll join us in a drink, enjoy a joke and a laugh, which is exactly as it should be'. Enid Morgan adds: 'She's very good with them, and even though they wind her up a bit, Christine's very tactful in the way she responds. As a choir we're very, very lucky'. Quite a few of the members don't read music, so it takes longer to learn a new piece. 'But once they've got it, they've got it,' she asserts. 'Then at concerts, it's strictly: no copies allowed!'

'We've been singing at quite a few weddings lately,' says Meurig. Usually they sing appropriate songs as people come into church and again during the signing of the register. 'It's the bride's parents who choose the pieces: often it's something they've heard at one of our concerts,' says Meurig, 'they've made a note about their favourites, then come and ask us to sing their chosen pieces.' Enid says that the small fee they get is a valuable help towards choir expenses, 'new copies for the choir, now forty-two in number, can cost hundreds of pounds. The days have long gone when they could be bought for one and sixpence a copy, and what's more they can't even be photo-copied due to copyright.'

Originally it was called the Cedewain Gleemen, then in 1951 becoming known as the Newtown and District Male Voice Choir. 'The first conductor was Hubert Evans, followed by Mrs Davies,' says Meurig Jones, 'then by Tommy Evans who was the conductor at the time I joined. He was of a very musical family, belonged to the Newtown Band and was always connected with music.' He worked in the Education Office in Newtown and retired when the office was closed down. Later he suffered a slight heart attack and gave up conducting but remained a regular choir member. The baton was then passed on to choir member, Bryn Jones, the possessor of a beautiful tenor voice, who was manager of the local Astons Furniture Shop. He was a native of Rhos near Wrexham and a close friend of musical maestro Colin Jones, who was for many years the choir's piano accompanist at their annual celebrity concerts. Suzanne Edwards was the one who next came briefly to the rostrum, a young lady of great musical ability, and commitments with other choirs, who left when she got married. Suzanne was followed by Theo Owen who had been associated with the choir for many years as accompanist and deputy conductor; sadly Theo did not enjoy good health and was forced to relinquish her position as a result. The one who then took over was the choir's accompanist and deputy director for many years, Christine Roberts, their present conductor.

Reflecting on trends and policy, Meurig Jones says that during Tommy Evans's tenure they were a mainly competitive choir. But a decision was taken during Bryn Jones's time leading the choir, that they would concentrate on concerts. 'Our concert programme varies each year as we learn new pieces.' It seems to be a decision well taken. 'When we're preparing for a concert we're rehearsing pieces we enjoy learning,' he asserts. This is evidently pleasing local audiences because concert engagements, particularly during the two months leading to Christmas, makes for an exceptionally busy schedule. And their annual celebrity concerts with guest artistes such as Iwan Parry from Dolgellau and Aled Wyn Davies from Llanbrynmair regularly attract an audience of six hundred people at the Newtown Baptist Chapel. When the choir celebrated its Golden Jubilee in 2001 with a special Anniversary Concert the audience was eight hundred, 'an event the choristers will remember for a very long time'. It's a popular choir with a tremendous local following. When they go to the Massed Choir Concert at the Royal Albert Hall, an event they've joined twelve times, they also have a mass following of three coach loads of supporters. Likewise when they go to St David's Hall Cardiff to join in a massed choir of three hundred voices in the November Remembrance Service, the community goes too!

Apart from their performances at many chapels and churches in aid of charitable organizations, and seasonal caroling at hospitals and nursing homes, the choir has also completed two tours abroad. The first in the 1970s took in exchange visits with a choir from Schinveld, Holland and in April 2003 to Les Herbiers, Newtown's twin town in France. Similar tours in the UK have been with the High Wycombe Male Voice Choir, and in June 2008, a memorable visit to Plymouth highlighted by a concert at All Saints Church, Holbeton.

The Choir

Catchment: Montgomery, Clun, Bettws, Kerry, Trefeglwys, Berriew, Newtown, Mochdre, Llanidloes, Llandinam and Aberhafesp.
Officials
President: George Jones
Chairman: Meurig Jones
Vice Chairman: Carlisle Scott
Secretary: Enid Morgan, Hazel Grove, Newtown, Powys SY16 4JS. Tel. 01686 626894
Treasurer: Les Roberts
Musical Director and Conductor: Christine Roberts
Deputy Conductor: Gill Owen
Accompanist: Peg Morris
Compere: Griff Evans

Rehearsals are held at the United Reform Church (Schoolroom)
Newtown on Sunday nights from 7:00 until 9:30.

Côr Meibion y Penrhyn
Penrhyn Male Voice Choir

'Historically the Penrhyn Male Voice Choir belongs to two periods,' says Emyr Vaughan Evans, who in 2007 is midway through his stint as the choir's chairman, but since joining in 1983 'has done every other job with the choir!'

The first part belongs to the time when it went to the 1893 World Fair in Chicago. 'It was a particularly flourishing period for the Penrhyn slate quarries at Bethesda five miles south west of Bangor,' he says, 'and each quarry section would have its own choir.' So the choir which braved the Atlantic Ocean then was a very big one. Those were the glory days, before the long and extremely bitter strike in the slate quarries took its toll on the area, compounded by the equally stressful Great War (1914-18).

Emyr dates the second period to the Llanllechid Eisteddfod of 1934 when the adjudicator Dr Caradog Roberts of Rhos urged the local quarry section (bonc) choirs to join together to form Côr y Penrhyn. It has to be remembered that each 'bonc' (section) sported its own choir, though admittedly by then the slate quarries were in gradual decline. So the choir which was formed in 1935 is the renowned Côr Meibion y Penrhyn of today with its compliment of sixty-five members. Names associated with the early years of the renewed choir include David Jones, Rachub conductor, and Ffrancon Thomas ARCO accompanist, who took them to National Eisteddfod success at Caernarfon after but eight months.

In the late forties they were getting into their golden age, sweeping aside all opposition, with Ffrancon Thomas now as conductor and Arnold Lewis accompanist, winning at the National Eisteddfod three years in succession, at Colwyn Bay (1947); Bridgend (1948) and Dolgellau (1949). In the sixties earning a well deserved reputation on radio's 'With Heart and Voice' Sunday programme. Menai Williams (who subsequently went on to successfully direct two other local choirs: Côr Meibion y Traeth and Côr Meibion Caernarfon) joined them in the seventies giving them a further boost when membership peaked at eighty. She was followed by Margaret Owen (wife of Prof. J. Bryn Owen), Alun Llwyd, John Eifion Jones a renowned National Eisteddfod soloist who is now with Côr Meibion y Brythoniaid, Mary Jones of Adlais and in 2004 Owain Arwel Davies, their present conductor. A native of Mochdre near Colwyn Bay, he attended Ysgol Y Creuddyn then went on to University of North Wales Bangor where Gwyn Davies and John Hywel were strong influences on his musical destiny. While at Bangor he took a conductors course. He's also an instrumentalist having played the trombone in several orchestras under famous conductors including Owain Arwel Hughes. Now head of music at Ysgol Tryfan Bangor, Owain came to the rostrum as a twenty-five year old and his powers to motivate is attracting new members.

Choir practices are taken each Monday night, two hour sessions starting at 7.15, in Ysgol Pen y Bryn – the Bethesda junior school. It's a competitive choir, and they thrive on the hard rehearsals that this requires. Rather modestly Emyr emphasises the importance of this, because after all, 'the choristers are amateurs in terms of reading music and historically they come from a quarrying tradition'. And so he argues the merit of the competitive ethos in developing the choir; receiving a constructive critique and appearing on stage improves their confidence and performance. And with the guidance of a good conductor they aspire to a high level of achievement.

They are also strong as a touring choir; during Emyr's time they have been to Germany, Canada, America – on one occasion to Chicago in 1993 to celebrate the centenary of their visit to the World Fair, Finland; Hungary (three times), Ireland and Brittany. But Emyr feels that touring is becoming increasingly difficult because 'the age of choir members is younger than the usual male voice choirs and therefore work and family commitments often make it difficult for all the choir to go on an extended tour to the more distant parts'. Consequently, without a full choir complement, voice balance is lost and the quality of their performance is impaired.

The Penrhyn Choir is very much community minded and closely identifies with Bethesda and its chapel going tradition. Emyr reckons that the choirs started in the chapels and that the singing spread outwards into the slate quarries. Indeed the eisteddfodau were usually held in the chapels, where standards of singing were perfected through their customary rehearsals after evening service. Chapel going may have waned in Bethesda, but Emyr asks whether there is a role-reversal and that the community is now becoming choir centred. He sees the choir performing pieces from Handel's Messiah or even complete oratorios involving the entire community. The choir itself is very much a social entity, providing friendship and goodwill perpetuated through its own golf, bowls and rugby tournaments.

Emyr Vaughan Evans is brimful of ambition for the choir and its part in the community. 'We have a responsibility to promote our culture,' he says. 'In the future we may do less foreign concert tours and rather, get people here to see what we have to offer.' He doesn't rule out Welsh choirs pooling their resources and employing agents to arrange tours of the large

English towns. 'When we perform at Llandudno or at the Pritchard Jones Hall in Bangor the audiences go wild!' he says.

The Choir

CDs and Tapes: See Website: corypenrhyn.org
Catchment: General area around Bethesda.
Officials
President: Tom Morgan
Chairman: Emyr Vaughan Evans, Aber Menai, Lôn Ddewi,
Caernarfon LL55 1BH
Secretary: Garem Jackson. Tel. 01248 355082
Treasurer: Maldwyn Pritchard
Accompanist: Frances Davies MR
Musical Director and Conductor: Owain Arwel Davies B.Mus., PDCE

Rehearsals are held at Ysgol Pen y Bryn, Bethesda Junior School
each Monday night 7.15 – 9.15.

Côr Meibion Penybontfawr
Penybontfawr Male Voice Choir

Could this village with a long sounding name in North Powys, home to a choir which is rapidly gaining countrywide fame, be the most isolated in Wales? Search your guide books and it scarcely gets a mention: yet more and more people are discovering it tucked away in the Tanat Valley, its beauty enhanced by the Berwyn Range. Bards and songsters talk nostalgically of how the Berwyns keep calling them back, writers are inspired by its hallowed isolation, hill farmers work their flocks here.

It's here every Wednesday night in the village hall, Canolfan Pennant, at about eight o clock that the choir meets for rehearsals and some socialising. Singing practice will go on till half past nine, with a ten minute half time break to discuss a possible concert destination or an eisteddfod commitment. All forty choristers will have a chance to talk through choir plans. Chairman Dei Jones holds firm to that. He holds firm on other things too such as a 'no copies policy'. 'How can you follow the conductor's directions with your nose stuck in the copy,' he reasons, 'and besides the voices are projected better without copies.'

'Canolfan Pennant is not acoustically satisfactory,' says Dei but argues that 'if you can sing well there, you can sing well anywhere!' There is great pride in giving a good performance. Secretary Arwel Watkins, a farmer and time served carpenter has made a mobile stage for the choir, to make quite sure that wherever the concert venue, they will certainly stand above audience level, and therefore sing to better effect.

Many of the choristers are farmers, but they also have a vicar, undertaker, accountant, doctor, builder, cabinet maker, professional wood turner, an expert sheep sheerer and a sheep breeder amongst their number. The latter being farmer Tegwyn Jones, their conductor, who excels as a baritone soloist. He's a keen eisteddfod man including a personal first in the baritone under twenty-five class at the National Eisteddfod (Rhos 1961) and he's done a solo turn at the Albert Hall Massed Choir Concert. He was first persuaded to sing as a soloist by Phyllis Dryhurst Dodd when he was a member of Llanfair Caereinion Male Voice Choir from 1956 until 1968. As a young man in his early twenties he had gone to Oswestry for weekly singing lessons from Winifred Steel of Ruabon who held voice training sessions in those days. For thirteen years from 1975 he conducted Côr Aelwyd Penllys, a choir of youngsters. This was a choir established originally by the Rev. Elfed Lewis when he held the pastorate of Llanfihangel-yng-Ngwynfa; Tegwyn had taken over when the minister moved to South Wales. He joined Penybontfawr Male Voice Choir in 1969 and was appointed conductor in 1995. In 1983 on two occasions he conducted the local community hymn singing for the Welsh television programme 'Dechrau Canu, Dechrau Canmol'. So apart from sheep farming his four hundred ewe flock and fifty suckler cows at Llanfihangel-yng-Ngwynfa, singing and choirs have been his adult life passion. And at his best singing old favourite solos like Cân yr Arad Gôch and Guide me o thou Great Jehofa.

At the rostrum on practice night however he's not averse to bringing new pieces such as African Trilogy into their portfolio, or learning 'set' pieces for the National Eisteddfod: they're up for the challenge whenever it comes to the north! Over the years they've done it four times since they were first formed as a choir in 1951 – at Flint (1969), Ruthin (1973), Wrexham (1977) and at Machynlleth (1981). And locally they've had a fair share of success at the annual two-day Powys Eisteddfod too. 'Learning new pieces and competing keeps us on top of our form,' says Dei Jones.

The choir was formed originally as a party of twelve in 1951 conducted by E. Spuriel Evans, who farmed locally at Peniarth Isa, with his wife K.A. Evans as accompanist. But the numbers soon 'swelled' into a fully fledged choir. This was a village with a singing tradition which could once boast three choirs and a railway terminus. Mr Evans tenure continued up to his death in 1968. He had taken the choir to a 'first' at the Powys Provincial Eisteddfod in Machynlleth and a Highly Commended Performance at the Royal National Eisteddfod of 1967 in Bala. Emyr Lloyd Jones succeeded him as conductor. Emyr was an accountant with an evident musical talent both as an organist and a Cymanfa Ganu, Hymn Singing Festival, conductor. Mrs K.A. Evans continued her role as accompanist, later followed by Mrs Sylvia Griffiths and then in 1974 by Lynda Williams. Lynda, a farmer's wife, was a niece of Spuriel Evans, the choir's founder. As a teacher she had achieved great eisteddfod successes with her school choir and instrumentalists at the Urdd (Welsh League of Youth) National Eisteddfodau. A grand concert tribute to Emyr on his retirement was held in the village in 1994: under his baton the choir had scaled new heights of achievement, four 'firsts' at the National Eisteddfod and there had been appearances at the Albert Hall Thousand Voices Concerts. A fitting accolade to team work of a high order betwixt conductor, accompanist and choir.

This was when Tegwyn Jones who had been deputy conductor took over at the rostrum. Under his baton the choir was to spread its wings even more. The Choir's links with the London Welsh Society through their chairman Berwyn Evans, whose family came from the Tanat Valley, meant they became part of the Autumn concerts in the Albert Hall held every two years. They were the only North Wales Choir to be there, thus joining up with other selected choirs from South Wales and England, as well as the London Welsh Male Voice Choir.

Similarly their fame spread to two London appearances in 1999 and 2002 at the Farmers Club in Whitehall for their St David's Day Dinner celebrations.

And three separate performances on the Concourse at the Royal Agricultural Show held annually at Stonleigh in Warwickshire. So this choir from its relative isolation responds to a challenge whether it's at St David's Hall in Cardiff singing with the Cardiff Arms Park Choir; in the Midlands at the Birmingham Symphony Hall with the Canoldir Male Voice Choir, or when called to entertain Welsh Communities in Huddersfield and Morecambe. It's a choir that responds to concert invites, but still has high regard for Eisteddfodic challenges.

The Choir

Catchment Area: Oswestry, Llanfyllin, Llanymynech, Llangynog, Llansilin and Penybontfawr.
CDs/Tapes: *Y Flwyddyn Aur* (The Golden Year) (2001)
Officials
President: Dr Richard Griffiths
Vice Presidents: Vera Field MBE, Ieuan Jones
Chairman: David Jones
Vice Chairman: Philip Ellis
Admin Secretary: Arwel Watkins, Bank Farm, Rhydycroesau, Oswestry, Shropshire SY10 7JE. Tel.01691 791255
Concert Secretary: Howard Owen, 37 Maes y Foel, Llansantffraid, Powys SY22 6TN. Tel. 01691 828427
Treasurer: Alwyn Williams
Musical Director and Conductor: Tegwyn Jones
Deputy Conductor: Gwylfa Jones
Accompanist: Lynda Thomas
Compere: Trevor Foster

Rehearsals are held every Wednesday evening
at Canolfan Pennant, Penybontfawr from 8 until 10.

Côr Meibion Powys
Powys Male Voice Choir

There had once been a male voice choir in Machynlleth associated with British Rail (the Great Western Railway), years before Tecwyn Jones came there. It was conducted by Ifan Maldwyn Jones the notable musician and voice trainer who had earlier conducted Côr Meibion Machynlleth when they won at the Cardiff National in 1938: but in 1963 when Tecwyn came there to work as a Crosville driver, there was a void. The nearest male voice choir was 13 miles away in Aberystwyth and, in Dinas Mawddwy, 12 miles north, a cerdd dant party – in Machynlleth there was nothing. For Tecwyn Jones, fresh from Llanuwchllyn, a musical hotbed where the redoubtable Tom Jones was king, it was unthinkable. Back there Martin Jones who conducted the congregational singing and Tom Jones a deacon at Peniel, the Welsh Independants, thoroughly drilled the rudiments of music into the youngsters on Sundays– and at other times too! On Saturdays when the lads much preferred to watch or play football in Bala, Tom Jones would insist on them coming back afterwards for singing practice – sometimes half past ten at night. Occasionally he would organise as a special treat; a trip to see the 'Swans' playing at home on the Vetch where Alchurch and John Charles were the Beckams of the day. Tom Jones too liked his soccer, but he made sure, while on the bus, that they went through their musical paces! It was he too with his great charisma who conducted Côr Godre'r Aran, which was to scale the heights of musical achievement. For fourteen years Tecwyn Jones had been part of that experience. Added to that there had been the robust eisteddfodic tradition where his mother Annie Jones would sometimes conduct the proceedings, or compete in solo events or duets with her sister. So Machynlleth of '63 must have seemed like a barren desert for Tecwyn Jones.

Llanuwchllyn was his template for Machynlleth, and by 1969 the Powys Male Voice Choir was born in the town, his dream fulfilled. He thanks friends in the fledgling North Wales Association of that time – people like Meirion Jones of Côr Meibion Y Brythoniaid and Wyn Roberts of Côr Meibion Trelawnyd and Islwyn Jones – Ifan Maldwyn's son, conductor of Runcorn Male Voice Choir who was president and is still a close confidante, for their help. For the first 30 great formative years Tecwyn Jones was their conductor and inspiration taking them to dizzy heights. 'We went to the Albert Hall 1000 Voices Concert seven times,' he says. Once they sang there on their own in the Albert Hall Burma Star Concert of 1978 in the presence of Earl Mountbatten. 'It was probably the first time for a postman to conduct a choir there,' he says. There was a strong connection locally with the Burma Star veterans led by Major General Lewis Pugh, and it was by his invitation that Côr Meibion Powys took part at their concert in London.

Tecwyn Jones's memories of those years are a roller-coaster of events: they went to the low countries three times through the good offices of Oswald Davies who ran the Brigade of St John at Cemaes Road, and on one unforgettable occasion two choir members stood on the famous dam ('Dam Busters') to sing their greetings, the first anyone had done do so since 1944.

'We've sung in a variety of places; at Hedd Wyn's grave which was truly moving, at Ypres singing *Mi Glywaf Dyner Lais* to the tune Sarah, we stopped the traffic for half an hour,' he says. 'We even sang in a Circus once and one wag was to joke rather irreverently that never before had they seen so many clowns in one place!' The circus experience came about when they were invited to the naming of a carriage on the Rheidol Narrow Gauge Railway at Aberystwyth, arranged by Prys Edwards of the Wales Tourist Board. The carriage was officially named by the Welsh celebrity actress Myfanwy Talog, who attended with her partner David Jason: the carriage name and the song they sang, appropriately, was *Myfanwy*. But nearby the circus in the town also had a particular naming event, which was the christening of the ringmaster's baby daughter and, responding to the vicar's special request, the choir sang there too in the big marquee.

During most of Tecwyn's tenure as conductor he had the very experienced pianist, Mrs Briwnant Jones, a former school mistress at Corris, as accompanist; she was first choice at the local eisteddfodau and was the official accompanist at the 1937 National Eisteddfod in Machynlleth. Tecwyn Jones well remembers on one of the choir's London visits, when she played on the grand piano in the Albert Hall, seeing Mrs Briwnant Jones afterwards engaged in a tête-à-tête with Princess Margaret in a private corner.

Mr Tecwyn Jones was succeeded as conductor by Gwennan Thomas from Llwyngwril, one of the eminently musical Gwanas family. Following her five year stint the baton was been taken up by Otto Freuenthal, a Swedish national who now lives in Corris, a good musician and wonderful instrumentalist. The choir's long standing tenor soloist is John Francis Jones from Glantwymyn. Choir practices are held every Monday evening in the Tabernacle, a Wesleyan Chapel until 1985, it is now acoustically probably the best concert hall in Wales – frequently used by recording companies.

The Choir

Officials
Chairman: Gwynfor Jones
Secretary: Richard Withers, 2 Cae'r Ffynnon, Corris Uchaf, Powys.

At the time of writing the future of the choir is uncertain,
the conductor having left on health grounds
and the choristers down to 13.

Côr Meibion Prysor

'My love of Welsh poetry led to my interest in Cerdd Dant,' says Iwan Morgan, who then goes on to explain, 'Cerdd Dant is the presentation of poetry through music.' So you can rightly deduce that he is both a poet and a musician. At home in Llan Ffestiniog the numerous bardic chairs won with his poetry indicate the extent of his interest. He still dabbles, at the merest prompting he will easily run out a poem (set to a musical arrangement) for his choir, Côr Meibion Prysor. But it's a long while since he's sent anything to an eisteddfod. His wife Alwena has drawn the line. 'There's no room for any more chairs in this house,' she says. But concedes, 'when you start winning tables and three piece suites you can start competing again!'

But seriously his music goes back very much further than that; fact is it goes back in the genes. His grandfather Gwilym Morgan, a test concert tenor soloist in his day, had a brother John who, although he'd lost the fingertips on his left hand in a slate quarrying accident, could still play the piano and organ, and also played the violin. He was nicknamed 'Handel.' Iwan's father, Luther, was a moderately good singer, and could certainly read the tonic sol-fa notation. While his mother Gwyneth, also of good musical stock, played the organ at the Rehoboth chapel for sixty years, although she'd had little formal training. 'We were a family who simply enjoyed music,' says Iwan.

Home was at Corris between Dolgellau and Machynlleth where singing rehearsals for the Gymanfa, with his mother at the chapel organ or at home on the piano, were commonplace. After the local junior school, he went to Tywyn High – fifteen miles away, and from there to Trinity College in Carmarthen to do a teacher's training course. There he studied Welsh and the art and technique of drama. Here he was influenced by arguably the top people in Welsh culture – people like Norah Isaac, Carwyn James and former chief poet and Archdruid Dafydd Rowlands. Noel John too, of 'Bois y Blacbord' fame, sensing Iwan's interests gave him examples of his 'cerdd dant' settings and told him to 'take them for further study'. All this was the purest elixir for a young man of Iwan's musical desire.

On leaving college in 1972, his first teaching post was at Dyffryn Ardudwy near Harlech where cerdd dant exponent Owen Thomas Morris urged him on. 'You know all the elements, you can read music and you're a good singer, you understand poetry better than I, so it's now time for you to do cerdd dant settings,' he declared. That was all that was needed,

Iwan was on his way. In 1979 he responded positively to an invitation to form and conduct Parti Meibion Dyfi, a role he played briefly because he left the area on becoming headmaster at Ganllwyd, near Dolgellau in 1981 (the year that he married Alwena from Rhewl in the Vale of Clwyd).

So it was in 1983 that he started singing with Côr Meibion Prysor which was, to Iwan's delight, a choir which sang a variety of songs including Cerdd Dant. It had been formed originally in 1966 as a male voice Cerdd Dant choir to compete at the National Eisteddfod to be held at Bala in 1967. The first conductor was Dafydd Roberts of Hendre, Cwm Hermon – a small-holding in the hills between Llanfachreth and Trawsfynydd – a notable eisteddfod adjudicator and cerdd dant connoisseur in his day, who with his wife Elizabeth Mary Roberts as accompanist had founded the choir. It was based at Trawsfynydd and could claim great singers amongst its number; people like William Jones – 'Prysor' – who was a Blue Ribband winner on two occasions at the National Eisteddfod. His twin brother Edward was later to succeed Dafydd Roberts as conductor.

During the eighties we see Edward and another notable local musician, Gerallt Rhun – who became deputy head teacher at the village school – at the conductor's rostrum, taking the choir to entertain in 'nosweithiau llawen' around North Wales. Eisteddfodic achievements were also attained in Cerdd Dant circles, and Gerallt Rhun's mother, another notable cerdd dant exponent – Heulwen Roberts of Rhydymain, near Dolgellau, steered the choir into the top award at the Gŵyl Gerdd Dant in 1984 (the National Cerdd Dant Festival held at Corwen). 'That was a good win,' Iwan recalls 'because there were ten choirs competing and the set piece, a Cerdd Dant setting of Y Genedl by Gerallt Lloyd Owen, suited male voices perfectly.'

Following this, more concerts were on their agenda, both in the United Kingdom and abroad. 1986 saw them on a visit to Brittany where they had concerts around Brest with choir member Alun Vaughan Jones (a Blue Ribband winner at Porthmadog in the following year), as their star soloist. In July 1989 they visited the Isle of Man for the Celtic Festival and concerts at Port Erin and Ramsey, with musical accompaniment by Elizabeth Mary Roberts and Iona Mair on the piano and Gerallt Rhun with guitar.

'We went to Plas Maenan Llanrwst in 1990 to entertain members of a New Jersey gardening club,' says Iwan. 'They enjoyed our singing so much that they invited us to go to the States to stay with them and do a concert tour.' This led to a fortnight concert stay with families in New Jersey followed by visits to New York – 'we went to the top of one of the

Twin Towers' – then to Baltimore and an open air concert on the quay followed by two days in Washington before going on to Philadelphia.

In January 1991 Iwan Morgan was appointed headmaster of Penrhyndeudraeth junior school and a year later, invited to become the conductor of Meibion Prysor. And it was also in 1992 that he led them on possibly their most poignant overseas tour: a visit to France and Belgium to celebrate the life of Trawsfynydd's most famous poet, who was killed in the Battle of Pilkem Ridge on July 31st 1917, just days before being adjudged the Bardic Chair winner at the National Eisteddfod held that year in Birkenhead. At the Menin Gate, Ypres and at his graveside in Artillery Wood, they sang R. Willliams Parry's elegy to him, *Y Bardd Trwm Dan Bridd Tramor* as well as Hedd Wyn's carol *Dyma'r dydd y gwelwyd Iesu*. Four coach-loads had made that journey from Trawsfynydd with the choir to pay homage on the seventy-fifth anniversary of the poet's death – arranged by John Isgoed Williams, one of Trawsfynydd's longest serving ambassadors.

Their next overseas tour was to Galway and Connemara in 1995. Singing to a large congregation in the Jesuit Church in Galway, while their second concert at Connemara was not so well attended. 'There was more of us on stage than in the audience,' says Iwan. 'But they were very warm hearted towards us when they realised we were there.' And one of their number had the good grace afterwards to dig a hundred punts out of his pocket, and handing it over, in the broadest Irish brogue said, 'Go and buy your lads a Guiness, Iwan'.

Easter 2004 gave the choir members an opportunity to take part in a Latin 'Requiem' composed by one of Wales's most talented contemporary musicians – Brian Hughes. The requiem was commissioned by 'Trawsnewid' – a co-operative society established to guard and promote the benefits and inheritance of the Trawsfynydd area. The requiem was to commemorate the Catholic Martyr Saint John Roberts of Rhiwgoch (1577-1610). Appearing at St Madryn's Church and Moreia, Capel y Fro with such renowned singers as tenor, Rhys Meirion, the Brian Hughes Group and marimba expert Dewi Ellis Jones was an experience never to be forgotten.

In 2007 came an invitation from the Ontario Welsh Society to go to St Paul's Anglican Church in Kingston for the North American Gymanfa Ganu: Iwan conducting the huge audience with 'my little choir behind me'. This itinerary included concert tours to Toronto and Ottawa, and visits to Niagara Falls and Niagara on the Lake.

Wherever the choir went, so too went their greatest character of all, Glyn Heddwyn. As a young man he had contracted diabetes, which ultimately left him totally blind. Ailing health and medical treatment meant he was frail of physique. Yet as the choir's master of ceremonies he was unbeatable, audiences really loved him. Despite poor health he managed to spread rays of happiness wherever he went. Iwan recalls how Glyn would appear on stage and go through his patter with his back to the audience, until Iwan turned him around to face in the proper direction! 'Oh, so that's where you are,' he'd say, pointing at the audience – and their cue for tumultuous applause! His last appearance on stage with the choir was at their concert at Porth y Rhyd, Carmarthen during the winter of 2006-07. His last cheery farewell, as at every concert he went to was to 'Keep on singing, keep on smiling – life will make sure that you cry your share . . . Nos da!' Glyn died in May 2007, he was 54. Now Iwan has written some strict metre verses which he has set to Cerdd Dant counter melodies to celebrate the life of a very dear friend which will get an airing at Trawsfynydd's two Eisteddfodau.

The Choir

CDs: *Pan Gwyd yr Haul*
Catchment: Trawsfynydd and district (with a few coming from Harlech and from Dolgellau and beyond).
Officers
Chairman: Gareth Williams
Secretary: Derfel Roberts, 6 Rhesdai Tŷ Llwyd, Steshon, Trawsfynydd
Treasurer: Kevin Lewis
Accompanist: Iona Mair
Harpists (on the CD): Einir Wyn and Elain Wyn Jones
Guitarist: Gerallt Rhun
Musical Director and Conductor: Iwan Morgan
Deputy Director: Derfel Roberts
Compere: Phil Mostert

*Rehearsals are held every Thursday night 8.30 until 10
at Y Capel Bach, Trawsfynydd.*

Côr Meibion Y Rhos

Rhosllanerchrugog, a village of 9000 people about 5 miles south west of Wrexham is awash with music. It has two male voice choirs, a mixed voice choir, a ladies choir, and each of its schools has a choir.

Gareth Pritchard Hughes, a member of Rhos Male Voice Choir since 1957, knows more than most about that musical tradition. 'It was the Bersham and Hafod Collieries which made Rhos into a close knit mining community, and together with the Welsh chapels, stimulated the choral custom,' he says. The chapels – reputedly there were twenty-six in Rhos – were centres of culture, most of them had their eisteddfod and drama competitions, and the other important element was their 'ysgol gân' (singing classes). Within this environment, by the turn of the twentieth century, we see a growth in the choir culture. At Capel Mawr, during the 1910s, E. Emlyn Davies, the chapel's gifted organist and choirmaster performed sacred works by Elgar, Mendelssohn, Handel and Mozart, whilst at Bethlehem, the Congregational Chapel, Dan Roberts held sway with his 150 strong chapel choir giving annual performances of sacred works by Dvorak, Rossini, Verdi, Mozart, Handel, Bach and Mendelssohn to the organ accompaniment of the conductor's nephew, the renowned musician/composer, Dr Caradog Roberts. *Stabat Mater*, *Samson*, and the *Creation* were their meat and drink as they strove to set new standards.

At Salem Chapel in Pen y Cae, the neighbouring village, there was a further flurry of interest inspired by three generations of musically gifted people: Owen Jones, John Owen Jones and John Owen Jones (Junior), the latter coming to national pre-eminence and subsequently conductor of Côr Meibion y Rhos.

Before all this, whilst the musical enthusiasm was evident, there was a lack of discipline as everyone intoned by ear. Joseph Owen, who came to Rhos as the headmaster of the newly opened British School in 1865 is credited with laying the foundations of the Rhos Choral tradition by establishing sol-fa classes which was to change the musical concept. Classes of up to two hundred singers became the norm, turning out pupils of an exceptionally high standard. Many going on to professional careers in music: people like James Savage the baritone who sang 40 leading opera roles with Carl Rosa and was possibly the first Welsh professional opera singer, and William Davies the composer who was principal tenor at St Paul's Cathedral, while others were to lead the singing in local chapels. With choristers now able to read music at first sight, they could raise their game and tackle more ambitious pieces.

In 1863, the amalgamation of two chapel choirs, Capel Mawr and Bethlehem, established the first Rhos Mixed Choir under the direction of Hugh Griffiths. It was a choir which achieved considerable success at eisteddfodau, and it is related that at such an event at Capel Tabernacle, Cefn Mawr in 1871, Richard Mills from Llanidloes, an adjudicator of considerable repute became greatly enamoured of the Rhos voices. He was a member of the famous Mills family from Llanidloes and musical editor of the publishing house Hughes a'i Fab, (Hughes and Son) Wrexham, prestigious in its day for producing high quality musical scores, the works of Joseph Parry in particular. It was to lead to great things. Richard Mills now married and living in Johnstown where he had set up a printing and publishing business, took over the Rhos Choral Union from Hugh Griffiths and led them very successfully from 1873 until 1876.

The choir then went through a period of repose in the 1880s, emerging revived once more in 1891 as Rhos Mixed Choir with Richard Mills at the helm. It was from the male voice section of this mixed choir that the Rhos Male Voice Choir was formed in December 1892 and gave its first public performance in January 1893. The accompanist was Dan C. Owen, Richard's brother-in-law, founder and conductor of the Rhos Orchestral Society. On one occasion, in May 1893, the choir and orchestra gave a memorable performance at the old Public Hall in the village. Later in 1893 it gained its first eisteddfod success at Llanfyllin singing the *Pysgodwyr* (Maldwyn Price), a piece which went on to give them many eisteddfod successes. These were the beginnings of extremely heady days in the annals of the choir and all the circumstances ensured that the enthusiasm continued.

So Richard Mills is the acclaimed founder of the choir in 1892. Because of ill-health, Richard Mills relinquished his role as conductor in 1895 and his deputy, Henry Stephen Jones, successfully directed the choir from 1895 until 1897. The accompanist at this time was Dr Caradog Roberts who continued in that role when Wilfrid Jones, a native of Arthog, took up the baton in 1897. Wilfrid Jones was a composer, soloist and conductor; as a fourteen year old he was the band master at Corris before going on to the Royal Academy of Music in London. Following a successful career as a baritone soloist he came to Wrexham. He was acknowledged as one of the finest voice trainers in the country and was appointed voice trainer at Wrexham and Ruabon Schools. Under his guidance the choir's singing gained poise and refinement. In 1898 they won at the National Eisteddfod in Blaenau Ffestiniog; and as such in 1899 they were invited to sing in St James's Hall London. Wilfrid Jones relinquished his role as conductor sometime between 1900-1902 but returned to lead the choir to a notable victory at a competition held at the Queen's Hall in London against stiff opposition from five South Wales Choirs! 'They were on the stage in London at eleven o'clock before making a hasty dash to Paddington Station, arriving back in Rhos at seven o'clock the following morning.'

The Evan Roberts religious revival of 1904-05 hit Rhos as all other parts of Wales, and Gareth Pritchard Hughes surmises that the revivalist meetings took over to the exclusion of all else. This meant the choir together with other communal activities were suspended. From 1908 – 10 the choir was reconvened with Emlyn Davies FRCO, who was reckoned to be 'one of the most brilliant organists of his day', as conductor. He later became the organist at Westminster Chapel London.

Between 1911-13 the choir had disbanded and despite efforts to form a male voice choir to compete at the Wrexham National Eisteddfod in 1912 with Samuel Evans (brother of Ben Evans who later played a key role in the destiny of the choir) as conductor, nothing came of it.

Next to take the rostrum was Ben Evans: during his forty-two years association with the choir – mainly during the first half of the twentieth century, he really marched his men to glory. Côr Meibion y Rhos was virtually 'Côr Benny' (Ben's choir); under his direction they were awarded 'two hundred and fifty major prizes, twelve silver cups, five chairs, five gold watches, eight Rose Bowls and a baton'. He was an extremely active person on the Rhos musical scene – he also conducted the Aelwyd Choir (Youth Choir), which is all the more astonishing since 'he'd had no formal musical education, other than simply pursuing Tonic Sol-fa examinations'.

By the 1950s Ben Evans had conducted the choir for three separate periods (1913-1917; 1924-1936; 1946-1955), now Llangollen beckoned and the choir, always a highly competitive one under Ben's directorship, wanted to tackle that too. But since the choir was way over the sixty chorister limit for the International Eisteddfod, a decision was taken to split the choir into two: Choir A (directed by Ben Evans) and Choir B conducted by Jerry Hughes (father of the composer Brian Hughes). The musical accompanists during this time were Tom Morris, Llew S. Hughes, Jerry Hughes and Colin Jones.

During the intervening years there had been other very notable people conducting and playing an important role in progressing the choir. Dan Roberts from 1917 to 1924 broadened their repertoire with extended works for male voice choirs by Schubert, Meander and Mendelssohn and also won notable victories at eisteddfodau, gaining 21 first prizes and 4 second prizes in 29 competitions. He was ably assisted as accompanist by

John Williams FRCO an eminent organist, pianist, extramural tutor and composer at the University of North Wales Bangor. John Williams is credited with the 'discovery' of the great Welsh tenor David Lloyd at an eisteddfod in Lixwm and actively urging him to go on to the Guild Hall in London.

Another significant influence on the choir was John Owen Jones (the younger), of the musically gifted family from Pen y Cae, previously referred to. John Owen Jones was a figure of national stature and a frequent National Eisteddfod adjudicator. Amongst his pupils were Ivor Novello, Mansell Thomas, Arwel Hughes, Gilmor Griffiths and Lottie Williams Parry. It was John Owen Jones who took the choir to a glorious National Eisteddfod victory at Cardiff in 1938, beating off the formidable Morriston Orpheus by one mark! The following Sunday morning celebration at Rhos was ecstatic. John Owen Jones (the younger) seated with his father led the cavalcade in an open top car. They were followed by three Crosville motor coaches which carried the choir. And everywhere excited crowds lined the streets cheering, waving flags and throwing confetti. And finally a rousing celebratory concert in the evening at the 'Miner's Institute'.

1946 to 1955 was Ben Evans's third and final period as conductor, with Edward Jones conductor of the Rhos Choral United mixed voice choir, as his deputy and Colin Jones his accompanist. A Spanish tour with the choir in 1948 and at the last, in 1954, a competitive event in the Central Hall, London was Ben's swan song; he died in 1955. Edward Jones took over at the rostrum until 1957. At this time the choir was going through a difficult period and had lost several members. As a matter of report this was when the Rhos Orpheus Male Voice Choir was formed with John Raymond Williams FRCO, M.Mus., organist at Bethlehem Chapel, as conductor, originally formed to compete at the International Eisteddfod at Llangollen.

In 1957 we see Colin Jones becoming the conductor of Côr Meibion y Rhos with John Tudor Davies as accompanist. The impeccable credentials of Colin Jones are noted elsewhere in this book, John Tudor Davies also a native of Rhos was head of music at Grove Park Grammar School, a noted Welsh composer – his hymn tune *Gwahoddiad* is probably an all time favourite – and an accomplished conductor. Between them this was a partnership, which for the following thirty years, brought further glory and success to the choir. Winning in the National Eisteddfod at Llanelli in 1962, Flint 1969, Bangor 1971 and Portmadoc in 1987; Winning the 'BBC Radio Choir of the Year' award in 1984 and 1985. Overseas concert tours aplenty: Germany in 1960 and 1967; the United States in 1983, 1985 and

1986 and whilst there, appearing on the Ed Sullivan Coast to Coast Show. 'During Ben Evans time, the main activity of the choir was competing at eisteddfodau, but during Colin's era, concerts and concert tours became more and more important and they performed at St David's Hall, Cardiff; Chicago Opera House; the Royal Albert Hall; the Free Trade Hall, Manchester; the Glasgow Guild Hall; the Liederhalle, Stuttgart and in 1975 a Royal Command performance at the London Palladium.'

When Colin Jones left the rostrum in 1987, John Tudor Davies became the choir's conductor with Haydn Bowen as accompanist, and again further accolades: in 1991 and 1992 they won the won the 'HTV Choral Trophy'. Tudor Jones, the deputy conductor, took the baton when John Tudor Davies retired in 1992, a position he held for three years. He was well chosen because of the wealth of his experience: he had previously conducted the Rhos Silver Band and had formed the Rhos Singers, a mixed voice choir. During his tenure the choir went on to win at the Bro Colwyn National Eisteddfod in 1995 as well as at the Llangollen International Eisteddfod in 1997 and the Gold Award for the best choir at the Glarner Music Festival in Switzerland where they defeated 112 other choirs. Their accompanists during 1993-1995 were Haydn Bowen and Llyr Williams, the latter now acknowledged as an accompanist and concert pianist of international fame.

The conductor from 2005, when Tudor Jones left, until 2008 was John Daniel who joined them after successfully conducting Côr Meibion Froncysyllte for many years, which included two first prizes in the male voice competition at the International Eisteddfod at Llangollen.

He was succeeded in 2009 by Aled Philips, a music graduate of the University of Wales Bangor where, studying music, he specialised in performance, conducting and composing, and for ten years studied privately with Brian Hughes, the internationally acclaimed chorus master, vocal consultant and composer. Aled, a native of Rhos was born in 1976, and awarded a scholarship by the Association of British Choral Directors in 2006, given to him as one of the most promising young conductors in Britain. During this time he had the opportunity of working alongside many of Great Britain's leading conductors and ensembles including the Liverpool Philharmonic and the RTE National Orchestra of Ireland. The choir's accompanist and assistant musical director is Kevin Whiteley B.Mus. (Hons), ALCM, MBA. A native of Wrexham, Kevin is Head of Music at Rhosnesni High School. All of which portents continued success for the choir.

The Choir

Catchment: Rhos, Chester, Wrexham, Oswestry, Shrewsbury.
CDs/Tapes: See Website at www.rmvc.co.uk
Officials
President: David Ethelston
Chairman: David Thomas
Vice Chairman: Harold Richards
Secretary: J. Raymond Jones. Tel.01978 845219
Treasurer: David Scott
Musical Director and Conductor: Aled Phillips BA (Hons)
Deputy Conductor: Kevin Whiteley B.Mus. (Hons), ALCM, MBA
Accompanist: Kevin Whiteley B.Mus. (Hons), ALCM, MBA
Music Associate: Lewis Davies
Compere: Harold Richards
Choir Website: www.rmvc.co.uk

*Rehearsals are held at the Hafod Club on Monday and
at the Stiwt Theatre on Thursday evenings at 7.30.*

Rhos Orpheus Male Choir
Côr Meibion Orffiws Y Rhos

The Rhos Orpheus Male Choir was formed in 1957 with the specific purpose of competing at the Llangollen International Eisteddfod on a long term basis. The founder conductor was John Raymond Williams, M.Mus. FRCO, a brilliant musician, and organist at the local Bethlehem Chapel. While his accompanist during the early years was another local young man, J. Brian Hughes, now acknowledged as one of Wales most accomplished and often performed composers. Between them they set the standard of high quality music which is still the Choir's hallmark.

The Choir came into being according to Bryan Dodd, a long serving second bass with the choir and for twenty-five years its membership secretary, when the (other) Rhos Male Voice Choir at a low point lost several members. This triggered off a few singers to approach Raymond Williams with a view to setting up the 'Orpheus'. So for nine years (1957 to 1966) Raymond was the one who set the standard of excellence which was to carry the choir forward, during which time they competed several times at Llangollen.

John Glyn Williams, head master at the local Wern School, took over as conductor in 1966. A man of enormous talent, he was a music teacher and organist at Capel Mawr, the Rhos Welsh Presbyterian Church, and conductor of the Aelwyd Choir as well as the Rhos Light Opera Choir. He was also in great demand as a guest conductor, and on three occasions went on to conduct the Thousand Voices Massed Male Voice Choir held biennially at the Royal Albert Hall. By now Brian Hughes, their accompanist, had gone to Cardiff University and was replaced for a time by Hayden Bowen. He was followed by Anne Phillips ALCM, who in 2008 is still the accompanist after forty-one years!

When John Glyn Williams LRAM, ALCM, retired in 2004 the Choir made him Emeritus Director of Music, and in the Queen's Birthday Honours List he was awarded the MBE for his services to music. During his tenure there had been several successful overseas concert tours, many occurring as the result of friendships struck up with other choirs while competing at Llangollen. European visits were made to Norway, Sweden, Holland, Belgium and several times to Markischer Kreis, Wrexham's twinning area in Germany. Canada and the USA have been visited five times including to Phoenix Arizona. While in Milwaukee, they performed to their biggest audience ever of over 45,000, when singing at Brewers Field Baseball Ground.

In 1992 they were invited to Israel, to perform Cherubini's Requiem in D minor with the Haifa Symphony Orchestra, and gave a series of five performances to packed theatres. But probably their most memorable tour was to China in 1980, the first time for a choir from the West to go there after the Cultural Revolution, when they sang in Shanghai and Canton. It's an experience they still talk about. Bryan Dodd recollects how the Chinese would stand about outside the theatre until two or three minutes before the performance began, and then, in a rush, they would all pile in! And even more remarkable, the choristers had been forewarned, if the audience talked during the performance, it was a sure sign that they were thoroughly enjoying the concert! 'That really took a bit of getting used to,' says Bryan. They certainly got on well with the Chinese; the food was very good, 'much tastier than you get at Chinese take-aways in this country'. The people were friendly and rowdily approved their rendering of the Chinese National Anthem which the Welsh choir sang at the end of every concert. At the Shanghai Conservatire of Music, where they sang, the Chinese students responded by singing our very own *Llwyn Onn*!

As with many choirs the 'Orpheus' supports charities such as the Royal Lifeboat Institution through country wide concerts and the sales of CDs with an ocean-going sea shanty flavour.

When John Glyn retired in 2003 the conductor's baton was taken by Eifion Wyn Jones, the deputy director since 1989. He'd been a member of the choir since he came along as a fourteen year old with his father. Eifion, up to his retirement in 2003, a surveyor with Ordnance Survey, was a personal friend of John Glyn and shared his musical passion. There had been close collaboration between the two friends at the Rhos Aelwyd Choir and Rhos Light Opera. As a twenty-three year old Eifion was musical director of the Rhos Girls Choir and had been director of Cefn Mawr Amateur Operatic Society and the Rhos Aelwyd Amateur Operatic Society. Under his direction the Rhos Orpheus Male Voice Choir's concert repertoire has been further enhanced to fulfil a busy touring schedule which has included a visit to Ireland, Cornwall and Worcester (where they sang with the Grenadier Guards Band), as well as a series of celebrity concerts to commemorate the Choir's Golden Jubilee in 2007. In the choir's fifty years there had been only three conductors and at the celebration date all three were still alive.

The Choir has a membership of fifty-five with rehearsals held twice weekly, on Monday and Wednesday evenings, in the 'Stiwt' Theatre (formerly the Miners Institute) at 7.30. Rather surprisingly, 'only six of the members come from the village, whereas at the outset most would be from Rhos'. Now the singers come from a wide spread of the outlying villages including Holt, Overton and Coedpoeth; two members come from Eglwys Bach in the Conwy Valley and they have some from Stoke-on-Trent as well as Wrexham, Chester and the Wirral. At Monday night rehearsal the bass section will receive their training in one room with Eifion while the tenors, in another room, will rehearse with Anne Philips, the accompanist. At half time both sections will come together as one under the conductor's baton. Bryan Dodd says that recruiting new members is a continuing process and with this in mind, they occasionally change the rehearsal venue to village halls outside Rhos. Members of the public are invited to these events, which include a half time cup of tea and chat, with an invitation in the second part of the evening for anyone interested to come and join in the choir practice. They have successfully attracted new members in this way, and are particularly keen to attract a younger element. The camaraderie, as with all choirs is superb, and Bryan says that men who have lost their wives through bereavement often find great solace in the choir's company.

The Choir

CDs/Tapes: *Carolau Nadolig* (Cambrian) 1967
Souvenir of Wales (Cambrian) 1967
Music of Wales
There's a Coach Coming In
Calm is the Sea
For Those in Peril
Voices from the Land of Song
Good News
Catchment: Rhosllanerchrugog, Wrexham, Holt, Overton, Coedpoeth, Eglwys Bach (Conwy) and Stoke-on-Trent.
Officials
President: Arthur Edwards.
Vice Presidents: Alex Humphreys, Merfyn Jones, Mrs Margaret Slade
Chairman: Gus Harper
Vice Chairman: Marc Williams
Secretary: Brynley Jones, 25 Cavendish Crescent, Alsager, Stoke-on-Trent. Tel. 01270 882616
Stage Manager: Harry Jones
Treasurer: John Oldknow
Musical Director: Eifion Wyn Jones

Accompanist: Anne Philips ALCM
Deputy Accompanist: Rachel Philips
Choir Website: www.rhosorpheus-mc.co.uk

*Rehearsals are held on Monday and Wednesday evenings
in the Stiwt Theatre, Rhos at 7.30.*

Côr Meibion Trelawnyd
Trelawnyd Male Voice Choir

The choir is based at Trelawnyd, a tiny village on the A5151 road between Dyserth and Holywell in north east Wales. Here at the Memorial Hall every Sunday and Tuesday evening, the choir of a hundred voices regularly meet for their practice, under the baton of Geraint Roberts their conductor since 1981. Oswestry born in 1957, the son of the late Reverend Clifford Roberts, Geraint is a former pupil of Ysgol Gyfun Glan Clwyd where he excelled as a musician and his natural talents encouraged, not only as a singer but also as a pianist and harpist. He then went to the Royal College of Music where he graduated as GRSM and ARCM, then to London University where he gained his MTC. Formerly for twenty years Head of Music at Ysgol Emrys ap Iwan, Abergele, he is now Assistant Head Teacher there since 2001. Geraint is highly regarded as a charismatic professional musician, 'of piercing wit he has the ability to cajole choristers to greater effort'. Under his baton he has led the choir to their seventh triumph at the National Eistcddfod of Wales, held at Mold in 2007. Geraint also won in the reality TV rugby programme 'Codi Canu' when non musicians were brought together to form a choir and trained under his baton in a competition held at the Millennium Stadium Cardiff in 2008 which was judged by Owain Arwel Hughes. His conducting experience has included work with the Welsh League of Youth as well with general congregational singing. In March 2009 invited to Melbourne Australia to conduct Australian Welsh choirs in a St David's Celebration Concert followed by a Welsh style Cymanfa Ganu (Hymn Singing Festival) there. 'Experience, discipline and a sense of fun' are all ingredients he has brought to the Trelawnyd rehearsal sessions ensuring a first rate concert performance.

Trelawnyd as a centre has an enviable musical reputation, because at the outset of World War 1 in 1914 it could claim to have three successful choirs, a male voice, a mixed, as well as a children's choir. Inevitably the war years briefly disrupted the tradition before evidence of a revival came about when William Humphreys of Prestatyn formed a choir of about forty men at Gwaenysgor (the village adjoining Trelawnyd) at the end of hostilities. It was of a short three year duration, due to the failing health of Mr Humphreys who had been seriously war wounded. But in 1923 the same William Humphreys was appointed to be a schoolmaster at Trelawnyd, and in 1933 we see the old pre-war male voice choir re-convened with him as conductor.

It is of interest here to note that the choir was referred to as Côr Niwmarcid, Newmarket Choir, at that time, Newmarket being the village's name since 1700. Various forms of the name Trelawnyd have occurred since 1086 when it was referred to as Rivelenoit but by 1699 it had evolved to Rhelownwyd. Archdeacon D.R. Thomas relates that in 1700 Squire John Wynne of Coppa'rleini, now known as Gop Farm 'who rebuilt most of the town, established several branches of industry, and procured for it a weekly market and an annual fair, obtained a faculty from the Bishop's Registry to change the name to Newmarket'. He was evidently a generous village benefactor because we see 'in a codicil to his will dated 17th of October 1713 that he left a school house, buildings, and garden, together with forty pounds per ann. chargeable on his property, for the following uses: schoolhouse, buildings, garden, and ten pounds per ann., to the schoolmaster, who was to teach twenty free boys from Newmarket, and one from each of seven neighbouring parishes . . . ' The conditions of the will were belatedly fulfilled 'in the building of a new school and master's house which were opened in 1860 with an endowment of eighty pounds per ann.'.

This was the schoolhouse which schoolmaster William Humphreys came to on his appointment in 1923. *(The village's name changed to Trelawnyd in 1954).*

Rhys Jones's father, Robert John Jones, a road length-man who never received a music lesson in his life, but conducted both the children's choir and the mixed choir in the village, was one of the choir's founder members. With Ernie Evans he was allotted the job of finding choristers, Ernie enrolled the bases while Robert John found the tenors.

'William Humphreys, father of the novelist Emyr Humphreys, was my teacher at Trelawnyd when I first went to school there in 1931,' says Rhys Jones, 'but I was really scared of him! I believe he'd been gassed in the first war and that may have had its effect. It's said that he delighted in Welsh poetry and hymns but we never saw that side of his personality.' Ednyfed Williams, the choir's compere at concerts who wrote a commemorative book on the choir's fiftieth anniversary in 1983, gave this thumb-nail sketch: 'William Humphreys always appeared in breeches and shiny leather leggings, and almost invariably addressed the virtually all Welsh speaking choir in English. A stickler for discipline he spent much time on good voice production and tone. He was often abrupt when he felt unwell'. Rhys Jones says, 'His strength as a choir master was his ability to maintain discipline; choir members had immense respect for him. He was able to bring out points in the pieces that they learnt that would enthuse members, in addition, as the head master, he'd had better education than most of them. Many were manual workers on farms or pit workers at Point of Air Colliery, a few had left school at twelve years old. He therefore had that higher platform of understanding to inspire their imagination.'

During the Choir's 74 years existence there have only been five choir masters: William Humphreys 1933-1939; Elford Roberts 1946-1955; Neville Owen 1955-1969; Goronwy Wynne 1970-1981; Geraint Roberts 1981-

About the conductors:

Elford Roberts was a schoolmaster in Trelawnyd. 'He used to run his fingers through his hair when frustrated by the Choir's slowness to pick up a point, until it stood up on end like an angry hedgehog. The blue eyes would flash, and he would lapse into Welsh from his more customary English, as if we were far too stupid to understand. "Ond 'dach chi ddim yn cofio, hogia – double piano". When the sound was pleasing he would draw in his breath noisily through his teeth, close the blue eyes, and join in with us in what was, truth to tell, a rather raucous tenor voice!'
Neville Owen, possibly the most insistent of all on musical accuracy. 'Some of us remember being heartily sick of Kodaly and his strange rhythms during the weeks leading up to the National Eisteddfod at Bala in 1967, but Neville ploughed inexorably on in his relentless search for correctness'. He has been described as a very good musician, an excellent pianist, but in public a rather shy person.

Goronwy Wynne was by training a botanist and scientist: in his period as conductor, utterly precise in his preparation. 'A strange mixture of style and nerves on stage. We recall the white dinner jacket, the buttonhole and the long unmistakable baton for style. But we also recall the inevitable routine before each public performance . . .

Spectacles out of case – case back in top pocket – polish spectacles with handkerchief – pause – place spectacles on nose – shuffle copies on stand so that pages don't stick – pause – hitch up trousers, wipe forehead with handkerchief and return to pocket, and finally after a lengthy fidget – raise baton and off we went . . .

At rehearsal total dedication, his favourite saying, "Please don't talk across me gentlemen . . . we're here to work".'

The loyalty of the Trelawnyd choristers is never better illustrated than in the anecdote about a particular incident after one of their annual events at the Memorial Hall in the village, when they are joined by a top class London soloist in a celebrity concert. Over a cup of tea after one such event, Bob Jones of Railway Terrace, a founder member and as devoted to Trelawnyd as ever they come, earnestly tried to persuade the famous soloist to come and live locally so that he could join the Trelawnyd Male Voice Choir! Bob is no longer with us but his widow Gladys, Auntie Gladys to all the choir, still has them in for tea and cake after their annual performances.

What more could you wish for in dedication!

The Choir

CDs/Tapes: See Website

Catchment: The members are drawn from the North East Wales coastal area and hinterland, from Abergele to the west, across eastward as far as Holywell and Flint on the Dee Estuary. Inland the membership is drawn from a region which includes Bodelwyddan, St Asaph, Denbigh and Ruthin.

Officers

President: Dr Goronwy Wynne

Chairman: Graham Thomas

Vice Chairman: John Morris

Secretary: J. Vince Roberts, Rhandir Mwyn, Allt Goch, Trefnant, St Asaph, Denbs. LL17 0BW. Tel. 01745 730059

Treasurer: Brian Lewis

Conductor and Musical Director: Geraint Roberts GRSM, ARCM, MTC

Accompanist: Angela Roberts BA

Compere: Ednyfed Williams and Ray Lewis

*Rehearsals are held at the Memorial Hall Trelawnyd
every Sunday and Tuesday at 8pm.*

Côr Meibion y Traeth
Traeth Male Voice Choir

Magdalene Jones wasn't a willing collaborator in forming Côr Meibion y Traeth. Cledwyn Rowlands and Owen John Jones weren't easily put off, although the first reaction had been a 'no-no', their dogged perseverance paid off – eventually! At last she relented by pointedly telling them, 'I'll be your conductor, if you will find the singers. But remember you asked me to do this, I'm not the instigator'. This was a very fair comment because she must have known that she was walking on egg shells. At Benllech there had been a long tradition of singing emanating from the congregational music at the chapel with its emphasis on sol-fa practice. There J.C. Parry had been the moving spirit with male voice and mixed voice ensembles. Often in the 40s and 50s the lads would meet in the square after chapel and burst forth into song where visitors and friends would listen in amazement. So her reticence was understandable.

It was the prestigious Môn Eisteddfod coming to Bro Goronwy that had set the lads thinking about a local male voice choir to compete. That is how the choir came into existence in 1969 with Eunice Parry as accompanist. And the recruiting began, finding the right voices and a meeting place for rehearsals. They reckoned Pentraeth would be a good location, there were some good tenor singers there – so Pentraeth School became their first home. From the original squad of about 15 the choir rapidly grew, first to 20 then 30, eventually peaking at a hundred. Soon they had outgrown their meeting place, which prompted their move to more suitable premises at Benllech School. Looking back it was a motley crowd, some had no idea whether they could sing at all. Francis Griffiths a builder from Llanfair PG reckoned he was a soprano! 'Come along and we'll make a tenor out of you,' said the lads. And for 30 years while his health held out Francis's fine tenor voice rang true and he never missed a single practice. Practices were fun too. Still remembered is the occasion when the choristers found Magdalene doubled up in fits of laughter during a practice session. The reason for her mirth was one of the front row singers in his shirt sleeves, his thumbs firmly placed under his braces, with all he was worth singing 'Dana, Dana'. And with each Dana beat his thumbs would emphasise the rhythm, so that with each Dana, Dana, Dana, up and down went his trousers in tune with the song. Soon everyone was in tucks!

And how proudly they wore their uniforms – blazers, white shirts, maroon ties and grey trousers, their dress on stage, when they took the first prize for six years in succession at the Butlins Eisteddfod at Pwllheli (in its time the finest eisteddfod in North Wales). One member Elias Parry was often even seen about town in Amlwch wearing the smart stage apparel and on his head a working cap, until told that it was for very special occasions only!

Once on a visit to the Aberteifi Festival they were caught short. Billed for a choral competition for choirs of forty and over in number, they only had 38 on board. So what was to be done? They would be counted as they went on stage, and faced with only two short in the contingent meant they would be ruled out of the event. Luckily Dewi, Magdalene's husband was with them, as was Grês Pritchard's (accompanist) husband, there was nothing for it they would quickly don the spare blazers and mime their bit in the back row. Result: first prize against all South Wales had to offer!

As with most choirs there is always a sense of fun and excitement. Witness their London escapade in 1988 when they hired the Duke of York Theatre in the West End to do a Sunday night concert with guest soloist Patricia O'Neil. Four coach-loads of Anglesey supporters went along with them to stay the night at the Hilton Hotel. When they came out to go to the theatre, just imagine their surprise when they saw a huge crowd waiting with autograph books at the ready. They just couldn't believe that they were so famous. But there is a slight down side to this story, the screaming youngsters were out there waiting for Matt of the chart topping Bros pop group who were also staying at the hotel. But Côr y Traeth were totally unfazed, they promptly invited Matt to be a vice-president and choir supporter, which he was delighted to accept!

Concert tours abroad have had their moments too. Hong Kong in 1988 as guests of the Welsh Society there was also fun charged with a choir member jumping into the China Sea in his long-johns and finding out after a swim around, that on emerging, said long-johns were full of sea water and weighted down around his ankles. So there have been moments of both culture and frolics. A visit to Vienna representing Wales at the International Music Festival to mark the bi-centenary of Mozart's birth was a tremendous experience as they sang his works in his own church. In August 1998 and 2006 Brittany for the Lorient Festival; Milwaukee for the Welsh Association of North America Gymanfa Ganu in 1997 and interspersed with all that, forays to Ireland, Denmark, France and Germany and in 2003 Canto Del Garda for the International Sacred and Secular Music Festival fulfilled a fairly heavy overseas commitment.

Meanwhile their successful National Eisteddfod appearances include the top accolades at Llangefni (1983); Llanrwst (1989); Bala (1997) and Mold (2006).

The choir have been blessed with outstanding conductors. And amongst those who followed Magdalene Jones, reference must be made to Bryan Powell (Assistant Director of Education for Gwynedd LEA) who conducted the choir for an interim period in 1981 following a time as deputy. Roland Wyn Jones came to the helm from 1981 until 1982 by which time Powell had been promoted to Cardiff. Roland Wyn Jones was Head of the Musical Department at the Normal College of Education with a well proven record conducting choirs. Another worthy of special mention was Gwyn L. Williams, a BBC Music Producer at Bangor. He conducted the choir for two separate periods and made Côr Y Traeth a truly formidable one. He went on to direct the Llangollen International Eisteddfod and later took a key organisational role with the London Olympics. Twenty-two years old David Julian Davies from Bethesda who followed him on to the rostrum in 1995 was not at first very highly regarded, 'he was just a young lad' and the choristers didn't think he was much use, that was until they heard him play the organ in the Pritchard Jones Hall, Bangor to tumultuous acclaim! 'He was brilliant,' from that moment 'they realised what the little fellow was made of'. At that time he was newly graduated BA (Oxon.) and an ARCO specialising in orchestration and performance, and was the Assistant Organist at St Asaph Cathedral. Later he was to give recitals at Westminster Abbey and Westminster Cathedral. He led them on an American concert tour which included Wisconsin. When he left the area to further his career in America and later as an organist at Truro Cathedral, Gwyn L. Williams returned for his second period with the choir.

When Gwyn L. Williams left at the turn of the century he was succeeded in 2001 by Annette Bryn Parri, better known as Wales' best known piano accompanist. Since her first appearance in that capacity on the stage of the Anglesey National Eisteddfod in 1983, and her decision then to go professional, she had gone on to provide piano accompaniment for leading artistes such as Bryn Terfel, Rhys Meirion, Gwyn Hughes Jones and Rebecca Evans. But she was also already an experienced conductor too. For seven years she had conducted the ladies choir Côr Alawon Menai, now known as Côr Cofnod. And back as a schoolgirl at Bryn Refail Grammar she had earned her spurs as team captain of Elidir House organising and conducting choirs, singing parties and pop groups.

Music was her life from very early childhood. As a three year old her mother had asked what she wanted from Santa Clause and her answer came back in a flash in classical kiddie-babble: 'I want a "panano"!' She can't remember a time when she wasn't strumming away at a 'panano'. And when their chapel in Deiniolen held their annual eisteddfod, she was there competing as a five year old. The children's session was in the afternoon, while the evening was for the adult competitions. When she went hand in hand with her father Ifan Bryn to the evening event, and later climbed on the stage and went to the piano, the Rev. Wynn, the minister, called her back. 'You've been competing this afternoon Annette bâch, now it's your daddy's turn to sing.' She replied: 'I know, that's why I'm here, I've come to play the piano for him to sing now.' And then played *Bwthyn Bach Melyn Fy Nhad*. The chapel eisteddfod and the junior school at Deiniolen were important: for Annette they encouraged her to fulfil her dreams. Success in a musical feature for the Urdd under the guidance of Maud Williams qualified her to play the piano in a St David's Day Concert at the Albert Hall before she was twelve years old! Bryn Refail Grammar School furthered her ambitions where Gwyndaf Parry, the head of music, 'persuaded' her to play the piano for morning service. From there with good 'A' levels she was accepted for a further five years study at the Royal Northern College of Music in Manchester. Meanwhile back home in Wales each weekend, she refined her musical talent, responding to calls on her services as eisteddfod accompanist. Calls to all parts: from Anglesey to Machynlleth and Barmouth to Abergynolwyn, polished her skills and enhanced her reputation.

The phone call from J.O. Roberts, famed compare with Côr y Traeth, inviting her to be their conductor propelled her into yet another career decision. She had often thought perhaps some day she would like to conduct a male voice choir, but not yet. Her first thought was that the opportunity had come too soon, on the other hand this was a chance not to be dismissed. A hurried discussion with Gwyn, her husband, quickly focussed her mind. Yes, she would do it if Gwyn could come too to join the baritone section. In the event she went one step better, she would bring her dad, Ifan Bryn, who lives in Dinorwic, just five minutes down the road along as well! Looking back now her decision to lead the choir was well made and the fine traditions of Côr y Traeth are safe in her hands.

The Choir

CDs and Tapes: (Sain) 1083D and C583 *Côr y Traeth* (1977)
(Sain) 1244 D and CH44 *Jubilate* (1982)
(Black Mountain) DM164
CDM1064 *Gorwelion – New Horizon* (1988)
(Black Mountain) CDM2020 *Ar Frig y Don* (1990)

(Black Mountain) XCDM2071 *Byd Newydd* (1992)
(Priory) PRCD658 *Côr Meibion y Traeth 1995 i 1998* (1998)
(Sain) SCD2104 *Goreuon Côr y Traeth 1977 i 1997.*
Catchment area: Benllech, Beaumaris, Holyhead, Llangefni,
Menai Bridge, Moelfre, Talwrn and Valley.
Officials
President: Magdalene Jones
Chairman: Glyn Jones
Vice Chairman: Gwyn Davies
Secretary: Glyn Owen Tel. 01248 600848
Treasurer: Derek Williams
Accompanist: Grês Pritchard ALCM, LLCM
Musical Conductor and Director: Annette Bryn Parri GRNCM
Deputy Conductor: Gwilym Charles Lewis M.Mus., LRAM, ARCM
Compere: J.O. Roberts and Gwyn Parri

Choir rehearsals are held at Ysgol Goronwy Owen School
Benllech on Monday evenings 7.30-9.30

The Welsh Association of Male Voice Choirs

The Welsh Association of Male Voice Choirs was formed in 1962 under the patronage of His Royal Highness, Prince Charles, Prince of Wales. It was formed as a non profit, amateur organisation to bring all the Welsh Male Voice Choirs together under one umbrella. Its basic remit, to provide advice on performing rights, copyright rules, the services of an honorary solicitor and a policy of insurance for its members. The Association's executive officers pledge to promote male voice choral music and to liase with educational and cultural agencies world-wide to stimulate a high standard of performance. The South Wales Branch was established in 1962 to address the needs of twenty-six choirs.

The North Wales Branch was born in 1969, staging its first major concert at the Royal Albert Hall in 1981.

Several Massed Male Voice Festivals have been organised since at other venues, which have included the International Pavilion, Llangollen; Deeside Leisure Centre; British Aerospace, Broughton; Chester Cathedral; Chester Leisure Centre; Liverpool Philharmonic Hall and St David's Hall, Cardiff. All of which have brought choral singing to the forefront for the overall enjoyment of a discerning public. Wales is a country where the fortunes of choirs are followed with an intensity not known in any other part of the world.

The South Wales Branch has also arranged Massed Male Voice Festivals at St David's Hall, Cardiff; the International Arena, Cardiff; Bristol; Swansea; Bournemouth and the Royal Albert Hall, London. The North and South Wales branches together, held their first combined Massed Festival at the Albert Hall on October 2nd, 2004, which marked a hugely successful new beginning. They have now agreed to hold all future festivals together as the Welsh Association of Massed Festival of Male Choirs to be organised biannually, the next to be held in March 2009.

These events are immensely successful, at the close of each Albert Hall Concert tickets are already being snapped up for the next time, two years hence! Holiday people package the festival as part of a superb London experience, companies see it as an exquisite way to entertain important clients; as each event comes around there's a tingle of excitement. The Albert Hall experience is the culmination of two years of exacting rehearsal; the programme drawn up by the Association's executive committee will already be in the choir master's hands well in advance, and is designed to entertain as well as demonstrate the virtuosity of the choirs. For most of the choirs this will be a peak experience, their musical directors will insist on nothing short of a gold standard performance. So for the choirs which have elected to join in the festival, an event which is also open to associate members outside Wales such as the choir from Northern Ireland or Oxford where émigré Welsh people relocated to work in the motor industry and formed their choirs, will be involved in a rehearsal flurry.

During the lead up to the Festival, the North Wales Choirs will come together for joint practices; in 2008 these rehearsals were held at The Corwen Pavilion and Prestatyn Church in North East Wales under the direction of Alwyn Humphreys. Mr Humphreys, among the most experienced conductors in Wales, will demand a high standard of excellence, choristers will be word perfect – he will insist on that. Likewise he will put the South Wales choir through their paces, but inevitably the eight hundred voices won't come together as an entity until the morning prior to the concert in London. This will be the very first time for both North and South to be singing together as one choir and will provide the final proof of the success of all the preparatory work. For all the choristers it will be the most magical experience of their lives; for Alwyn too, an event to savour as he contemplates the evening and bringing the Albert Hall thousands to their feet.

John Hughes Roberts, a retired primary school head master of Sychdyn near Mold and many times chairman of the Association, has often been at the centre of the preparations. 'For most of them it will mean a two night stay in London,' he says, and the first consideration will be the seating arrangements for the choristers. 'Often they will want to be next to their usual partner, because this makes for a better musical blend and will increase their confidence.' The programme will contain eighteen pieces, specially selected for an audience who will want to hear the old familiar classical standards as well as new pieces by modern composers. Interlaced with this, the executive will bring in up and coming young Welsh musicians who have shown outstanding promise at the major Welsh Eisteddfodau, thus providing them with a prestige platform for their talent.

'The staging arrangements are the province of the Association,' says Mr Roberts which includes introducing the artistes by the chairman of the Association. 'Ushering the audience to their seats is done by experienced volunteers.' And so the seemingly impossible is achieved: raising standards in choral music by bringing male voice choirs from all parts of Wales, where the venues are usually chapels and churches, to the finest and largest UK auditorium, The Royal Albert Hall.

John Hughes Roberts, with his twenty year experience with the association and participation as a member of Llangollen Male Voice Choir, is very well aware of the financial undertaking. Travelling from remote parts of Wales and staying in London for two days is not cheap, music copies for the concert are now over two pounds each and photocopying, not allowed under rules of copyright, is a mortal sin! And when all is said and done the male voice tradition in Wales is an amateur one largely reliant on enthusiastic unpaid volunteers. The redeeming factor however with the Albert Hall Concert is that when the resounding applause has died down, the bills settled and the takings reckoned – the profit will be shared between the choirs. But that pales into insignificance because singing in that massed choir is a treasured experience which is beyond price.

The North Wales Branch of Welsh Male Voice Choirs

Patron: HRH Prince Charles, Prince of Wales
Chairman: Gwilym Lewis
Secretary: Emyr Williams, 29 Llwyn Gwgan, Llanfairfechan,
Conwy LL33 0UT. Tel. 01248 681159
Treasurer: H.B.R. Davies
Executive Committee: John Hughes Roberts ex-officio, Charles Cooksley, G. Evans, L. Lloyd Jones, Emlyn P. Thomas, Myfyr Williams, K. Slater
Guest Conductor: Alwyn Humphreys

Royal Albert Hall Concert March 2009.

Bibliography

Roberts, Ernest, *Bargen Bywyd Fy Nhaid* (Llyfrau'r Dryw) 1963

Roberts, Ernest, *Cerrig Mân* (Gwasg Gee) 1979

Roberts, Ernest, *Ar Lwybrau'r Gwynt* (Llyfrfa'r MC) 1965

Jones, Elfed, *Côr Meibion y Penrhyn Ddoe a Heddiw* (Gwasg Gee) 1984

Edwards, Hywel Teifi, *Eisteddfod Fawr y Byd – Chicago 1893*
   (Gwasg Gomer) 1990

Williams, Gwladys Lloyd, *Hanes Cerddoriaeth yn Nyffryn Ogwen*
   (Llyfrfa'r MC)

Trevor, Alun, *Cofio Cantorion – The Welsh Imperial Singers*
   (Gwasg Carreg Gwalch) 1991

Tomos, Dewi, *Eryri* (Gwasg Carreg Gwalch) 2005

Davies, Aled Lloyd, *Canrif o Gân* (Y Gymdeithas Cerdd Dant) 2000
   Gwasg Carreg Gwalch

Edited by Peter Crossley-Holland, *Music in Wales*
   (Hinrichsen Edition Ltd) 1948

Jones, J.E., *Swyn y Tannau* (Adran Meirionydd o Undeb
   Cenedlaethol yr Athrawon)

Edited by Guto Roberts, *Tom Jones Llanuwchllyn*
   (Pwyllgor Cofio Tom Jones) 1991

Edwards, Einion (Nerius), *Mi glywes 'nhad . . .* 2002

Edited by R.H. Evans, *Hanes Henaduriaeth Dyffryn Clwyd*
   (Henaduriaeth Dyffryn Clwyd) 1986

Williams, Ednyfed, *Côr MeibionTrelawnyd* 1983